11/05

PENGUIN

The Ro

Hermann Broch was born in Vienna in 1886. He managed his father's textile firm and was almost forty before he studied philosophy and mathematics at Vienna University. He published the three parts of *The Sleepwalkers* trilogy (*The Romantic*, *The Anarchist* and *The Realist*) in 1931–2, and *The Unknown Quantity* in 1933. He was briefly imprisoned by the Nazis when they invaded Austria in 1938, but the help of friends such as James Joyce and Willa and Edwin Muir led to his emigration to America that year, where he remained until his death in 1951. *The Death of Virgil* was published to great acclaim in 1945, and *The Guiltless* in 1950. His last work, *The Spell*, an incomplete fragment, was published posthumously in 1953.

During his lifetime Broch's work brought him great praise as an innovative visionary writer, comparable to Joyce, Thomas Mann and Robert Musil. He was admired by Aldous Huxley, who wrote of *The Sleepwalkers*, 'We are haunted by the strange and disquieting feeling that we are at the very limits of the expressible ... Broch performs with an impeccable virtuosity.'

Milan Kundera's novels include *The Unbearable Lightness of Being* and *Identity*.

John J. White is Professor of German and Comparative Literature at King's College, London. After studying at the Universities of Leicester, Berlin (Free University), Alberta and London, he taught at Westfield College before being promoted to a Readership in German at King's College London in 1977. He is the author of *Mythology in the Modern Novel* (1971), *Literary Futurism: Aspects of the First Avant-Garde* (1990) and a study of Brecht's *Galileo* (1997), and co-editor of volumes on Grass, Kafka, Musil, Group 47 and the image of Berlin in German literature.

The Sleepwalkers is a trilogy whose component novels can be
read completely independently of one another.

Each novel is set in a different year – *The Romantic* in 1888,
The Anarchist in 1903 and *The Realist* in 1918.

HERMANN BROCH

The Romantic

Translated by Willa and Edwin Muir

Introduced with a Biographical Note by John White
and an Essay by Milan Kundera

PENGUIN BOOKS

PENGUIN BOOKS

Published by the Penguin Group
Penguin Books Ltd, 27 Wrights Lane, London w8 5tz, England
Penguin Putnam Inc., 375 Hudson Street, New York, New York 10014, USA
Penguin Books Australia Ltd, Ringwood, Victoria, Australia
Penguin Books Canada Ltd, 10 Alcorn Avenue, Toronto, Ontario, Canada m4v 3b2
Penguin Books (NZ) Ltd, Private Bag 102902, NSMC, Auckland, New Zealand

Penguin Books Ltd, Registered Offices: Harmondsworth, Middlesex, England

First published in German as *1888. Pasenow oder die Romantik* 1930
This translation first published in the USA by Little, Brown, and Company, 1932

Published in Penguin Classics 2000
1 3 5 7 9 10 8 6 4 2

Copyright © The Estate of Hermann Broch
Introduction and biographical note copyright © John White 2000

Translation by Willa and Edwin Muir used by permission of Alfred A. Knopf, Inc.
Essay by Milan Kundera taken from *The Art of the Novel* and reproduced by
permission of the author
All rights reserved

The moral right of the author of the introduction and biographical note
has been asserted

Printed in England by Clays Ltd, St Ives plc

Except in the United States of America, this book is sold subject
to the condition that it shall not, by way of trade or otherwise, be lent,
re-sold, hired out, or otherwise circulated without the publisher's
prior consent in any form of binding or cover other than that in
which it is published and without a similar condition including this
condition being imposed on the subsequent purchaser

Contents

Introduction

In July 1932, the year in which the final volume of Hermann Broch's monumental trilogy came out in German, T. S. Eliot's *Criterion* published what it introduced as 'two sections from a long novel, *The Sleepwalkers*, which will shortly appear in English'. The choice of material was Broch's own: two untypically demanding extracts from the 'Disintegration of Values' essay inserted into *The Realist*, the third part of *The Sleepwalkers*.[1] As Broch had confessed in October 1931 to Edwin Muir, he considered the 'Disintegration of Values' material to be 'by far the most important part of *The Sleepwalkers*'.[2] So anxious was he, in fact, for the English public to receive with due respect the novel's sections dealing with the philosophy of history informing the entire work that Broch, an insatiable reviser at the best of times, reworked them to a far greater extent than any other part of the trilogy. It is clear that he would have ideally liked to place the entire theoretical essay in an English literary magazine, but two sample extracts – one on the modern pluralism resulting from partial value-systems and the other a historical excursus positing the collapse of the unified Catholic value-system as a result of the Reformation (a choice calculated to appeal to Eliot) – were deemed sufficient to give a potential English readership some sense of the theoretical construct underlying the work's sweeping diagnosis and interpretation of the causes of the *malaise* affecting the last thirty years of the Wilhelmine Empire.

Muir, who as publisher's reader for Secker had been one of the first foreigners to set eyes on the manuscript, wrote enthusiastically to the author: 'I really think it has given me the deepest experience I have ever had from an imaginative work, since the time, in my 'teens, when I discovered poetry. You have done something decisive for my generation – lost though it may be.'[3] In an earlier letter to Sydney Schiff, Muir had expressed himself equally positively ('really first rate, and very beautiful', a work of 'great truth and psychological subtlety'[4]). Moreover, Muir reported that he had decided to postpone translating Kafka's *The Trial* for the time being in order to devote himself to working with his wife, Willa, on an English version of *The Sleepwalkers*.

Although *The Death of Virgil* (1945) is usually thought of as Broch's 'lyrical novel' *par excellence*, *The Sleepwalkers* is, as Muir had observed, also a work with numerous lyrical sequences, many of them of far greater beauty than the rather mediocre poetry occasionally inserted into the 'Story of the Salvation Army Girl in Berlin' in *The Realist*. It is also a work rich in memorable episodes and populated by a whole gamut of strikingly individualistic characters, so much so that many of the trilogy's admirers would probably have chosen to present some of these, rather than densely argued theoretical material, to readers of the *Criterion*. However, as can be seen from the 'Methodological Prospectus' he issued to publishers to explain what he was attempting with *The Sleepwalkers*, by the time he was working on the third volume of the trilogy, Broch had become wont to underestimate his undoubted strengths as storyteller, psychologist and observant chronicler and analyst of contemporary Europe. As a result he tended to view the work exclusively as a novel of ideas: as a 'polyhistorical' or 'epistemological' novel, to use two of his favourite terms. His correspondence of the time makes it patently clear that he considered the trilogy's story-telling element – which makes up nine-tenths of the narrative – to be primarily a vehicle for the fictional embodiment of his epistemological concerns. For similar reasons, the whole Balzacian cavalcade of colourful characters to whom we are introduced and the presiding spirit of the three novels' diverse settings (the Junker estates of West Prussia, Wilhelmine Berlin, the Rhineland of the shipping industry and small business enterprises, and a sleepy Moselle community, so close to and yet so cocooned from the reality of the Western Front) were all for the author first and foremost quasi-allegorical illustrative material, the primary task of which was to mediate a complex and systematizing philosophy of history. No wonder Broch at one stage felt that the work should simply be given the uncompromising title 'Historical Novel'. Fortunately, his German publisher, Daniel Brody of the Rhein-Verlag, disabused him of this unworldly idea, but Broch clung persistently to his conviction that what was most important in *The Sleepwalkers* was not detail but the grand plan.

And a grand plan there certainly was behind almost every feature of the work. From the outset, *The Sleepwalkers* had been conceived as a kind of Naturalist *roman expérimental*: a triptych, with each volume moving forward fifteen years to a different part of the Imperial Germany of the late nineteenth and early twentieth centuries and to a fresh milieu, in both the geographical and the sociological senses. The three constituent novels span the entire period of Kaiser Wilhelm II's reign, from his accession to the imperial throne in 1888 to his hasty departure during the tumultuous year 1918, a time-frame which Broch saw as 'representing the final stages of the old European values and attitudes'.[5] Each of the three novels marks an attempt to convey the *Zeitgeist* and representative style of these sample moments in time as experienced between the spring and autumn of one particular year, and each concentrates on a single paradigmatic figure: a 'romantic', an 'anarchist' and a 'realist' (although they are all 'sleepwalkers' in Broch's idiosyncratic understanding of the metaphor). With each successive novel we move progressively farther westwards and the narrative mode becomes distinctly more modernist. In all probability, Broch chose Germany rather than his native Austria as the setting for his chronicle of the disintegration of values because he perceived the process to be more advanced there than anywhere else in Europe. Yet *The Sleepwalkers* is not merely some gloomy counterpiece to Oswald Spengler's *Decline of the West*: *The Realist* – above all in its 'Epilogue' – also suggests that by 1918 the country was beginning to show signs of potential renewal as well as symptoms of imminent collapse.

The obvious fact that *The Sleepwalkers* begins by focusing on the life and values of a professional soldier and ends in the Armistice month of November 1918 has to be interpreted with a modicum of caution. Admittedly, the very first part of the 'Disintegration of Values' essay seeks to present the mindless carnage in the trenches on the Western Front as the epitome of a modern world of atomized values:

Is this distorted life of ours still real? is this cancerous reality still alive? the melodramatic gesture of our mass movement towards death ends in a shrug of the shoulders, – men die and do not know why; without a hold on reality they fall into nothingness . . . .

The unreal is the illogical. And this age seems to have a capacity for surpassing even the acme of illogicality, of anti-logicality: it is as if the monstrous reality of the war had blotted out the reality of the world. . . . How could a man take a gun in his hand, how could he march into the trenches, either to die in them or to come out again and take up his work as usual, without going insane? How is such adaptability possible? How could the ideology of war find any kind of response in these men, how could they ever come even to understand such an ideology and its field of reality, not to speak of enthusiastically welcoming it, as was not at all impossible? Are they insane because they did not go insane? (*The Realist*, chapter XII)

At one point, in response to a war-casualty patient's complaint that nowadays all doctors seem to want to do is 'cut things off', Dr Flurschütz replies: 'Can't be helped; this century has been devoted to surgery and rewarded by a world-war with guns' (chapter VI). Yet as Broch was quick to point out in response to what he held to be a misguided review, neither the four-hundred-year-long process analysed in the 'Disintegration of Values' essay nor the thirty-year timespan upon which the narrative concentrates can be meaningfully read as simply the prehistory of the First World War: 'the process of cultural development which includes the War is emphatically a far larger phenomenon; the catastrophic War is only a subsidiary matter, a side-effect' (Letters, 127). In this respect, *The Sleepwalkers* is comparable to both Thomas Mann's *The Magic Mountain* and Robert Musil's *The Man without Qualities*, works whose timescale overlaps substantially with that of the trilogy. The truth of the war's only marginal causal relevance is intuitively grasped by Hanna Wendling in one of the parallel stories in *The Realist*: 'The war is not the cause', she thinks to herself, 'it's only a secondary thing' (chapter LXIV). However, like most other characters in Broch's trilogy, she is unable to explain how what *The Sleepwalkers* calls the 'disintegration of values' had come about.

The original German titles for the three novels that make up *The Sleepwalkers* (first published as three separate volumes, as they are once again in the present edition) bring out the principle of representativeness more explicitly than do their English counterparts. A more literal translation of the German titles would be:

1888. Pasenow or Romanticism
1903. Esch or Anarchy
1918. Huguenau or Realism

Broch deliberately puts the date first because everything we encounter in the individual narratives is interpreted, within the context of a rigorously schematic philosophy of history spelled out in the final volume, as a product of what he and his contemporaries would have thought of as the *Zeitgeist*. As the full titles show, the work's concern is with various abstract concepts as manifestations of that *Zeitgeist*: romanticism *per se* (not just one particular romantic) and so on. Broch explained in a letter to Willa Muir that, as he perceived things, there was 'a suprapersonal, collective logic to events, and progress in intellectual achievement is inexorably determined ... within a margin of error of a few years, the railway engine *had to be* invented in about 1820, the car around about 1890' (Letters, 142f.). Moreover, he was implying, history's parallel cultural timetable dictated that a James Joyce and even a Hermann Broch were predestined to write in the way they did at approximately the time they did. In *The Sleepwalkers*, with its markedly changing literary style from novel to novel, it is not just the techniques of writing that are the products of determinism; architectural features (the presence or absence of ornament), ways of killing, how one rationalizes one's behaviour or conceives of one's relationship to the world around one are all historically motivated. More crucially, for this is the main theme of *The Sleepwalkers*, values themselves, far from being absolutes, remain subject to comparable processes of conditioning, distortion and eventual disintegration. As one character puts it: 'Honour is by no means a mere convention ... once upon a time poison-gas would have been rejected as a weapon of warfare' (*The Realist*, chapter XXXIX). Along with the technology of modern combat, war's ultimate rationale thus also changes. By the time of Wilhelm II's reign, 'the warrior is no longer concerned with absolute war, such as took concrete shape in the Crusades, but with earthly squabbles carried on with new-fangled and unchivalrous weapons' (chapter LV). Yet the clocks of European history are by no means fully synchronized. Thus, while by 1918 'The logic of the soldier demands that he shall throw a hand-grenade between the legs of his enemy' (chapter XLIV), the Moselle Memorial Association (in *The Realist*) still goes through the charade of commemorating its war-dead by laying in tribute a wreath of oak-leaves anachronistically inscribed 'From the Fatherland to its brave soldier' (chapter LII). Broch's purpose is to uncover the processes by which the world reached such a schizophrenic situation. *The Sleepwalkers* is consequently part contemporary diagnosis, part ambitious etiology and part implied cure, although Broch preferred the sleepwalking image to the rhetoric of sickness and apocalypse so prevalent in the work of Thomas Mann and many of his contemporaries.

Apart from the generic 'Historical Novel', Broch mooted a number of other titles for his work-in-progress. 'Huguenau': because the main protagonist of the final novel, a man totally lacking in ethical values was, of all figures in the trilogy, the 'adequate child of his times'.[6] 'Bertrand': because in Broch's eyes Bertrand, as the man who steps back from the events to observe the other sleepwalking participants from a vantage-point of splendid isolation, was 'the passive main figure of the entire novel'.[7] However, whether the title would have simply been a reference to the Eduard von Bertrand of the first two novels or to Dr Bertrand Müller in *The Realist* or both as *Doppelgänger* of one another remains unclear. Eventually, the collective but more elusive sleepwalking image was chosen as the umbrella title. At the time, Broch was elaborating a personal aesthetic which associated symbols very much with the realm of the irrational, and the novel's whole system of balances and counter-balances between rational and irrational elements was of vital importance to him during the genesis of *The Realist*, in particular. Clearly, *The Sleepwalkers* abounds in symbolic images and objects, including, most notably, Pasenow's uniform and its various reprises in the later novels, Esch's miniature symbols of freedom (his replica Statue of Liberty and copy of the Schiller monument at Mannheim), a whole series of symbols of redemption through sacrifice (Ilona's part in the knife-throwing act being the most striking one), as well as the harbingers of death and threatening sexuality which so often intrude upon the secure rational realms of the male protagonists. Broch had turned from philosophy to creative writing in the late 1920s due to his dissatisfaction with the way in which the logical positivists of the Vienna Circle had sought to exclude the irrational, the mystical and the religious from modern philosophy. *The Sleepwalkers* was intended to redress the imbalance. The trilogy's collective title thus had the attraction of consonance with this general aesthetic of the irrational: both as one among many symbols and leitmotifs holding the vast narrative together and also because of its deliberately imprecise associations.

Sleepwalking is a happy metaphor for the state in which virtually all of the trilogy's characters find themselves – and indeed have to, if Broch's rigid conception of the *Zeitgeist* is to remain convincing. Nevertheless, because of the sheer variety of people and situations it is applied to, it tends to have different connotations at various junctures. Frequently, 'sleepwalking', i.e. moving in a realm between the mental states of sleep and being awake, functions as a symbol of the way in which characters are caught somewhere in between an earlier familiar and protective world of accepted values and a battery of irrational experiences that leave them uncertain of themselves and trapped between fear and seduction. The way such a predicament is depicted in *The Romantic* makes it clear that things are not happening of the characters' own volition, but as if in a dream. They have descended below the level of the reassuringly rational and controllable to a realm of libidinous urges and hidden fears. On the whole, one gains the impression that many of the novel's figures are sleepwalkers who would prefer to wake up again. As the somnambulism image also implies, they appear to be going through the motions of normal behaviour, yet as if in a trance. It may be dangerous to wake them up and they have no clear sense of where they are heading. Some, like Esch and the later Pasenow, have quixotic dreams of setting the world aright, but only have quirky notions about how to embark upon the task. (Tellingly, in the volatile revolutionary mood of the trilogy's conclusion, some of the crowd are singing 'La Marseillaise', others 'The Internationale'.) Some dream of personal salvation through the erotic realm or via self-sacrifice. Others merely dream of revenge or survival.

To be sleepwalking is to be in the realm which Broch's 'Methodological Prospectus' to the novel called 'the "no longer" and the "not yet"'. We see this most vividly in the case of the young Joachim von Pasenow in *The Romantic*. The Pasenow whom we meet at the beginning of the trilogy seems to be not merely a soldier by profession, but one by ideological conviction. He feels faintly unreal in civilian clothing; he mistrusts civilians and even dislikes walking through those parts of *fin-de-siècle* Berlin which he associates with civilian life. However, such appearances are deceptive. For most of *The Romantic* Pasenow is in fact progressively coming under siege from various irrational quarters. Certain early incidents (the fact that his brother Helmuth's pony has to be put down, Helmuth's own death in a duel a few years later, his parents' mention of the need for him to marry) remain for Pasenow irrational threats associated with the feeling that 'some pillar or other of life had become shaky' (chapter I). Caught off-guard by Helmuth's death, all he can do is respond with a misplaced cliché: 'He died for honour, for the honour of his name' (chapter I). His father's mental decline becomes another major challenge to Pasenow's assumption that he had succeeded in creating a rational, ordered regime within which to live out his entire life. His friend Eduard von Bertrand undermines an already wavering confidence by ridiculing the military ethos and subsequently resigning his commission ('deserting', as Pasenow sees it), in order to transfer his allegiances to the civilian world of big business. To cap it all, in a re-enactment of the return of the repressed, Pasenow's affair with Ruzena, an echo of nineteenth-century literature's stereotypical dark Bohemian *femme fatale*, rapidly becomes too threatening to be contained within the parameters of his military code of conduct. Pasenow takes desperate measures to solve his dilemma; he breaks with Ruzena, soliciting Bertrand's help with the organizational niceties, and agrees to marry someone from his own class, Elisabeth von Baddensen. But his impotence at the end of the first novel, symbolized in his inability to take off his officer's uniform – which he had always seen as a bulwark against the irrational – and get into bed with his new bride, suggests that his attempts at putting his life in order have been no more than what Broch once dismissed as 'semi-solutions which bring about no emancipation from the realm of the dreamlike, but instead introduce the ethical into the sphere of the dark and libidinous'.[8] The major role played by the irrational in all three parts of *The Sleepwalkers* is the hallmark of a novel of consciously deployed depth-psychology. Nevertheless, the 'psychological subtlety' which had so impressed Edwin Muir on first reading was only a subservient part of the work's overall method. For Broch had confessed that he wished to write an '*epistemological novel* instead of a psychological one, a work in which we penetrate beneath and beyond psychological motivation to basic epistemological attitudes and to the actual logic and plausibility of values' (Letters, 93). This, he observed wistfully, used to be the domain of philosophy, now it has become the modern novel's task. What Broch meant by the epistemological novel – in contradistinction to the novel of 'psychologism' – can best be appreciated if we bear in mind the way the image of Pasenow in *The Romantic* is retrospectively reassessed in the 'Disintegration of Values' essay.

That Pasenow was, in Broch's idiosyncratic interpretation of the term, 'a romantic' had already been established within the first few pages of *The Sleepwalkers*. Here, in an abstract passage which begins with the ironic observation that 'On the theme of the military uniform Bertrand could have supplied some such theory as this', we encounter the apodictic pronouncement that 'when the secular exalts itself as the absolute, the result is always romanticism' (chapter I). (Such philosophizing passages,

Broch noted, serve to break through the pastiche of nineteenth-century *mésalliance* fiction and open up a window on to the more philosophical treatises to come (*Letters*, 90).) Put less ponderously, Pasenow has raised his circumscribed military value-system to the status of a private religion. The reader might object that Pasenow's obsession with the protective powers of the uniform and his tendency to measure everything using the yardstick of the military's value-system is essentially a defensive ploy. Only by reductively rationalizing experience in this way can he master it. Anyone capable of the thought that 'everything connected with being born, sleeping, loving and dying – in short, everything civilian – was a matter of underclothing' (chapter I) sounds as if he is in need of professional help. But behind the psychological portrait of an individual, *The Sleepwalkers* is at pains to highlight factors that can only be understood within a wider historical framework: an epistemological one. Perhaps as a concession to the reader, the more philosophical aspects of Broch's epistemological apparatus are deferred to the final volume, and, even there, are only phased in gradually in a manner contriving not to alienate anyone who has by now grown accustomed to the methods of *The Romantic* and *The Realist*.

The stereotypical choice between the dark woman Ruzena and the genteel Aryan Elisabeth, the all-too-familiar triangular love situation, the overworked city/country and military/civilian antitheses all make *The Romantic* come across, at least superficially, as being a deliberate pastiche of a certain kind of nineteenth-century novel. What Broch is showing with this appropriation of an anachronistic genre, however, is the horizon of expectation of Pasenow and his kind, and the 'style' – both logical and cultural – in which they would receive and process their own experiences. Working within such a conventional paradigm, the narrative also inevitably lays itself open to a straightforward Freudian reading (Broch was under analysis at the time he was writing his trilogy) whereby Pasenow's super-ego attempts to assert its control over the various libidinous forces which have erupted into his tranquil life. Again in Freudian terms, most of his fanciful thinking about a uniform's ability to provide 'its wearer with a definitive line of demarcation between his person and the world' (*The Romantic*, chapter I) could be dismissed as a form of 'compensation', a bulwark against the irrational forces he fears are beyond his control. Without a doubt, Pasenow fetishizes his officer's uniform. Hiding initially behind the defensive assumption that 'This is what

Bertrand might have said' on the subject, he pronounces that 'it is the uniform's true function to manifest and ordain order in the world, to arrest the confusion and flux of life' (chapter I). (Later sleepwalking characters will substitute other nouns for 'uniform', but think in the same way.) Yet what began in *The Romantic* as a psychological portrait of a man with an inadequate value-system struggling to come to terms with irrational experiences gradually widens into a case-history begging for another kind of interpretive model.

The two sections of the 'Disintegration of Values' essay which take the analysis of Pasenow's motives and responses implicitly beyond the capacities of the modern psychological novel are chapter XXXI ('Disintegration of Values (4)') and chapter XLIV ('Disintegration of Values (6)') of *The Realist* . The second of these might at first appear to approach Pasenow's military *déformation professionelle* typologically, as just one among many examples of modern forms of blinkered, compartmentalized ethics: what it criticizes as the logic of the soldier, the businessman, the politician, the bourgeois climber and the self-preoccupied artist ('*l'art pour l'art*'). Each type is content to live according to a closed code of behaviour, what the novel terms a 'partial value-system' (chapter LXXXVIII), which has been raised in an act of false consciousness to the status of a personal absolute. The result is a kind of private faith-system with such mantras as 'war is war' or 'in politics there's no room for compunction, business is business' (chapter XLIV). Such ethical myopia, a kind of self-serving tunnel vision, leads to a situation where values have been degraded to the level of what the essay castigates as 'the non-values of our age'. True, it may be difficult to recognize in Joachim von Pasenow an illustration of the claim that 'the logic of the army demands in general that all military resources shall be exploited with the utmost rigour and severity, resulting, if necessary, in the extermination of peoples, the demolition of cathedrals, the bombardment of hospitals and operating-theatres'. Pasenow is too much of an anachronism, too much a man on the defensive for this to sum him up adequately. Rather, it is a picture of what one imagines Huguenau the soldier must have been like before his decision to desert: an amoral fighting machine. And this is the novel's point: with the gradual secularization and atomization of once coherent ethical values, our world is moving from Pasenow's last-ditch values to Huguenau's. And if we ever needed to remind ourselves, *The Sleepwalkers* was written at a time substantially nearer to the Second World War than to the cessation of hostilities in 1918.

If we also try to think of Esch in terms of the conception of a 'partial value-system', we recognize that he too is hardly a paradigmatic illustration of the fact that underlying the principle 'business is business' is a 'ruthless logic directed on the object and on the object alone', an ethos according to which the end justifies the means and 'immanent Being has been analysed into pure function' (*The Realist*, chapter XLIV). Like Pasenow, Esch, with his noble intentions, is also caught between the worlds of the 'no longer' and the 'not yet'. In fact, in a manner reminiscent of Mann's *Buddenbrooks*, *The Sleepwalkers* measures the whole process of cultural change by the criterion of what is presented as the justification for good business practice. And in both instances, a ruthless present is contrasted with a Utopian Christian past: 'The dictum "Business is business" was not permitted to the medieval merchant, competitive struggle being forbidden to him.' In the medieval world, 'faith was the point of plausibility in which every line of inquiry ended', and hence the underlying rationale for all activity.

One might have expected Huguenau to be presented as the trilogy's epitome of anarchy; but within a further idiosyncratic interpretation of a key concept, the 'anarchy' of Esch, who is repeatedly referred to as 'an impetuous man', consists in not retreating into his protective partial value-system, as Pasenow had done in *The Romantic*, but actively applying his book-keeper's scheme of values to the world and trying to set things right. If, with his distorted, vaguely religious notions of sacrifice, atonement and the need for some new kind of leader-figure, Esch is in his own peculiar way still intuitively trying to reassert some form of moral order, Huguenau, the man totally bereft of ethical values, represents one horrible direction in which the disintegration of values may possibly be leading. Huguenau is categorized as 'the realist', although the German noun 'Sachlichkeit' has overtones of 'matter-of-factness', rather than pragmatic realism. Huguenau the opportunist, the value-free man, is conceivably the logical end of a process which all forms of retreat into partial value-systems have been unable to halt and have in actual fact probably accelerated. Whereas the Middle Ages shared a common 'point of plausibility' no matter what activity one has in mind, the world of the sleepwalkers has 'rendered impossible at one stroke the binding of all single value-systems to a central value' (*The Realist*, chapter XLIV). God, the justificatory point of reference, is no longer there. As a consequence of centuries of fragmentation occasioned by the Renaissance and the sectarianism represented by the Reformation, values have become largely secularized and pluralistic. Fanatical logic has excluded the irrational in both its positive and negative manifestations and those in search of help have turned to a whole rabble of false prophets.

Towards the end of Chapter XLIV of *The Realist*, the reader is offered a diagnosis of the world which the final volume is designed to reflect, both in its content and stylistically:

> the abstract ruthlessly invaded the logic of every single value-making activity ... [and] has also radicalized so thoroughly the single value-systems that these, being thrown back on themselves and referred to the Absolute, have separated from one another, now run parallel to each other, and, since they can no longer combine in the service of a supreme value, claim equality one with the other: like strangers they exist side by side ... each autonomous, each 'in and for itself,' each 'unfettered' in its autonomy, each resolved to push home with radical thoroughness the final conclusions of its logic and to break its own record.

The images of a world in which competing value-systems are *thrown back on themselves*, exist *like strangers side by side*, with each, '*unfettered*' in its autonomy, seeking to *push home with radical thoroughness the final conclusions of its logic*, express the predicament in such human terms that they could just as well be referring to the main characters of *The Realist*.

When Broch declared that 'revolutionary content calls out for a new form' (Letters, 136), even claiming that new cognitive insights were only possible within new structures, he was thinking above all of *The Realist*: 'in many respects a *novum* in the genre of the novel' (Letters, 138). This is the most fragmentary (disintegrated and disintegrating) of the three novels – a multi-strand narrative juxtaposing a whole series of parallel stories, some first written as a whole and then cut up and folded into various parts of the complex. From the outset, it was Broch's intention to bring together Pasenow and Esch from the previous two novels and to confront them with his new main figure: Huguenau 'the realist'. But now, he felt, the *Zeitgeist* also made it necessary for him to intercalate:

> a whole series of stories all acting as variations on the same theme, i.e. man's confrontation with loneliness – a ... consequence of the disintegration of values ... These individual stories, interwoven like a tapestry, each depict a different level of consciousness: they rise up from the level of the completely irrational (the story

of the Salvation Army girl) to the complete rationality of the theoretical (the dis-integration of values essay). The other stories take place between these two poles on graduated intermediary levels of rationality. By this means the overall mean-ing of the trilogy will be achieved. (Letters, 144)

What Broch called the 'additive method' of *The Realist* (Letters, 186), i.e. the accretion of a series of sub-plots and parallel actions to the main story of Huguenau's manipulative rise to power in a small Moselle township, was to some considerable extent indebted to recent international experi-ments in modern fiction. 'Have you already read the new Dos Passos?', he asked Daisy Brody in September 1930; 'He's no Joyce, but he writes with virtuosity' (Letters, 102). Already familiar with *Manhattan Transfer* (1925), Broch appears to have been reading *The 42nd Parallel* within months of its appearance in the USA in 1930 (while completing work on *The Realist*). 'Who', Broch asked disingenuously, 'could write a com-parable European book to put alongside Dos Passos' cross-section of America?' (Letters, 137). *U.S.A.*, according to the work's foreword, offers 'the slice of a continent', presented in the various dialects of 'the speech of the people'.[9] As such vocabulary suggests, the method owes a distinct debt to Zola's *tranche de vie* paradigm of Naturalist fiction, organized to offer a cross-section of life as it is in the raw and not intrusively organized according to some externally conceived aesthetic principle. Much as he felt encouraged in his experiment by Dos Passos's method, Broch had certain misgivings. Like Döblin's *Berlin Alexanderplatz* (1929), the urban epic juxtaposing a series of parallel stories with only occasional, loose plot connections technically represented for him little more than a 'broaden-ing of the old Naturalistic novel'. It remained too unquestioningly 'in the realm of the empirical', with surface reality failing to be 'spiritually penetrated' ('durchgeistigt' (Letters, 137): a term Thomas Mann was also fond of using of his particular form of symbolic realism). If *Manhattan Transfer* and *The 42nd Parallel* could be thought of as enriching the tech-nical repertoire of the modernist novel, they did so in an essentially cumulative way, not qualitatively. Broch's description of the montage of discourses and sub-plots included in *The Realist* reveals major differences between his strategy (the narrative threads, he stresses, have been 'inter-woven like a tapestry') and Dos Passos's more random, slice-of-life sequences. By contrast, the various fragmentary parts of Broch's third novel are conceived of as existing on a broad spectrum, with the totally irrational at one end counterbalanced by the extreme rationality of the 'Disintegration of Values' sections at the other. This is also mirrored in the work's stylistic spectrum: the sixteen lyrical chapters evoking the love of the Salvation Army soldier Marie for the Jew Nuchem standing in a contrapuntal relationship to the abstract philosophy of history in the theoretical essay; and all this interleaved with a series of sub-plots. The two extremes (the lyrical and the philosophical) were added at a late stage in the novel's composition, producing a grid for the other case studies of a loneliness symptomatic of the disintegration of values.

An important contributory factor to the manner in which *The Realist* is structured was Broch's dissatisfaction with the way in which most contemporary 'philosophical novels' incorporated their intellectual material in the form of often stilted conversations between an improbable array of intellectuals. Citing Gide, Mann and Huxley as culprits, Broch complained about the polyhistorical novel's predilection for 'dreadfully cerebral discussions': intellectual padding composed of random fragments chipped rather amateurishly off the 'crystal block' of knowledge and clumsily accommodated in poorly motivated dialogue (Letters, 148). To avoid the trap of thinking of the intellectual novel as being by definition a novel about garrulous intellectuals, Broch resorted to a dual strategy. First, the underlying scholarly ideas (and in the case of *The Sleepwalkers* this meant, above all, the philosophy of history and the novel's epistemological assumptions) were to be placed 'immanently in the action and the figures' themselves, not just talked about. This is particularly the case with virtually all of *The Romantic* and *The Anarchist*. Broch's second solution was to incorporate what he called 'living science', the theory behind the fiction, in an unapologetically 'naked' form (again, his word) into the body of the fiction. In other words, he refused to have it masquerading as conversational material or smuggled in in the guise of the ruminations of a fictive author who happens to be working on a novel bearing striking similarities to the work in which he appears (e.g. Edouard in Gide's *The Counterfeiters* or Philip Quarles in Huxley's *Point Counter Point*). In 1918, Broch had written a story entitled 'Methodological Novella' in which he had proceeded inductively, via a series of narrative hypotheses, from a theoretical construct to an illustrative piece of fiction. He was clearly anxious that the theory in *The Sleepwalkers* should not appear to be in the same mode. The 'Disintegration of Values' essay should not give the impression of existing like 'a crystal block *alongside* the novel', but had to '*come into being*, continually deriving its existence from the novel itself' (Letters, 152). The theory must appear to be generated by the accompanying fiction. Thus, while it was not to be integrated into the fiction at plot-level, it had to come across as far from autonomous.

Given the boldness of the move to put non-fictionalized theory into *The Sleepwalkers*, why does Broch eventually reveal Dr Bertrand Müller to be the author of this material? The most persuasive answer is to be found in Chapter LXXIII of *The Realist*: 'Disintegration of Values (9): *Epistemological Excursus*'. It is not by chance that Broch informed Edwin Muir that this was 'the most important chapter' in the entire work (Letters, 158). It may be that the chapter's paramount importance was emphasized because its starting-point is a question that in a sense lies behind the whole project: whether Hegel's optimistic philosophy of history has been invalidated by the events of the First World War. The answer for the author of the '*Epistemological Excursus*' is self-evidently 'yes', but for him this does not matter, inasmuch as many other phenomena had already proved Hegel wrong. However, rather than merely dismiss the whole question of the contemporary legitimacy of rival optimistic and pessimistic teleologies of history, the '*Epistemological Excursus*' lives up to its name by turning its attention to underlying methodological questions raised by what it terms 'the logical possibilities of this emergent antideductive reality'. Now if Broch thought of this chapter as the jewel in the crown of *The Realist*, which he already saw as the crowning glory of the trilogy, he must have been acutely aware that few of his readers would have the philosophical training or stamina to follow him down all the avenues of the following excursus. Even a cursory reader will nevertheless observe that the Three Theses which are at the core of the excursus stress the centrality of a value-concept to all historiography; they harness the Kantian conception of the world as the product of the intelligible Self to a process of unlimited semiosis whereby 'the world is not an immediate but a mediate product of the Self, it is "a product of products," "a product of products of products," and so on in infinite iteration'. On a more pragmatic level, the reader will recall the extent to which the world is shaped by – is a 'product' of – the individual's perspective and his value-centre has been illustrated throughout the entire trilogy. Reality is perspectival, a series of 'products', in the philosophical sense. The excursus relates this most strikingly to the modern conception of relativity, while underlying the final paragraphs of the excursus is the fundamental question of where this leaves God, the absolute, or what Broch likes to call 'the Platonic idea'. The reader will find the theoretical section's answer to that question near the end of the excursus (and taken up in the narrative's 'Epilogue'). But the problems delineated here also have repercussions for the status of the entire 'Disintegration of Values' material within Broch's narrative. The theory cannot be absolute, any more than the rest of the novel could be permitted to come across as the product of an independent omniscient narrator. The essay has, by the same token, to be a 'product', hence it needs to be given an identifiable authorial source: namely Dr Bertrand Müller. If not, the trilogy would be an exception to what it has been showing, or, failing that, it would have to have been narrated by the God of the medieval world. To be sure, the narrative repercussions of this theorizing are not spelled out to the reader. Just as one is left with the task of establishing connections between the various parts of *The Realist*, so too one has to relate episte-mological questions pertaining to the philosophy of history to features of the novel's narrative strategy. Broch points us in the right direction, but refuses to take us by the hand.

No doubt influenced by Gide's conception of the structure of *The Counterfeiters* as analogous to musical form and Huxley's *Point Counter Point*, Broch conceived of *The Realist* as a work with a musical structure. He speaks, for example, of 'the entire contrapuntal system upon which *The Realist* is constructed' (Letters, 187) and alerts a fellow writer to the work's 'somewhat complicated counterpoint' (Letters, 145). Yet such metaphors remain loose enough to apply either to the contrapuntally arranged extremes of irrationality and rationality or to the relationship between the major characters in the Huguenau–Esch–Pasenow main strand and the various minor figures in the subordinate parallel stories. Elsewhere, when Broch uses the phrase 'architectonic polyphony' for the end-effect, he seems to be referring to the varieties of perspective and resultant styles in which the individual tales are told. 'Polyphony' seems little more than a figurative way of referring to modern pluralism, but what it and the epithet 'architectonic' seem calculated to emphasize is that there is a grand design, a coherence to the organization of the various narrative strands of *The Realist*. Contrary to the assumption of many early readers, more was at stake than simply finding an experimental correlative for the theme of 'disintegration'. Broch's notion of form as cognition encourages the reader to search further than that.

Broch, who had met Georg Lukács in Vienna in 1920, was profoundly influenced by his *Theory of the Novel*, a work which argued that the modern novel's legitimacy rested on its ability to depict the world in its totality. This is not the place to consider the various respects in which *The Sleepwalkers* attempts to convey such an impression. Although there are occasional gestures towards the notion of totality in the narrative ('We feel the totality to be insane', the first part of the 'Disintegration of Values' essay declares (*The Realist*, chapter XII)), the sense of totality has to be mainly conveyed by various structural means. The cross-sections of history, the sense of a spectrum of representative figures and plots, the concomitant stylistic spectrum and the theory's ability to extend backwards in time and outwards to more abstract considerations are all part of this rhetoric of totality. What Broch is attempting, however, is not merely a totality which consists of the sum of the trilogy's parts. It is a larger, implied totality: Broch himself spoke of the 'hypothetical synthesis that he was attempting' (Letters, 187), and he imagines the reader engaged in a comparable project. The reading process will inevitably run parallel to the narrative strategy of *The Realist*: the challenge of bringing together the irrational elements and the logical theoretical sections will, Broch surmised, be rather like the bricklayer Gödicke's piecemeal attempt at retrieving the coherence of his soul. Modern literary theory has been fascinated by the stratagems by which readers piece together *their* text from the fragments of information put at their disposal. In the case of *The Sleepwalkers*, Broch saw this as a spiritual quest, not merely an act of what Wolfgang Iser would call 'consistency-building'.

The 'new problem', a spiritual one, that Broch felt *The Sleepwalkers* confronted was formulated in his letter of 10 April 1930 to G. H. Meyer, the *eminence grise* of the Rhein-Verlag: 'where is this yearning to be awakened and saved leading, if it cannot achieve its goals in a period of the collapse and dissolution of old values and attitudes? Can a new ethics arise from the slumber and dreams of the darkest of days?'[10] Like Mann's *The Magic Mountain*, which concludes with a similarly impassioned yet desperate question, *The Sleepwalkers* leaves the matter for the reader, or history, to resolve. (And, sadly, there is little evidence in the trilogy that Broch could foresee just what history's answer would be.) Unlike Mann, of course, Broch really appears to be asking whether some form of religious renewal, not just a replacement secularized ethics, is possible. The eighth section of the 'Disintegration of Values' essay begins with the declaration that 'Religions rise out of sects and in their decadence lapse again into sects', a thesis broad enough to encompass an interpretation of Protestantism as 'the first great sect-formation in the decay of Christianity' (*The Realist*, chapter LXII). There is repeated evidence of growing sectarianism in *The Sleepwalkers*, above all in some of the sub-plots of *The Realist*. Not just in the activities of Esch and his Bible group, but in the Salvation Army girl Marie's proselytizing in Berlin and in Pasenow's zealous turn to religion. The novel's continual play with the leitmotif of 'no longer' and 'not yet', which is to re-emerge in a less ambiguous guise in Broch's later novel *The Death of Virgil*, leaves open the question of whether such sectarianism is a terminal symptom or a sign of renewal. However, the words with which the entire trilogy ends, culminating in a passage from chapter 16 of the Acts of the Apostles, make Broch's own position abundantly clear. A voice is heard:

not the voice of dread and doom; it falters in the silence of the Logos and yet is borne on by it, raised high over the clamour of the non-existent; it is the voice of man and of the tribes of men, the voice of comfort and hope and immediate love: 'Do thyself no harm! for we are all here!' (chapter LXXXVIII)

We are left in no doubt why Broch was never tempted to use such a negative phrase as 'The Disintegration of Values' as the title for his entire trilogy.

Writing in the financially traumatized world of the early 1930s at a time when he was having to defend the last-minute expansion of *The Realist* through the incorporation of the 'Disintegration of Values' material, Broch remarked that 'if someone wants to spend money on a book these days, he must be given a heroic piece of reality as a reward for his act of despair' (Letters, 155). *The Sleepwalkers*, he reminded Brody, was not something to be bought at a station kiosk and perused on the train. No doubt the word 'heroic' implied that the reader had to have the temerity to embark on such an expedition; words like 'risk', 'boldness', and the slogan 'no concessions to the reader' abound in Broch's discussions of the work's innovativeness. The trilogy's early reception in the English-speaking world assured him that such intrepid readers existed among his intellectual peers. While Nazi propagandists were already initiating their campaign against such anti-military modernist literature, Broch was receiving plaudits from gratifying quarters: Aldous Huxley, Stephen

Spender, Herbert Read, James Joyce and Thornton Wilder, and he was
particularly excited to hear that Bertrand Russell had promised to read
his work. Without the equally heroic service rendered the text by his
translators, Broch's exile years would have been very different – indeed,
without their aid he might not even have been able to leave his home
country in the wake of the *Anschluß*. The Muirs were tireless in their
efforts to draw attention to Broch, but of course their greatest single act
of homage was the translation of his *magnum opus*. Broch's early confidence that Kafka's English translators would stand him in good stead as
he launched his new literary career was well placed. He wrote to Willa
Muir in 1932: 'I think I shall have to translate *The Sleepwalkers* back into
German from the English, then I will have a good book' (Letters, 174).

NOTES

1. Hermann Broch, 'Disintegration of Values', *Criterion: A Literary Review*,
II: 45 (July 1932), 664–75. The extracts chosen were Chapters XLIV
('Disintegration of Values (6)') and LV ('Disintegration of Values (7):
Historical Excursus').

2. Broch's fascinating correspondence with his editor, his translators and
a number of fellow writers has yet to be translated into English. Unless
otherwise indicated, all quotations from Broch's correspondence in the
Introduction (page number preceded by 'Letters') are from Hermann
Broch, *Briefe I (1913–1938)*, *Kommentierte Werkausgabe*, ed. P. M. Lützeler
(Frankfurt a. M., 1981), vol. 13/1, p. 158. Translations are my own.

3. *Selected Letters of Edwin Muir*, ed. with an Introduction by P. H. Butter
(London, 1974), p. 76.

4. Ibid., p. 69.

5. *Hermann Broch–Daniel Brody. Briefwechsel 1930–1951*, ed. Bertold Hack
and Marietta Kleiß (Frankfurt a. M., 1971), col. 15.

6. Ibid., col. 38.

7. Ibid., col. 16.

8. Ibid., col. 16.

9. *U.S.A.: The 42nd Parallel, Nineteen-Nineteen, The Big Money* (London, 1950),
p. vi.

10. *Hermann Broch–Daniel Brody. Briefwechsel*, col. 15.

Further Reading

OTHER WORKS BY BROCH IN ENGLISH TRANSLATION

The Unknown Quantity [*Die unbekannte Größe*, 1933], trans. Willa and Edwin Muir (London and New York, 1935).

The Death of Virgil [*Der Tod des Vergil*, 1945], trans. Jean Starr Untermeyer (New York, 1945).

The Guiltless [*Die Schuldlosen*, 1950], trans. Ralph Manheim (New York, 1974).

The Spell [*Der Versucher*, 1953, republished as *Die Verzauberung*, 1976], trans. H. F. Broch de Rothermann (New York, 1987).

Hugo von Hofmannsthal and His Times: The European Imagination 1860–1920 [*Hofmannsthal und seine Zeit. Eine Studie*, 1955], ed. and trans. Michael P. Steinberg (Chicago, 1984).

GENERAL STUDIES OF BROCH'S WORK (IN ENGLISH)

Hannah Arendt, *Men in Dark Times* (New York, 1968).

Stephen D. Dowden (ed.), *Hermann Broch: Literature, Philosophy, Politics. The Yale Broch Symposium 1986* (Columbia, SC, 1988).

Ernestine Schlant, *Hermann Broch* (Boston, 1978).

Theodore Ziolkowski, *Hermann Broch* (New York, 1964).

STUDIES OF *THE SLEEPWALKERS* (IN ENGLISH)

Dorrit C. Cohn, *'The Sleepwalkers': Elucidations of Hermann Broch's Trilogy* (The Hague and Paris, 1966).

William P. Hanson, 'Broch's "Geschichte des Heilsarmeemädchens in Berlin', *Quinquereme*, 2 (1979), 1–9.

Henry Hatfield, 'Hermann Broch's *The Sleepwalkers*', in *Crisis and Continuity in Modern German Fiction: Ten Essays* (Ithaca, NY, 1969), pp. 109–27.

Paul Michael Lützeler, 'Success and Failure of *The Sleepwalkers*: 1930–1932', in *Hermann Broch: A Biography*, trans. Janice Furness (London, 1987), pp. 75–91.

Ernestine Schlant, 'The Mechanics and Metaphysics of Sleepwalking', in *Hermann Broch* (Boston, 1978), pp. 40–67.

Martin Swales, 'Story, History, Discursiveness: On Hermann Broch's *Die Schlafwandler*', in A. Stevens *et al.* (eds.), *Hermann Broch. Modernismus, Kulturkrise und Hitlerzeit* (Innsbruck and London, 1994), pp. 45–75.

Michael Tanner, 'Introduction' to Hermann Broch, *The Sleepwalkers*, trans. Willa and Edwin Muir (London, Melbourne and New York, 1986), pp. iii–viii.

Theodore Ziolkowski, 'Hermann Broch and Relativity in Fiction', *Wisconsin Studies in Comparative Literature*, 8 (1967), 365–76.

Theodore Ziolkowski, 'Hermann Broch: *The Sleepwalkers*', in *Dimensions of the Modern Novel: German Texts and European Contexts* (Princeton, 1969), pp. 138–80.

The Romantic (1888)

I

In the year 1888 Herr von Pasenow was seventy, and there were people who felt an extraordinary and inexplicable repulsion when they saw him coming towards them in the streets of Berlin, indeed, who in their dislike of him actually maintained that he must be an evil old man. Small, but well made, neither a shrivelled ancient nor a pot-belly, he was extraordinarily well proportioned, and the top-hat which he always sported in Berlin did not look in the least ridiculous on him. He wore Kaiser Wilhelm I. whiskers, but cut somewhat shorter, and on his cheeks there was none of that white fluff which gave the Emperor his affable appearance; even his hair, which had scarcely thinned yet, showed no more than a few white strands; in spite of his seventy years it had kept its youthful fairness, a reddish blond that reminded one of rotting straw and really did not suit an old man, for whom one would have liked to imagine a more venerable covering. But Herr von Pasenow was accustomed to the colour of his hair, nor in his judgment did his monocle look in the least too youthful. When he gazed in the mirror he recognized there the face that had returned his gaze fifty years before. Yet though Herr von Pasenow was not displeased with himself, there were people whom the looks of this old man filled with discomfort, and who could not comprehend how any woman could ever have looked upon him or embraced him with desire in her eyes; and at most they would allow him only the Polish maids on his estate, and held that even these he must have got round by that slightly hysterical and yet arrogant aggressiveness which is often characteristic of small men. Whether this was true or not, it was the belief of his two sons, and it goes without saying that he did not share it. For, after all, sons' thoughts are often coloured by prejudice, and it would have been easy to accuse his sons of injustice and bias in spite of the uncomfortable feeling which the sight of Herr von Pasenow aroused, a really remarkable feeling of discomfort that actually increased when he had passed by and one chanced to look after him. Perhaps that was due to the fact that his back view made one doubtful of his age, for his movements were neither like those of an old man,

3

nor like those of a youth, nor like those of a man in the prime of life.
And as doubt gives rise to discomfort, it is possible that some chance
stroller might have resented as undignified the man's style of progression,
and if he should have gone on to characterize it as overweening and
vulgar, as feebly rakish and swaggering, one would not have been surprised. Such things, of course, are a matter of temperament: yet one can
quite well imagine some young man, blinded with hatred, hurrying back
to thrust his cane between the legs of any man who walked in that way,
so as to bring him down by hook or by crook and break his legs and put
an end for ever to such a style of walking. Herr von Pasenow, however,
went straight on with very quick steps; he held his head erect as small
men generally do; and as he held himself very erect too, his little belly
was stuck slightly forward, one might almost have said that he carried it
in front of him; yes, that he was carrying his whole person somewhere
or other, belly and all, a hateful gift which nobody wanted. Yet as a
simile really accounts for nothing, those ill opinions would have remained
without solid foundation, and perhaps one might even have grown
ashamed of them until one noticed the walking-stick accompanying his
legs. The stick moved to a regular rhythm, rose almost to the height
of his knees, returned with a little sharp impact to the ground and rose
again, and the feet went on beside it. And these too rose higher than
feet should do, the toes shot out a little too far as if they were presenting
his shoe-soles in contempt to approaching pedestrians, and the heels
were deposited again with a little sharp impact on the pavement. So
the two legs and the walking-stick went on together, suggesting the
involuntary fancy that this man, had he come to the world as a horse,
would have been a pacer; but the horrible and disgusting thing was that
he was a three-legged pacer, a tripod that had set itself in motion. And
it was horrible, too, to realize that the three-legged purposiveness of the
man's walk must be as deceptive as its undeviating rapidity: that it was
directed towards nothing at all! For nobody who had a serious end in
view could walk like that, and if for a moment one involuntarily thought
of a profiteer inexorably conveying himself to some poor man's house to
collect a debt, one saw at once how inadequate and prosaic was such
a notion, and one was terrified by the intuition that it was a devil's walk,
like a dog hobbling on three legs—a rectilinear zigzag . . . enough: for
anyone who analysed Herr von Pasenow's walk with loving hate might
have discovered all this and more. Most people, after all, lend themselves

to such experiments. There is always something that will fit. And if Herr von Pasenow did not really lead a busy life, but on the contrary expended ample time in fulfilling the decorative and other obligations which a quietly secure income brings with it, yet—and that too expressed his character—he was always bustling, and mere sauntering was far from his nature. Besides, visiting Berlin but twice a year, he had abundance to do when he was there. Just now he was on his way to his younger son, Lieutenant Joachim von Pasenow.

Whenever Joachim von Pasenow met his father, memories of his boyhood thronged up in him as was natural enough: but the most vivid of these were always the events preceding his entrance to the cadet school in Culm. True, it was only fragments of the past that fleetingly emerged, and important and trivial things flowed chaotically through one another. So perhaps it may seem idle and superfluous to mention Jan, the steward, whose image, though he was a quite secondary figure, obtruded itself in front of all the others. But this may have been because Jan was not really a man, but a beard. For hours one could gaze at him and meditate whether, behind that dishevelled landscape covered with impenetrable yet soft undergrowth, a human creature was concealed. Even when Jan spoke—but he did not speak much—one could not be certain of this, for his words took form behind his beard as behind a curtain, and it might as easily have been another who uttered them. But most exciting of all was when Jan yawned; for then the hairy superficies gaped at a pre-ordained point, substantiating the fact that this was also the place where Jan conveyed food into himself. When Joachim had run to him to tell him of his approaching entrance into the cadet school, Jan was having his dinner; and he sat there cutting bread into chunks and silently listening. At last he said: " Well, is the young master glad? " And then Joachim became aware that he was not in the least glad; he actually felt he wanted to cry; but as there was no immediate pretext for that, he only nodded and said that he was glad.

Then there was the Iron Cross that hung in a glass-covered frame in the big drawing-room. It had belonged to a Pasenow who, in the year 1813, had held a high position in the army. Seeing that it always hung on the wall, the great fuss that was made when Uncle Bernhard received one too was somewhat puzzling. Joachim was still ashamed, now in 1888, that he had ever been so stupid. But perhaps he had been embittered merely because they had tried to make the cadet school more palatable to him by dangling the Iron Cross before him. In any case his brother Helmuth would have been a more suitable subject for the cadet school, and in spite of the years that had passed Joachim still considered it a ridiculous arrangement that the elder son had to take to the land and the younger to the army. The Iron Cross had left him quite indifferent, but Helmuth had been filled with wild enthusiasm when Uncle Bernhard had taken part in the storming of Kissingen with his division, the Goeben. In any case he wasn't even a real uncle, but only a cousin of their father's.

His mother was taller than his father, and everything on the home farm was managed by her. Strange how little attention Helmuth and he had paid to her; they had been like their father in that. They had ignored her stubborn and lackadaisical: " Don't do that," and were only annoyed when she added: " Look out, or your father will catch you." And they weren't in the least daunted when she employed her final threat: " Well, I'm really going to tell your father this time," and scarcely minded even when she fulfilled the threat; for then their father only threw them an angry look and went on his way with his stiff, purposive stride. It was a just punishment on their mother for trying to side with the common enemy.

At that time the predecessor of the present pastor was still in office. He had yellowish white side-whiskers which were hardly distinguishable from the hue of his skin, and when he came to dinner on festival days he used to compare their mother with Empress Luise in the midst of her brood of children. That had been a little ludicrous, but it had made one proud all the same. Then the pastor had acquired yet another habit, that of laying his hand on Joachim's head and calling him " young warrior "; for all of them, even the Polish maids in the kitchen, were already talking about the cadet school in Culm. Nevertheless Joachim was still waiting at that time for the final decision. At table one day his mother had said that she didn't see the necessity of sending Joachim away; he could quite well enter later as an ensign; that was how it had invariably been done, and the custom had always been kept. But Uncle Bernhard replied that the new army required capable men and that in Culm a proper lad would soon find his place. Joachim's father had remained disagreeably silent—as always when his wife said anything, for he never listened to her. Except, indeed, on her birthday, when he clinked glasses with her, and then he borrowed the pastor's comparison and called her his Empress Luise. Perhaps his mother was really against his being sent to Culm, but one could put no dependence on her: she always finished by taking sides with his father.

His mother was very punctual. In the byre at milking time, and in the hen-house when the eggs were being collected she was never absent; in the morning one could always find her in the kitchen, and in the afternoon in the laundry, where she counted the stiff starched linen along with the maids. It was on one of these occasions that he had first heard the news. He had been with his mother in the byre, his nostrils were full of the heavy odour of the stalls, then they stepped out into the cold wintry air and saw Uncle Bernhard coming towards them across the yard. Uncle Bernhard still carried a stick; for after being wounded one was allowed to carry a stick, all convalescents carried sticks even when they had ceased to limp badly. His mother had remained standing, and Joachim had gripped Uncle Bernhard's stick and held it fast. Even to-day he still clearly remembered the ivory crook carved with a coat of arms. Uncle Bernhard said: " Congratulate me, cousin; I've just been made a major." Joachim glanced up at the Major: he was even taller than Joachim's mother and had drawn himself up with a little jerk, proudly yet as if at the word of command, and looked still more warrior-like and straight than usual; and perhaps he had actually grown taller; in any case he was a better match for her than Joachim's father. He had a short beard, but one could see his mouth. Joachim wondered whether it was a great honour to hold a major's stick, and then decided to be slightly proud of it. " Yes," Uncle Bernhard went on, " but now it will mean an end of these lovely days at Stolpin." Joachim's mother replied that it was both good news and bad news, and this was a complicated response which he could not quite understand. They were standing in the snow; his mother had on her brown fur coat which was as soft as herself, and under her fur cap her fair hair escaped. Joachim was always glad when he remembered that he had the same fair hair as his mother, for it meant that he too would become taller than his father, perhaps as tall as Uncle Bernhard; and when Uncle Bernhard nodded to him now, saying, " We'll soon be comrades in the King's uniform," for a moment he felt pleased at the thought. But as his mother only sighed and made no objection, submitting herself just as if she were standing before his father, he let go the stick and ran away to Jan.

He could not discuss the matter with Helmuth; for Helmuth envied him and talked like the grown-ups, who all said that a future soldier should be proud and happy. Jan was the only one who was neither a hypocrite nor a deceiver; he had only asked if the young master was glad, and had not behaved as if he believed it. Of course Helmuth and the others probably meant well and perhaps only wanted to comfort him. Joachim had never got over the fact that at that time he had been secretly convinced of Helmuth's treachery and hypocrisy; for though he had tried to make it good immediately by presenting all his toys to Helmuth, yet he could not have taken them with him into the cadet school, and so it was not a real expiation. He had given Helmuth also his half of the pony which the two boys shared in common, so that Helmuth possessed a whole horse to himself. These weeks had been pregnant with trouble, and yet good; never, before or afterwards, had he been so intimate with his brother. Then, it is true, came the accident with the pony. For the time being Helmuth had renounced his new rights, and Joachim was given full control of it. But of course that did not mean very much, for in these weeks the ground had been soft and heavy, and there was a standing prohibition against riding in the fields when the ground was in that state. But Joachim felt the superior right of one who would soon be going away, and as Helmuth was agreeable, rode out into the fields on the pretext of giving the pony exercise. He had only started on a quite short canter when the accident happened; the front leg of the pony was caught in a deep hole; it fell and could not get up again. Helmuth came running, and after him the coachman. The pony lay with its dishevelled head in the mire, its tongue hanging sideways out of its mouth. Joachim could still see Helmuth and himself kneeling there and stroking the pony's head, but he could not remember any longer how they had got home and only knew that he had found himself in the kitchen, which had suddenly become very still, and that everybody was staring at him as if he had committed a crime. Then he had heard his mother's voice: " Your father must be told." And then he was suddenly in his father's study, and it seemed to him that the punishment which his mother had menaced him with so often in that hateful sentence, was now, after being stored up and accumulated, about to fall on his head. But nothing happened. His father only kept on walking up and down the room in silence, and Joachim tried to stand straight, gazing at the antlers on the wall. Still nothing happened, and his eyes began to wander and remained fixed on the bluish sand in the frilled paper that covered the polished brown hexagonal spittoon beside the stove. He had almost forgotten why he was there; but the room seemed vaster than ever and there was an icy weight on his chest. Finally his father stuck the monocle into his eye: " It's high time that you were out of the house "; and then Joachim knew that they had all been duping him, even Helmuth himself, and at that moment he was glad that the pony had broken its leg; for his mother, too, had been telling tales on him so as to get him out of the house. Then he could see that his father was taking his pistol out of its case. And then he vomited. Next day he learned from the doctor that he was suffering from concussion, and that made him proud. Helmuth sat on his bed, and although Joachim knew that the pony had been shot by his father, neither of them said a word about it, and these were very happy days, strangely secure and remote from the lives of all the grown-ups. Nevertheless they came to an end, and after a delay of a few weeks he was deposited at the cadet school in Culm. Yet when he stood there before his narrow bed, so distant and remote from his sick-bed at Stolpin, it almost seemed to him that he had brought the remoteness with him, and at the beginning that made his new surroundings endurable.

Naturally there were a great number of things belonging to this time that he had forgotten, yet a disturbing residue remained, and in his dreams he sometimes imagined that he was speaking Polish. When he was made lieutenant he presented Helmuth with a horse which he had himself ridden for a long time. Yet he could not free himself from the feeling that he was still slightly in his brother's debt, and sometimes even thought of Helmuth as an importunate creditor. But that was all nonsense, and he very seldom thought of it. It was only when his father came to Berlin that those ideas awakened again, and when he asked after his mother and Helmuth he never forgot to inquire after the health of the nag as well.

Now that Joachim von Pasenow had put on his civilian frock-coat and between the two corners of his peaked stiff collar his chin was enjoying unaccustomed freedom, now that he had fixed on his curly-brimmed top-hat and picked up a walking-stick with a pointed ivory crook handle, now that he was on the way to the hotel to take out his father for the obligatory evening's entertainment, suddenly Eduard von Bertrand's image rose up before him, and he felt glad his civilian clothes did not sit on him with by any means the same inevitability as on that gentleman, whom in secret he sometimes thought of as a traitor. Unfortunately it was only to be expected and feared that he would meet Bertrand in the fashionable resorts he would have to visit with his father that evening, and already during the performance in the Winter Garden he was keeping an eye open for him and seriously considering the question whether he could introduce such a man to his father.

The problem still occupied him as they were being driven in a droshky through Friedrichstrasse to the Jäger Casino. They sat stiffly and silently, with their sticks between their knees, on the tattered black-leather seats, and when a chance girl on her beat shouted something to them Joachim stared straight in front, while his father, his monocle rigidly fixed, muttered: " Idiotic." Yes, since Herr von Pasenow had first come to Berlin many things had changed, and even if one accepted it, yet one could not close one's eyes to the fact that the innovating policy of the founder of the Reich had produced some very curious fruits. Herr von Pasenow said, as he was accustomed to say every year: " Paris itself isn't any worse than this," and when they stopped in front of the Jäger Casino the row of flaring gas-lamps before it, drawing the attention of passers-by to the entrance, excited his disapproval.

A narrow wooden stair led up to the first floor where the dancing-halls were, and Herr von Pasenow climbed it with the bustling, undeviating air which was characteristic of him. A black-haired girl was descending. She squeezed herself into a corner of the landing to let the visitors pass; and as she could not help smiling, it seemed, at the old gentleman's fussiness, Joachim made a somewhat embarrassed and deprecatory gesture. And once more he felt a compulsion to picture Bertrand either as this girl's lover, or as her bully, or as something else equally fantastic; and no sooner was he in the dancing-hall than he looked searchingly around for him. But of course Bertrand was not there: on the contrary Joachim found two officers from his own regiment, and now he remembered for the first time that it had been himself who had incited them to come to the casino, so that he might not be left alone with his father, or with his father and Bertrand.

In acknowledgment of his age and position Herr von Pasenow was greeted with a slight, stiff bow and a click of the heels, as if he were a military superior, and it was indeed with the air of a commanding general that he inquired if the gentlemen were enjoying themselves: he would feel honoured if they would drink a glass of champagne with him; where-upon the gentlemen made known their agreement by clicking their heels again. A new bottle of champagne was brought. They all sat stiffly and dumbly in their chairs, drank to each other in silence, and regarded the hall, the white-and-gilt decorations, the gas flames that hissed, surrounded by tobacco smoke, on the branches of the great circular chandelier, and stared at the dancers who were revolving in the middle of the floor. At last Herr von Pasenow said: " Well, gentlemen, I hope that you aren't refraining from the company of the fair sex on my account." Bows and smiles. " Some pretty girls here too. As I was coming upstairs I met a very promising piece, black hair, and with eyes that you young fellows couldn't remain indifferent to." Joachim was so ashamed that he could have throttled the old man to suppress such unseemly words, but already one of his comrades was replying that it must have been Ruzena, really an unusually pretty girl, and one couldn't deny her a certain elegance either; anyhow, most of the ladies here were better than might be ex-pected, for the management were very strict in selecting their girls and laid a great deal of importance on the maintenance of a refined tone. Meanwhile Ruzena had returned to the dancing-hall; she had taken the arm of a fair girl, and as they sauntered past the tables and boxes with their high coiffures and tight-laced figures they actually produced an elegant impression. As they were passing Herr von Pasenow's table they were asked jestingly whether Ruzena's ears had not been tingling, and Herr von Pasenow added that, to judge from her name, he must be addressing a fair Pole, consequently almost a countrywoman of his. No, she was not Polish, said Ruzena, but Bohemian, or as people said in this country, Czech; but Bohemian was more correct, for the proper name of her country was Bohemia. " All the better," said Herr von Pasenow, " the Poles are no good . . . unreliable. . . . Well, it doesn't matter."

Meanwhile the two girls had sat down, and Ruzena began to talk in a deep voice, laughing at herself, for she had not yet learned to speak German correctly. Joachim was annoyed at his father for conjuring up the memory of the Polish maids, but was forced himself to think of one of the harvest workers who, when he was a little boy, had lifted him up on to the wagon with the sheaves. Yet though in her hard, staccato pro-nunciation she made hay of the German language, still she was a young lady, stiffly corseted, who lifted her champagne-glass to her lips with a proper air, and so was not in the least like a Polish harvest worker; whether

the talk about his father and the maids were true or not. Joachim had
nothing to do with that, but this gentle girl wasn't to be treated by the old
man in the way he was probably accustomed to. All the same Joachim was
unable to envisage the life of a Bohemian girl as any different from that
of a Polish one—indeed even among German civilians it was difficult to
divine the individual behind the puppet—and when he tried to imagine
Ruzena as coming out of a good home, with a good matronly mother and
a decent suitor with gloves on, it did not fit her; and he could not get
rid of the feeling that in Bohemia life must be wild and low, as among
the Tartars. He was sorry for Ruzena, although she reminded him
somewhat of a humble little beast of prey in whose throat a dark cry is
strangled, dark as the Bohemian forests, and he longed to know whether
one could talk to her as one talked to a lady; for all this was so terrifying
and yet seductive, and in a way justified his father and his father's lewd
intentions. He was afraid that Ruzena, too, would see through these, and
he sought for an answer in her face; she noticed it and smiled to him;
yet she let the old man fondle her hand which was hanging languidly
over the edge of the table, and the old man did it quite openly, and tried
at the same time to summon up his scraps of Polish to erect a lingual
hedge round the girl and himself. Of course it was wrong of her to allow
him such liberties, and when at Stolpin they maintained that Polish
maids were quite unreliable perhaps they were right. Yet perhaps she
was only weak, and one's honour demanded that she should be protected
from the old man's advances. But that would be the duty of her lover;
if Bertrand possessed the slightest vestige of chivalry he was in duty
bound to appear now to put everything in order with a word. And
suddenly Joachim began to talk about Bertrand to his fellow-officers:
hadn't they heard any word of Bertrand lately and of what he was
doing; yes, a curiously reserved fellow, Eduard von Bertrand. But his
comrades, who had already drunk a good deal of champagne, gave him
confused answers and were beyond being surprised at anything, even at
the pertinacity with which Joachim harped on the theme of Bertrand; and
cunningly and persistently as he brought out the name in a loud and
distinct voice, not even the girls twitched an eyelash, and the suspicion
mounted within him that Bertrand might have sunk so low as to come
here under an assumed name; and so he turned directly to Ruzena and
asked whether she didn't know von Bertrand—until the old man,
keen of hearing, and officious as ever in spite of the champagne, asked

why Joachim was so hot on the track of this von Bertrand: " You're as
eager about him as if he were hidden somewhere in the place." Joachim
reddened and denied it, but the old man had been set going: yes, he
had known the father well, old Colonel von Bertrand. He had departed
this life, very likely it was this Eduard who had brought him to his
grave. When his waster of a son had chucked the army he had taken it,
people said, very much to heart; nobody knew why, or whether there
mightn't have been something shady behind it. Joachim became indignant.
" Pardon me, but that's only empty gossip—and the last thing that
Bertrand can be called is a waster! " " Gently, gently," replied the old
man, turning again to Ruzena's hand, on which he now pressed a long
kiss; Ruzena calmly permitted it and regarded Joachim, whose soft fair
hair reminded her of the children at the village school in Bohemia. " I
not will flatter you," she said in her staccato voice to the old man, " but
nice hair has your son." Then she seized the head of her friend, held
it pressed to Joachim's, and was delighted to see that the colour of the
hair was the same. " Would be beautiful pair," she declared to the two
heads, and ran her hands through their hair. The other girl shrieked,
because her coiffure was being disarranged; Joachim felt a soft hand
touching the back of his head, he had a slight sensation of dizziness and
threw his head back as if he wished to catch the hand between his neck
and his collar and force it to remain there; but then the hand slipped of
its own accord down to the back of his neck, and stroked it quickly and
timorously, and was gone. " Gently, gently! " he heard his father's dry
voice again, and then he noticed that the old man had taken out his
pocket-book, had drawn out two large notes, and was on the point of
pressing them on the two girls. Yes, that was just how he used to throw
marks to the harvest girls when he was in a good mood, and though
Joachim wanted to intervene now he could not prevent the fifty-mark
note from being pressed into Ruzena's hand, nor her from sticking it
gaily into her pocket. " Thanks, papa," she said, then she bettered her
words, " papa-in-law," and winked at Joachim. Joachim was pale with
rage: the old man would buy a girl for him for fifty marks, would he?
Quick of hearing, the old man caught Ruzena's quip and seized on it:
" So! It seems to me that my young rascal has caught your fancy. . . .
Well, you have my blessing. . . ." Swine, thought Joachim. But now the
old man was in full sail: " Ruzena, my sweet child, to-morrow I'll call
on you and fix up the match in proper style, all tip-top. What shall I

bring you as a wedding gift? . . . But you must tell me the address of your castle. . . . " Joachim looked away like one who at an execution does not wish to see the axe falling, but Ruzena suddenly stiffened, her eyes went blind, her lips quivered, she pushed away a hand that was stretched out in help or concern, and ran away to cry herself out beside the woman who attended to the lavatory.

"Well, well," said Herr von Pasenow, "but it must be quite late! I'm afraid we must be going, gentlemen." In the droshky father and son sat side by side, stiff and hostile, their sticks between their knees. At last the old man said: "Well, she accepted the fifty marks, all the same. And then she took to her heels." What a wretch, thought Joachim.

On the theme of the military uniform Bertrand could have supplied some such theory as this:

Once upon a time it was the Church alone that was exalted as judge over mankind, and every layman knew that he was a sinner. Nowadays it is the layman who has to judge his fellow-sinner if all values are not to fall into anarchy, and instead of weeping with him, brother must say to brother: "You have done wrong." And as once it was only the garments of the priest that marked a man off from his fellows as something higher, some hint of the layman peeping through even the uniform and the robe of office, so, when the great intolerance of faith was lost, the secular robe of office had to supplant the sacred one, and society had to separate itself into secular hierarchies with secular uniforms and invest these with the absolute authority of a creed. And because, when the secular exalts itself as the absolute, the result is always romanticism, so the real and characteristic romanticism of that age was the cult of the uniform, which implied, as it were, a superterrestrial and supertemporal idea of uniform, an idea which did not really exist and yet was so powerful that it took hold of men far more completely than any secular vocation could, a non-existent and yet so potent idea that it transformed the man in uniform into a property of his uniform, and never into a professional man in the civilian sense; and this perhaps simply because the man who wears the uniform is content to feel that he is fulfilling the most essential function of his age and therefore guaranteeing the security of his own life.

This is what Bertrand might have said; but though it is certain that not every wearer of uniform is conscious of such things, yet it may be

maintained that everyone who has worn a uniform for many years finds
in it a better organization of life than the man who merely exchanges
one civilian suit in the evening for another civilian suit during the day.
True, the soldier has no real need to think deeply of these things, for a
generic uniform provides its wearer with a definitive line of demarcation
between his person and the world; it is like a hard casing against which
one's personality and the world beat sharply and distinctly and are
differentiated from each other; for it is the uniform's true function to
manifest and ordain order in the world, to arrest the confusion and flux
of life, just as it conceals whatever in the human body is soft and flowing,
covering up the soldier's underclothes and skin, and decreeing that
sentries on guard should wear white gloves. So when in the morning a
man has fastened up his uniform to the last button, he acquires a second
and thicker hide, and feels that he has returned to his more essential and
steadfast being. Closed up in his hard casing, braced in with straps and
belts, he begins to forget his own undergarments, and the uncertainty of
life, yes, life itself, recedes to a distance. Then, after he has finished by
pulling down his tunic so that it stretches smooth and without a crease
over chest and back,—then even the child whom he sincerely loves, and
the woman in whose embrace he begot that child, recede into such a
civilian remoteness that the mouths which they present to him in farewell are almost strange to him, and his home becomes something foreign,
which in his uniform he dare not enter. Should he next proceed in his
uniform to the barracks or to his office, it must not be thought pride
that makes him ignore men otherwise clothed; it is simply that he can
no longer comprehend that such alien and barbarous raiment can clothe
anything even faintly resembling actual humanity as he feels it in himself.
Yet this does not mean that the man in uniform has become blind, nor that
he is filled with blind prejudices, as is commonly assumed; he remains
all the time a man like you and me, dreams of food and love, even reads
his newspaper at breakfast; but he is no longer tied to things, and as
they scarcely concern him any longer he is able to divide them into the
good and the bad, for on intolerance and lack of understanding the
security of life is based.

Whenever Joachim von Pasenow was compelled to put on civilian
clothes Eduard von Bertrand came into his mind, and he was always
glad that mufti did not sit on him with the same assurance as on that
man; yet he was very eager to know what Bertrand's views were on the

question of uniform. For Eduard von Bertrand had of course every reason to reflect on the problem, seeing that he had laid aside the uniform once for all and decided for the clothing of a civilian. That had been astonishing enough. He had been passed out of the cadet school in Culm two years before Pasenow, and while there had acted exactly like the others; had like the others worn white trousers in summer, had eaten at the same table, had passed his examinations like the others; and yet when he became a second lieutenant the incomprehensible thing happened: without ostensible cause he quitted the service and vanished into a kind of life quite foreign to him—vanished into the labyrinth of the city, as people called it, into a labyrinth from which he emerged only now and then. If one met him in the street one was always a little uncertain whether to greet him or not, feeling that he was a traitor who had carried over to another world and there offered up something which had been a common possession, and that in confronting him one was exposed and naked, while he himself gave away nothing about his motives and his life, and maintained always the same equable friendly reserve. But perhaps the disturbing factor lay simply in Bertrand's civilian clothes, in the fact that his white stiff shirt-front was so exposed that one really had to feel ashamed for him. Besides, Bertrand himself had once declared in Culm that no genuine soldier would ever allow his shirt-cuffs to appear below his sleeves, because everything connected with being born, sleeping, loving and dying—in short, everything civilian— was a matter of underclothing; and even if such paradoxes had always been characteristic of Bertrand, no less than the airy gesture with which he was accustomed, lazily and disdainfully, to disavow them afterwards, yet obviously he must have been troubled at that time by the problem of the uniform. And about the underclothing and the shirt-cuffs he may have been partly right: for instance when one reflected—and Bertrand always awakened such unpleasant reflections—that all men, civilians and Joachim's father not excepted, wore their shirts stuck into their trousers. For that reason Joachim actually did not like to encounter anyone in the men's barracks with his tunic open; there was something indecent about it, which gave one a vague inkling of the justification for the regulation that when visiting certain resorts and for other erotic purposes mufti must be worn; and more, which made it appear almost like an offence against the regulations that such beings as married officers and married non-commissioned officers should exist. When the married sergeant-major reported for morning service and opened two buttons of his tunic so as to draw out of the opening, which laid bare his checked shirt, his huge red-leather book, Joachim generally ran his fingers over his own tunic buttons, and felt secure only when he had certified that they were all in order. He could almost have wished that the uniform was a direct emanation of his skin, and often he thought to himself that that was the real function of a uniform, and wished at least that his underclothes could by a distinctive pattern be made a component part of the uniform. For it was uncanny to think that every soldier carried about with him under his tunic the anarchical passions common to all men. Perhaps the world would have gone off the rails altogether had not someone at the last moment invented stiff shirt-fronts for the civilians, thus transforming the shirt into a white board and making it quite unrecognizable as underclothing. Joachim recalled his astonishment as a child, when, looking at the portrait of his grandfather, he had recognized that that gentleman did not wear a stiff shirt, but a lace jabot. But then in his time men had had a deeper and more intimate faith, and did not need to seek any further bulwark against anarchy. Of course all these notions were rather silly and obviously only an overflow from the kind of things Bertrand said, which had neither rhyme nor reason; Pasenow was almost ashamed of thinking of them in front of the sergeant-major, and when they surged up he thrust them aside and with a jerk resumed his stiff, official bearing.

But even if he thrust aside those thoughts as foolish, and accepted the uniform as a decree of nature, there was more in all this than a mere question of attire, more than a something which gave his life style at least, if not content. Often he fancied that by saying " Comrades in the King's uniform " he could put an end to the whole question, and to Bertrand too, although in doing so he was far from desiring to express any extraordinary reverence for the King's uniform or to indulge an overweening vanity; he was rather concerned that his elegance of figure should neither exceed nor fall short of a definitely demarcated and prescribed correctness, and he had actually been a little flattered when once some ladies expressed the opinion, which was well grounded, that the straight, wooden cut of the uniform and the glaring colours of the bright cloth went but indifferently with his face, and that the brown-velvet jacket and flowing necktie of an artist would suit him far better. The fact that in spite of this the uniform meant much more to him may be explained by the obstinacy which he inherited from his mother, who always stuck immovably to a custom once formed. And sometimes it seemed that for him there could never be any other attire, although he was still full of resentment at his mother for submitting herself without a struggle to Uncle Bernhard's opinions. And now, of course, it had all been decided, and if one has been accustomed to wear a uniform from one's tenth year, sooner or later it grows into one's flesh like the shirt of Nessus, and no one, and least of all Joachim von Pasenow, will be able to specify then where the frontier between his self and his uniform lies. For even if his military vocation had not grown into him, as he into it, his uniform would still have been the symbol for many things; in the course of years he had fattened and rounded it with so many ideas that, securely enclosed in it, he could no longer live without it; enclosed and cut off from the world and the house of his father in such security and peace that he could scarce distinguish, scarce notice, that his uniform left him only a thin strip of personal and human freedom no broader than the narrow strip of starched cuff which was all that an officer was allowed to show. He did not like to put on mufti, and he was glad that his uniform protected him from visits to questionable resorts, where he pictured the civilian Bertrand in the company of loose women. For often he was overcome with the uncanny fear that he too might slip into the same inexplicable rut as Bertrand. And that also was why he bore a grudge against his father for his having to accompany him, and in mufti at that, on the obligatory round of the Berlin night haunts with which ended, in accordance with tradition, the old man's visits to the capital of the Empire.

When next day Joachim escorted his father to the train the latter said: " Well, as soon as you're a captain, and that won't be long now, we'll have to think of finding a wife for you. How about Elisabeth? The Baddensens have a nice little property over there at Lestow, and it will all go to the girl some day." Joachim said nothing. Yesterday he almost bought me a girl for fifty marks, he thought, and to-day he is trying to arrange a legitimate engagement. Or had the old man himself some hankerings after Elisabeth, as after the other girl, whose fingers Joachim could still feel on the back of his neck? But it was incredible to him that anyone at all should dare to think of Elisabeth with sensual desire, and still more incredible that any man should want to incite his son to violate a saint because he was unable to do it himself. Joachim almost felt like asking his father's pardon for the monstrous suspicion; but

really the old man was capable of anything. Yes, it was one's duty to
protect all the women in the world from this old man, Joachim thought
as they were walking along the platform, and while he saluted the departing train he was still thinking it. But when the train had disappeared
his thoughts returned to Ruzena.

And in the evening he was still thinking of Ruzena. There are evenings
in spring when the twilight lasts far longer than the astronomically prescribed period. Then a thin smoky mist sinks over the city and gives it
the subdued suspense of evenings preceding a holiday. And at the same
time it is as if this subdued, pale grey mist had netted so much light
that brighter strands remain in it even when it has become quite black and
velvety. So these twilights last very long, so long that the proprietors
of shops forget to close them; they stand gossiping with their acquaint-
ances before the doors, until a passing policeman smilingly draws their
attention to the fact that they are exceeding the regulation closing-time.
And even then a beam of light shines from many a shop, for in the back
room the family are sitting at their supper; they have not put up the
shutters as usual in front of the door, but only placed a chair there to
show that customers cannot be served; and when they have finished their
supper they will come out, bringing their chairs with them, and take their
ease before the shop-door. They are enviable, the small shopkeepers and
tradespeople who live behind their shops, enviable in winter when
they put up the heavy shutters so as to enjoy doubly the warmth and
security of the lighted room, through whose glass door at Christmas-
time the glittering Christmas-tree can be seen from the shop; enviable
in the mild spring and autumn evenings when, holding a cat, or stroking
the soft head of a dog, they sit before their doors as on a terraced garden.

Returning from the barracks Joachim walked through the streets of the
suburb. It was not fitting for one of his rank to do this, and the officers
always drove home in the regimental carriages. Nobody ever went walking here—even Bertrand would not have thought of it—and the fact that
he himself was doing so now was as disturbing to Joachim as if he had
made a false step. Was it not almost as if in doing so he were humiliating
himself for Ruzena's sake? Or was it an indirect humiliation of Ruzena?
For in his fantasy she now occupied quite definitely a suburban flat,
perhaps that very cellar-like little shop before whose dark entry greens
and vegetables were spread for purchase; and perhaps it was Ruzena's
mother who squatted in front of it, knitting and talking in her dark

foreign speech. He smelt the smoky odour of paraffin lamps. In the low
vaulted cellar a light shone out. It came from a lamp fixed into the dingy
wall at the back. He felt he could almost sit there himself with Ruzena
before the cellar, her hand ruffling his hair. But he was startled when
he became conscious of this thought, and to drive it away he tried to
imagine that over Lestow the same light grey dusk was settling. And in
the park, silent under the mist and already fragrant with dewy herbs,
he saw Elisabeth; she was walking slowly towards the house, from whose
windows the soft light of the paraffin lamps shone out into the falling
dusk, and her little dog was there too, and it, too, seemed to be tired
after the day. But as he thought more intently and intimately it was
Ruzena and himself that he saw on the terrace in front of the house, and
Ruzena's caressing hand was resting on the back of his head.

It went without saying that in those beautiful spring days one was in
good spirits, and that business was flourishing. Bertrand, who had been
in Berlin for a few days, felt this too. Yet in his heart he knew his good
spirits came simply from the success which, for years now, had followed
all his transactions, and conversely that his good spirits were needed to
bring about further success. It was like a propitious gliding with the
current, and instead of himself making towards the things he wanted
he saw them come floating towards him. Perhaps this had been one of
the reasons why he had left the regiment: there were so many things
which invited him and from which at that time he was excluded. What
did the brass plates of banks, solicitors and export firms mean to him
then? They were only empty words at which one did not look, or which
disturbed one. Now he knew a great number of things about banks,
knew what took place behind the counter, yes, understood not only all
that was connoted by the inscriptions discount, foreign exchange, deposits,
and so on, but knew also what went on in the directors' offices, could
size up a bank by its deposits and its reserves, and draw lively conclusions
from a fluctuation in shares. He understood such export terms as transit
and bonded warehouse, and all this had come very natural to him, had
become as matter of course as the brass plate in the Steinweg in Hamburg:
Eduard von Bertrand, Cotton Importer." And the fact that now a
similar plate could be seen in the Rolandstrasse in Bremen and the
Cotton Exchange in Liverpool actually gave him a feeling of pride.
When in Unter den Linden he met Pasenow, angular in his long

military coat with the epaulets, his very shoulders angular, while he himself was comfortably clad in a suit of English cloth, he felt quite elated, greeted Pasenow airily and familiarly as he always greeted his old comrades, and asked him without further ado if he had lunched yet and if he would come with him to Dressel's.

Taken aback by the sudden encounter and the quick cordiality, Pasenow forgot how much he had been thinking of Bertrand these last few days; once more he felt ashamed to be talking in his spick-and-span uniform to a man who stood before him naked, as it were, in mufti, and he would have been glad to evade the invitation. But all that he found himself saying was that it was a terribly long time since he had seen Bertrand. Oh, considering the monotonous and settled life he led that wasn't surprising, replied Bertrand. To himself, on the contrary, always harried and on the move as he was, it seemed only yesterday that they had worn their swords for the first time in Unter den Linden and had their first supper at Dressel's—by this time they had entered—and yet they had grown older meanwhile. Pasenow thought: " He talks too much," but because it pleased him to think that Bertrand possessed obnoxious qualities, or because he vaguely felt that his friend's previous taciturnity had always mortified him—in spite of his horror of being indiscreet he asked where Bertrand had been all this time. Bertrand made a slight deprecatory gesture with his hand as if he were dismissing something quite unimportant: " Oh, lots of places. I'm just back from America." Hm, America—for Joachim America was still the country where unruly or disinherited or degenerate sons were sent, and old von Bertrand must have died of grief after all! But again this thought did not seem to fit the assured and obviously prosperous man who sat opposite him. Of course Pasenow had heard often of such ne'er-do-wells working their way up over there as farmers and then returning to Germany to look for a German bride, and perhaps this fellow had come to fetch Ruzena; but no, she wasn't German but Czech, or rather, for that was the proper term, Bohemian. Yet, as the idea still stuck in his mind, he asked: " And you're going back again ? " " No, not immediately, I must go to India first." A mere adventurer, in fact! And Pasenow cast a glance round the restaurant, feeling embarrassed to be sitting there with an adventurer; yet there was nothing else for it but to see it through: " So you're always travelling, then ? " " Oh, it's only on business that I travel—but I like travelling about. Of course a man should always do

what his demon drives him to." And with that the cat was out of the
bag; now he knew; Bertrand had quitted the service simply to go into
business, from mere greed, mere avarice. But, thick-skinned as these
profiteers always were, Bertrand did not feel his contempt and went on
without embarrassment: " Look here, Pasenow! It's more and more
incomprehensible to me how you can stick it out here. Why don't you
at least report for colonial service, seeing that the country has provided
that amusement for you? " Pasenow and his comrades had never bothered
themselves about the colonial problem: that was the preserve of the navy;
all the same he felt indignant: " Amusement? " Bertrand had once more
that ironical curl to his lips: " Well, what else is there in it? A little
private amusement and glory for the soldiers immediately concerned.
All honour, of course, to Dr Peters, and if he had appeared earlier I
should certainly have been with him, but what other elements are there
except pure romanticism? It's romantic from every point of view—
except for the activities of the Catholic and Protestant missions, of course,
who are doing sober and useful work. But as for the rest—a joke, nothing
but a joke." He spoke so disdainfully that Pasenow was honestly indignant, but what he said sounded merely as if he were offended: " Why
should we Germans fall behind the other countries? " " I'll tell you
something, Pasenow: first, England is England; second, even in England
every day isn't a holiday; third, I shall always invest my spare capital
in English colonies rather than in German; so, you see, even from a
business point of view it's romantic for us to have colonies; and fourthly,
as I said before, it's only the Church that ever has a real palpable interest
in colonial expansion." Joachim von Pasenow's mortified admiration
grew, and along with it the suspicion that this Bertrand fellow was trying
to blind him and dupe him and lead him into a trap by his enigmatic
and conceited generalizations. In some way all this went with Bertrand's
hair, which was quite unmilitary, indeed almost curly. It was theatrical
in some way. The words, " the pit," " the bottomless pit," came into
Joachim's mind: why did this man keep on talking of religion and the
Church? But before he could gather himself together to reply Bertrand
had already noticed his astonishment: " Yes, you see, Europe has already
become a pretty dubious field for the Church. But Africa, on the other
hand! Hundreds of millions of souls as raw material for the Faith. And
you can rest assured that a baptized negro is a better Christian than
twenty Europeans. If the Catholics and the Protestants want to steal a

march on each other for the winning of these fanatics it's very understandable; for there's where the future of their religion lies; there will be found the future warriors of the faith who will march out one day, burning and slaying in Christ's name, against a heathen Europe sunk in corruption, to set at last, amid the smoking ruins of Rome, a black Pope on the throne of Peter." That's like Revelation, thought Pasenow; he's blaspheming now. And what did the souls of negroes matter to him? Slave-dealing had surely been abolished, although a man obsessed by greed for filthy lucre might even be capable of that. And Bertrand had just been talking of his demon. But perhaps he had only been joking; even in the cadet school one had never known when Bertrand was serious. " You're joking! And as for the Spahis and Turcos, we've settled with them for good." Bertrand could not but smile, and he smiled so winningly and frankly that Joachim too could not keep himself from smiling. So they smiled frankly at each other and their souls nodded to each other through the windows of their eyes, just for an instant, like two neighbours who have never greeted each other and now happen to lean out of their windows at the same moment, pleased and embarrassed by this unforeseen and simultaneous greeting. Convention rescued them out of their embarrassment, and lifting his glass Bertrand said: " Prosit, Pasenow! " and Pasenow replied: " Prosit, Bertrand! " whereupon they had both to smile again.

When they left the restaurant and were standing in Unter den Linden under the somewhat parched, motionless trees in the hot light of the afternoon sun, Pasenow remembered the reply which he had been too shy to utter when they were having lunch: " I really can't understand what quarrel you have with the faith of us Europeans. It seems to me that you people who live in cities don't have the proper understanding for that. When one has grown up in the country, like myself, one has quite a different attitude to these things. And our peasants out there are far more closely bound to religion than you seem to think." In saying this to Bertrand's face he felt somehow daring, like a subaltern trying to explain what strategy was to a Staff officer, and he was a little afraid lest Bertrand should take it badly. But Bertrand only replied cheerfully: " Well, then, probably everything will turn out splendidly after all." And then they exchanged addresses and promised that they would remain in touch with each other.

Pasenow took a droshky and drove out to the west end to the races.

The Rhine wine, the afternoon heat, and perhaps also the strangeness of his encounter, had left behind his forehead and at the back of his temples —he would have dearly liked to take off his stiff cap—a dark, flawed feeling, reminding him of the leather seat he was sitting on, which he was prodding with his gloved finger-tips; it was actually a little sticky, so hotly did the sun burn upon it. He was sorry he had not invited Bertrand to go with him, but he was glad at least that his father was no longer in Berlin, for he would certainly have been sitting there beside him. Yet on the other hand he was sincerely glad not to have Bertrand accompanying him in his civilian clothes. But perhaps Bertrand wanted to give him a surprise and had called for Ruzena now, and they would all meet at the races again. Like a family. But of course that was all nonsense. Not even Bertrand would show himself at the races with a girl like that.

When a few days later Leindorff, one of Joachim's fellow-officers, received a visit from his father, to Pasenow it was like a sign from heaven bidding him go to the Jäger Casino and be there before old Leindorff, whom he already saw mounting the narrow stairs with an undeviating, bustling air. He drove to his flat in the regimental carriage and put on his civilian clothes. Then he set out. At the corner he met two soldiers; he was about to bring up his hand perfunctorily to his cap in reply to their salute, when he noticed that they had not saluted him at all, and realised that instead of his cap he was wearing his top-hat. All this was somehow comic and he could not help smiling, because it was so absurd to think that old Count Leindorff, half paralysed as he was, thinking of nothing but his consultations with his doctors, should visit the Jäger Casino that evening. Probably the wisest thing would be simply to turn back, but as he could do that at any time he liked, he enjoyed the slight feeling of freedom this gave him and went on. Yet he would rather have gone for a stroll in the suburbs to see again the little cellar-like greengrocery-shop and the smoking paraffin lamp; but of course he really could not parade in the northern suburbs in his frock-coat and top-hat. Out there the twilight would probably be again as magical as on that other evening, but here in the actual centre of the city everything seemed hostile to Nature: above the noisy light and the innumerable shop-windows and the animated life of the streets, even the sky and the air seemed so urban and unfamiliar that it was like a fortunate and reassuring, yet disconcerting, rediscovery of familiar things when he found a little linen-shop, in whose narrow window lace, ruches and half-finished hand-worked embroideries picked out in blue were lying, and saw a glass door at the back which obviously led to a living-room. Behind the counter a white-haired woman—she seemed almost a lady—was sitting, and beside her was a young girl whose face he could not see; both of them were busied with hand-work. He examined the wares in the window and wondered whether it might not please Ruzena to present her with a few of those lace handkerchiefs. But this too seemed to him absurd, so he walked on, but at the first corner turned and went back again, driven by his desire to see the averted face of the girl. He bought three flimsy handkerchiefs without really deciding to give them to Ruzena, quite haphazardly, simply to please the old lady by buying something. The girl's looks, however, were indifferent; indeed she actually looked cross. Then he went home.

In winter during the Court festivities, to which without admitting it the Baroness looked forward, and in spring during the races and the summer shopping, the Baddensen family occupied a trim house in the west end, and one Sunday morning Joachim von Pasenow paid the ladies his duty call. It was seldom that he visited this outlying villa suburb, an imitation of the English model which was spreading rapidly, although only rich families accustomed to a permanent equipage could live here without being keenly aware of the disadvantage of its distance from the city. But for those privileged persons who could afford to qualify this spatial disadvantage the place was a little rustic paradise, and walking through the trim streets between the villas Pasenow was pleasantly and delight-fully penetrated by a sense of the superiority of the neighbourhood. During the last few days he had become uncertain about many things, and this in some inexplicable way was connected with Bertrand; some pillar or other of life had become shaky, and though everything still remained in its old place, because the parts reciprocally supported each other, yet along with a vague wish that the vaulted arch of this equilibrium might cave in and entomb beneath it all that was tottering and uncertain, a fear had arisen at the same time that the wish might really be fulfilled, and there had grown within him a longing for per-manence, security and peace. Well, this comfortable neighbourhood with its castellar edifices in the most excellent Renaissance, Baroque and Swiss

styles, surrounded by carefully tended gardens in which one could hear
the scrape of gardeners' rakes, the hiss of garden hoses and the splashing
of fountains; all this breathed out a great and insular security, so that one
could not really believe in Bertrand's dictum that even in England every
day was not a holiday. From open windows rang out *études* by Stephen
Heller and Clementi: the daughters of these families could devote themselves to their pianos in complete security: theirs was a safe and gentle
existence, filled with friendship until friendship should give place to
love and love once more die away into friendship. Far off, but not too
far off, a cock crowed as if he too wished to indicate the rusticity of this
well-planned suburb: yes, if Bertrand had grown up on the land he would
not be spreading insecurity, and had they allowed Joachim himself to
stay at home he wouldn't have been so susceptible to this feeling of
insecurity. It would be lovely to walk with Elisabeth through the fields,
and take the ears of the ripening corn between one's expert fingers, and
in the evenings, when the heavy odour of the byre was carried on the
wind, to cross the neatly swept yard and look on while the cows were
being milked. Elisabeth would stand there among the great rustical
beasts, far too slight for the ponderousness of her surroundings, and
what in his mother had seemed merely natural and homely would be
in her both homely and touching. But for him it was much too late for
all that, for him whom they had made an outcast, and he was—now the
thought struck him—as homeless as Bertrand.

And now the fold of the garden, whose railings were concealed by
hedges, enclosed him. The security of nature here was still further
enhanced by the fact that the Baroness had had one of the plush sofas
from the drawing-room brought out into the garden: it stood there like
something exotic reared in a hot-house, with its turned legs and swivelled
feet resting on the gravel, lauding the friendliness of a climate and a
civilized nature which permitted it such a station; its hue was a fading
damask rose. Elisabeth and Joachim sat on iron garden-chairs, whose
metal seats were pierced with stars like frozen Brussels lace.

After they had exhausted the excellences of the neighbourhood, which
were bound to appeal particularly to one accustomed to and fond of
country ways, Joachim was asked about his life in the town, and he
could not help expressing his longing for the country and trying to
justify it. He found that the ladies completely agreed with him; the
Baroness in particular assured him again and again that—he mustn't be

surprised—but often for days, yes, even for weeks, she never went into the centre of the town, so terrified, yes, terrified, was she of the hubbub, the noise and the tremendous traffic. Well, replied Pasenow, here she had a real haven, and the conversation flowed again for some time round the theme of the superior neighbourhood, until the Baroness, as if she had a delightful surprise in store, informed him almost with an air of secrecy that they had been offered the chance of buying the little house which they had come to love so much. And in the anticipatory joy of possession she invited him to look through the house, to make a *tour du propriétaire*, she added ironically and with a slight touch of embarrassment.

As usual the reception-rooms lay on the ground floor and the bedrooms upstairs. Yes, in the dining-room, which with its carved old German furniture breathed out an oppressive comfort, they were going to make a winter-garden with a fountain, and perhaps transform the drawing-room too. Then they climbed the stairs, at the top and the bottom of which were velvet hangings, and the Baroness went on opening door after door, passing over only the more intimate ones. Hesitatingly and with a slight blush Elisabeth's room was revealed to the masculine eye, but even the cloud of white lace with which her bed, window, washing-table and mirror were hung did not fill Joachim with such a painful and ashamed feeling as the bedroom of her parents; indeed he could almost have reproached the Baroness for making him free of the household and compelling him to be a co-witness of her shame. For now, before his eyes, before everybody's eyes, plainly displayed even before Elisabeth, whom he felt such knowledge confounded and violated, the two beds stood side by side, ready for the sexual uses of the Baroness, whom he now suddenly saw before him, not indeed naked, but unladylike and brazen: here was the double bedchamber, and now in a flash it seemed to him the central point of the house, its hidden and yet obviously visible altar, round which all the other rooms were built. And in the same flash he saw clearly that every house in the long row of villas which he had passed had as its central point a similar bedroom, and that the sonatinas and the *études* sent out through the open windows, behind which the spring breeze softly waved the lace curtains, were only intended to veil the actual facts. So everywhere towards evening the beds of the master and mistress were decked with the sheets that were folded with such hypocritical glossiness in the linen-room, and the servants and the children knew why this was done;

everywhere the maids and the children slept, chaste and unpaired, round the coupled central point of the house, they chaste and pure, yet at the service and command of the unchaste and the shameless. How had the Baroness dared, when she was lauding the advantages of the neighbourhood, to include among these the nearness of the church? Should not she enter it with humility, and as it were barefoot? Perhaps this was what Bertrand had meant when he spoke of the unchristian age, and it became intelligible to Joachim that the black warriors of God must fall on this abomination with fire and sword, so as again to restore true chastity and Christlikeness. He looked across at Elisabeth and thought he read from her glance that she shared his indignation. And that she should be fated to the same desecration, that indeed he himself should be the man chosen to perform that act of desecration, filled him with such compassion that he longed to steal her away, simply that he might watch before her door, so that undisturbed and unviolated she might dream for ever in a dream of white lace.

Affably conducted back to the ground floor by the ladies, he parted from them with the promise to return soon. In the street he became aware of the emptiness of his visit; he thought how dismayed the ladies would be if they heard Bertrand talking, and he actually wished that they could hear him for once.

When a man has adopted the habit of not noticing his fellow-creatures —in consequence perhaps of the caste-like seclusion of his life, and of a certain slowness in emotional reaction—he is bound to be surprised at himself if his eye should be attracted and held by two strange young men standing talking together near him. This is what happened to Joachim one evening in the foyer of the Opera House. The two gentlemen were obviously foreigners and not much over twenty; he was inclined to take them for Italians, not merely because of the cut of their clothes which was a little unusual, but because one of them, a black-eyed and black-haired fellow, wore an upward-curling Italian moustache. And although it went against Joachim's grain to listen to the conversation of strangers, he perceived that they were employing a foreign language which was not Italian, and he felt constrained to listen more carefully, until with a slight sensation of alarm he thought he could tell that they were speaking Czech, or more correctly, Bohemian. His alarm was quite unfounded, and still more unfounded seemed to him the feeling of infidelity to Elisabeth which supervened on it. Of course it was possible, if also unlikely, that Ruzena might be in the audience and that these two young men might presently visit her in her box, as he himself had often visited Elisabeth in hers; and perhaps there was really a resemblance between Ruzena and the young man with the little black moustache and the far too curly black head, and not merely in the colour of their hair; probably it was the slightly too small mouth and the lips which stood out too vividly from the olive face, the nose, too short and delicately chiselled, and the smile which was in some way challenging—yes, challenging was the right word—and nevertheless seemed to be asking for forgiveness.

Yet all this seemed preposterous, and it might well be that the resemblance was only a fancy of his; for when he thought of Ruzena now he had to admit to himself that her image had completely faded, indeed that he would not recognize her if he met her again in the street, and that he could see her only through the medium and in the mask of this young man. That reassured him and made the incident in some way safe, but without giving him any feeling of satisfaction, for at the same time and in some other layer of his mind he felt that it was somehow dreadful and unspeakable for the girl to be concealed behind the mask of a man, and even after the interval he could not rid himself of this feeling. They were presenting Gounod's *Faust*, and even the sugary harmonies seemed to him not so fatuous as the operatic convention on the stage, where no one, not even Faust himself, noticed that in the beloved lineaments of Margaret those of Valentine lay concealed, and that it was for this, and this alone, that Margaret had to suffer. Perhaps Mephistopheles knew it, and Joachim was glad that Elisabeth had no brothers. When after the performance he again ran into Ruzena's brother, he was thankful that now the sister too was set beyond his reach, and he felt so sure of himself that, in spite of his uniform, he turned in the direction of Jägerstrasse. And the feeling of infidelity, too, was gone.

It was only when he turned into Friedrichstrasse that he became conscious that he could not visit the casino in his uniform. He was disappointed and continued to walk along Jägerstrasse. What should he do? He turned round the next corner, came back to Jägerstrasse again, and caught himself peeping under the hats of passing girls, often half expecting to hear a few words of Italian. But when he was again approaching the Jäger Casino the voice he heard was not Italian, but hard and staccato. " But you not know me any more? " " Ruzena," Pasenow said reluctantly and thought at the same time: How painful! There he was standing in the open street in his uniform with this girl, he who only a few days ago had been ashamed of being seen with Bertrand in his civilian clothes, and instead of going away he was, forgetting all convention, almost happy, yes, completely happy, simply because the girl was going on talking: " Where is papa to-night? He comes not to-night? " She shouldn't have reminded him of his father: " No, nothing doing to-night, little Ruzena: the "—what had she called him?—" the old gentleman isn't coming to-night either." . . . Yes, and now he must hurry away. Ruzena gazed at him in dismay: " So long keep me waiting and now not . . ." But, and her face cleared, he must pay her a visit. He gazed into her apprehensively questioning face as if he wished to print it finally on his mind, but seeking at the same time to discover if her southern brother with the curled moustache was hidden in it. There was some resemblance; but while he was wondering whether a girl who bore her brother in her face could be anything to him, he remembered his own brother, fair-haired and masculine with his short beard, and that brought him back to actuality. Of course that was different; Helmuth was a country gentleman, a huntsman, and had nothing in common with those soft southern people; and yet it was a reassurance. His eyes still searched her face, but his aversion faded and he felt a need to do her a kindness, to say something comforting to her, so that she might cherish a happy memory of him; he still hesitated; no, he would not visit her, but . . . " But? " the word sounded anxious and expectant. Joachim himself did not know at first what was to follow the " but," and then he suddenly knew: " We could meet somewhere and have lunch together." Yes, yes, yes, yes; she knew a little place: to-morrow! No, it couldn't be to-morrow, but on Wednesday he had leave, and they arranged to meet on Wednesday. Then she stood on the tips of her toes and whispered into his ear: " You're good, nice man," and ran away, and vanished through the door over which the gas-jets were burning. Pasenow saw his father bustling up the stairs with his quick and purposive tread, and his heart contracted perceptibly and very painfully.

Ruzena was enchanted by the conventionally stiff courtesy with which Joachim had treated her in the restaurant, and in her delight she even forgot her disappointment that he had appeared in mufti. It was a cool, rainy day; yet she did not want to give up her programme, and so after lunch they had driven out through Charlottenburg to the Havel. Already in the droshky Ruzena had pulled off one of Joachim's gloves, and now, as they went along the river-path, she took his arm and pushed it under hers. They went slowly, walking through a landscape expectant in its stillness, and yet which had nothing to expect save the rain and the evening. The sky hung softly over it, sometimes united indissolubly to the earth by a veil of rain, and for them too, wandering through the stillness, there seemed to be nothing left but expectation, and it was as though all the life in them had flowed to their fingers, which, clasped and folded in upon each other, slept like the petals of an unopened bud. Shoulder leaning against shoulder, from the distance resembling the two sides of a triangle, they walked along the river-path in silence, for neither knew what it was that drew them together. But quite unexpectedly while they were walking along Ruzena bent over his hand, which lay in hers, and kissed it before he could draw it away. He looked into eyes that were swimming with tears, and at lips that twitched with sobs, yet managed to say: " When you meet me on stairs I say, Ruzena, I say, he not for you, never for you. And now you here. . . ." But she did not reach up her mouth for the expected kiss, but fell again, almost greedily, on his hand, and when he tried to free it, bit into it with her teeth, not sharply, but as gently and cautiously as a little dog playing: then looking at the mark contentedly she said: " Now let us walk on again. Rain matters not." The rain sank quietly into the river, and rustled softly on the leaves of the willows. A boat lay half-sunk near the bank; under a little wooden bridge a runnel poured more rapidly into the placid flow of the river, and Joachim too felt himself being floated away, as though the longing which filled him were a soft, light out-flowing of his heart, a breathing flood longing to be merged in the breath of his beloved, and to be lost as in an ocean of immeasurable peace. It was as though the summer were dissolving, so that the very water seemed light, rustling from the leaves, and hanging on the grasses in clear drops. A soft misty veil rose in the distance, and when they turned round it had closed them in behind, so that in walking they seemed to be standing still. When the rain came on more violently they sought the protection of the trees, beneath which the ground was still dry, a patch of unreleased summer dust almost pitiable in the release of everything

around. Ruzena pulled out her hat-pins, not only because their constraint
irked her, but also to protect Joachim from their sharp points, took off
her hat, and leant her back against him as if he were a protective tree.
She had bent back her head, and when he sank his, his lips touched her
brow and the dark curls that framed it. He did not see the faint and
slightly stupid furrows on her forehead, perhaps because he was too
near to distinguish them, perhaps because seeing had melted completely
into feeling. But she felt his arms round her, his hands in hers, felt as
if she were among the branches of a tree, and his breath on her brow
was like the rustling of the rain on the leaves; so motionless did they
stand, and so at one was the grey sky with the level waters, that the
willows on the little island seemed to float as in a grey insubstantial sea,
hanging or resting there, one did not know which. But then she looked
at the wet sleeve of her coat and whispered softly that they must turn
back.

Yet though now the rain beat on their faces, they dared not hasten,
for that would have dispelled the charm, and they only became sure of
themselves again when they were drinking coffee in the little inn. Now
the rain ran faster and faster down the panes of the rustic veranda, and
splashed thinly from the gutters. Whenever the landlady left the room
Ruzena set down her cup, took his out of his hand, and seizing his head
drew it quite close to hers, so close—and they had not yet kissed—that
their glances melted together, and the tension was quite unendurable in
its sweetness. But when, as in a dark cave, they sat in the droshky under
the covered roof with the rain-flaps let down, the faint soft drumming
of the raindrops on the stretched leather above them, seeing nothing
of the world save the coachman's cape and two wet grey strips of roadway through the opening on either side, and soon not even seeing that,
then their faces bowed towards each other, met, and melted together,
dreaming and flowing like the river, lost irrecoverably, and ever found
again, and again sunk timelessly. It was a kiss that lasted for an hour
and fourteen minutes. Then the droshky stopped before Ruzena's door.
Yet when he made to enter with her she shook her head, and he turned
to go; but the pain of parting from her was so great that after a few
steps he turned back, and driven by his own dread and drawn by hers,
seized her hand, which was still motionlessly outstretched in longing; and
as if already dreaming they ascended like sleepwalkers the dark stairs,
which creaked under their feet, crossed the dark entrance-room, and in

her bedroom, which lay in the gloom of the early rainy twilight, sank on the dark rug that covered the bed, seeking once more the kiss from which they had been torn, their faces wet with rain or with tears, they did not know which. But then Ruzena freed herself and guided his hands to the fastenings that held her dress at the back, and her singing voice was dark. " Open that," she whispered, tearing at the same time at his necktie and the buttons of his vest. And as if in sudden, precipitate humility, whether towards him or towards God, who can say, she fell on her knees, her head against the foot of the bed, and quickly unfastened his shoes. Oh, how terrible that was—for why should they not sink down together, forgetting the casings in which they were held? —and yet how grateful he was to her that she made it easier, and so touchingly; oh, the deliverance of the smile with which she threw open the bed into which they flung themselves. But the sharp-cornered starched plastron of his shirt, cutting against her chin, still irked her, and opening it and squeezing her face between the sharp angles she ordered: " Put that off "; and now they felt release and freedom, felt the softness of their bodies, felt their breathing stifled by the urgency of emotion, and their delight rising up out of their dread. Oh, dread of life streaming from the living flesh with which the bones are clothed, softness of the skin spread and stretched over it, dreadful warning of the skeleton and the many-ribbed breast frame which he can now embrace, and which, breathing, now presses against him, its heart beating against his. Oh, sweet fragrance of the flesh, humid exhalation, soft runnels beneath the breasts, darkness of the armpits. But still Joachim was too confused, still they were both too confused, to know the delight they felt; they knew only that they were together and yet that they must still seek each other. In the darkness he saw Ruzena's face, but it seemed to be flowing away, flowing between the dark banks of her hair, and he had to put out his hand to touch it and assure himself that it was there; he found her brow and her eyelids beneath which the hard eyeballs rested, found the satisfying curve of her cheeks and the line of her mouth opened for his kiss. Wave beat against wave of longing; drawn by the flood his kiss found hers; and while the willows of the river grew up and up, stretching from bank to bank, enclosing them as in a sacred grotto in whose profound peace the security of the eternal sea slumbers, it was—so faintly did he say it, stifled and no longer breathing, but only seeking for her breath—it was like a cry that she heard: " I love you "; and she opened, like a shell in the sea she opened, and he sank drowning into her.

Without warning the news reached him that his brother was dead. He had fallen in a duel with a Polish land proprietor. Had it happened a few weeks before Joachim might not have been so shaken. In the twenty years which he had spent away from home the image of his brother had faded more and more, and when he thought of him he saw only the fair-haired lad in his boy's suit—they had always been dressed alike until Joachim had been sent into the cadet school—and even now the first thing that came into his mind was a child's coffin. Yet immediately, side by side with it, rose Helmuth's masculine blond-bearded form, the same form which had come to him that evening in the Jägerstrasse when he had been afraid that he saw something more in a girl's face than was there: oh, then the clear eyes of the huntsman had rescued him from the nightmare into which another had wished to draw and entangle him, and those eyes which had been lent him then Helmuth had closed now for ever, perhaps in order that he himself might have them always. Had he required this of Helmuth? He had no feeling of guilt, yet it was as if his brother's death had come about for his sake; yes, as if he had been the cause of it. Strange that Helmuth had worn Uncle Bernhard's beard, the same short beard which left the mouth free; and now it seemed to Joachim that he had always held Helmuth respon-sible for the cadet school and his military career, and not Uncle Bernhard who was really to blame. Still, Helmuth had been allowed to stay at home, and besides he had played the hypocrite—that was probably the explanation; yet all this was very confusing, and the more so because Joachim had known for a long time now that his brother's life was not enviable. He saw the child's coffin before him again, and a feeling of bitterness against his father rose up in him. So the old man had succeeded at last in driving his other son out of the house too. It gave him an acrid feeling of relief to throw the responsibility for his brother's death on his father.

He returned to Stolpin for the funeral. When he arrived a letter from Helmuth was awaiting him: " I don't know whether I shall come alive out of this rather unnecessary affair. Naturally I hope so; still it is almost a matter of indifference to me. I recognize that there is something called a code of honour which in this shoddy life gives a hint of some higher idea to which one may submit oneself. I hope that you have found more value in your life than I have found in mine. I have often envied you your military career; in the army one serves at least something greater than oneself. I don't know, of course, how you think about it, but I'm writing you to warn you (in case I should fall) not to give up your career for the sake of taking over the estate. You'll have to do that sooner or later of course, but as long as father is alive it would be better, all things considered, for you to stay away, unless mother should need you. I send you lots of good wishes." Here followed a varied list of instructions for Joachim to carry out, and at the end, somewhat unexpectedly, the wish that he might be less lonely than Helmuth had been.

His parents were remarkably collected, his mother no less than his father. His father gripped his hand and said: " He died for honour, for the honour of his name," and with his sharp, purposive stride walked in silence from end to end of the room. Soon he repeated again: " He died for honour," and went out through the door.

They had laid the coffin in the big drawing-room. In the antechamber Joachim already could smell the heavy perfume of the flowers and wreaths: too heavy for a child's coffin—a stubborn and meaningless thought—and yet he remained hesitating within the heavily curtained door, and did not dare to look across, but stared at the floor. The floor he knew well, knew the triangular parquet which bordered the threshold, knew the recurring pattern that ran across the room, and when he followed it with his eyes, as he had often done as a child picking his steps along the geometrical figures, his glance reached the black cloth spread under the bier. A few leaves, fallen from the wreaths, were lying there. He had a longing to walk along the pattern again, took a few steps, and looked at the coffin. It was not a child's coffin, and that was good; but he still shrank from looking with his own seeing eyes into those dead ones, into eyes which must be so completely quenched that the face of the boy would be drowned in them, perhaps drawing himself after it, the brother to whom those eyes had now been given; and the fancy that he himself was lying there grew so strong that it was like a release and piece of good fortune when, stepping nearer, he saw that the coffin was covered. Someone said that the dead man's face had been mutilated by the bullet. He hardly listened to this, but remained standing beside the coffin, his hand resting on the lid. And seized by the impotence that overcomes human beings in the presence of the dead and the silence of death, where all accepted things recede and fall away, where the long familiar breaks and falls and is frozen in its fall, where the air becomes thin and incapable of supporting one, it seemed to him that he would never be able to move from his station beside the bier, and it caused him a great effort to remember that this was the big drawing-room, and that the coffin was standing in the place usually occupied by the piano, and that behind it there must be a strip of parquet never yet walked on; he went slowly over and touched the black-draped wall, felt under the gloomy hangings the picture-frames and the frame of the case where the Iron Cross hung, and this refound fragment of actuality transformed death in a novel and almost exciting way into a matter of drapery, accommodating almost cheerfully the fact that Helmuth in his coffin, decked with all his flowers, had been introduced into this room like a new piece of furniture, thus once more reducing the incomprehensible so radically to the comprehensible, the certain and assured, that the experience of those few minutes—or had it been only seconds?—passed over into a soothing feeling of quiet confidence. His father appeared accompanied by several gentlemen, and Joachim heard him once more saying repeatedly: " He died for honour." But when the gentlemen had left and Joachim thought he was alone, suddenly he heard again: " He died for honour," and saw his father, small and forlorn, standing beside the bier. He felt it his duty to go up to him. " Come, father," he said, leading him away. At the door his father looked into his face and said: " He died for honour," as if he wished to learn the words by heart, and wished Joachim also to do so.

Then a great number of people arrived. The village fire brigade were standing in the yard. The neighbouring military associations also put in an appearance, making an orderly show of top-hats and frock-coats on which not infrequently an Iron Cross was to be seen. Carriages from the houses in the vicinity drove up, and while the vehicles were being directed to a place where they could remain in the shade, Joachim had to greet the visitors and do the honours beside his brother's coffin. Baron von Baddensen arrived alone, for his wife and daughter were still in Berlin, and as Joachim greeted him he was seized by the thought, angrily dismissed at once, that this gentleman might well now regard the only remaining son at Stolpin as a desirable son-in-law, and he felt ashamed for Elisabeth. From the gable of the house a black flag hung motionlessly, almost reaching down to the terrace.

His mother descended the stairs on his father's arm. The visitors were astonished at her calmness, indeed admired her. But her calmness was probably due simply to the slowness of feeling that characterized her. The funeral procession formed up, and as the carriages turned into the village street, and the house of God lay before them, everyone was heartily glad that they could now step out of the dust and heat of the afternoon sun, which had burned fiercely on their thick mourning-suits and uniforms, into the cool white church. The pastor gave an address in which the quality of honour was much stressed and by adroit turns linked with the honour that is due to God: to the pealing of the organ their voices rose, acknowledging that from our loved ones we must part . . . with pain and smart, and Joachim kept waiting for the rhyme to see that it came. Then on foot they proceeded to the cemetery, over whose portal glittered in golden letters: " Rest in Peace," and the equipages followed slowly in a long-stretching cloud of dust. The sunny sky arched, a violet-blue, over the dry, crumbling earth that was wait-ing for them to give Helmuth's body into its keeping; though indeed it was not the earth, but only the family vault, a little open cellar, that was yawning as if in boredom for the newcomer. When Joachim had three times emptied the little spade into the hole he looked down, saw the ends of his grandfather's and his uncle's coffins, and thought that it was because they had to keep a place for his father that they had not buried Uncle Bernhard here. But then as the shovelled earth fell on the lid of Helmuth's coffin and the stony sides of the tomb, standing there with the toy shovel in his hand he could not help thinking of days spent as a child in the soft river-sand, and he saw his brother again as a boy, saw himself lying on the bier, and it seemed to him that the dryness of this summer day was cheating Helmuth not only out of his parents, but out of death itself. For Joachim thought of a soft rainy day for his own death, a day in which the heavens themselves would sink to receive his soul, so that it might flow away as in Ruzena's arms. Unchaste thoughts, out of place here, but it was not he alone who was responsible for them, but all the others to whom now he gave place at the graveside, yes, even his father shared in the blame for them: for all their religion was a sham, was brittle and dusty and at the mercy of the sun and the rain. Could one not almost wish for the negro host, so that they might sweep all this away, and the Saviour might arise in new glory and lead men back to His kingdom? A Christ hung on the marble

cross over the tomb, clothed only with the rag that covered His loins
and the crown of thorns from which the bronze blood-drops fell, and
Joachim too felt drops on his cheeks; perhaps they were tears that he
had not noticed, perhaps however it was only the oppressive heat; he
did not know, and went on shaking the hands that were held out to him.

The military associations and the fire brigade had accorded the
dead man the last honour of a march past and a sharp leftward turn
of their heads; their boots rang sharply on the gravel of the path, and
four abreast they marched stiffly out through the cemetery gates to
the curt, military commands of their officer. Standing on the steps of
the family vault, Herr von Pasenow with his hat in his hand, Joachim
with his hand to his cap, Frau von Pasenow between them, they acknowledged the march past. The other soldiers present stood at attention
with their hands raised in salute. Thereupon the equipages advanced,
and Joachim and his parents stepped into their carriage, whose door-
handle and other silver furnishings, no less than the silver of the harness,
had been carefully covered with *crêpe* by the coachman; Joachim
assured himself that the very whip had been decorated with a *crêpe*
rosette. Now his mother was crying, and Joachim, who could think of
nothing to say to comfort her, once more could not comprehend why it
should have been Helmuth, and not himself, who had been hit by the
fatal bullet. But his father sat stiffly on the black-leather seat, which was
not hard and tattered like the seats of the Berlin droshkies, but flexible
and well quilted with leather buttons. Several times his father seemed
on the point of saying something, something to sum up the line of
thought that obviously occupied and completely absorbed him, for he
made as if to speak, but then fell into blank silence again, only moving
his lips soundlessly; at last he said sharply: "They have accorded him
the last honours," lifted one finger as if he were waiting for something
more, or wished to add something, then laid his hand back palm
downwards on his knee again. Between the end of his black glove and
his cuff with its great black cuff-link a strip of reddish-haired skin
was visible.

The next few days passed in silence. Frau von Pasenow went about
her business; she was in the byre at milking time, in the hen-house
when the eggs were collected, in the laundry. Joachim rode out a few
times into the fields; it was the horse that he had given to Helmuth,

THE ROMANTIC   39

and to take it out now was like a service of love to the dead. At evening
the yard was swept and the servants sat on the benches before their
wing enjoying the soft, cool breeze. Once during the night there was a
thunderstorm, and Joachim realized with alarm that he had almost forgotten Ruzena. He had seen little of his father, who sat for the most
part in his study reading the letters of condolence or registering them
in a book. The pastor, who now arrived every day, often staying for
dinner, was the only one who spoke of the dead, but as he brought out
only a sort of professional platitudes they were but little regarded, and
his only listener seemed to be Herr von Pasenow, for he now and then
nodded his head and seemed on the point of saying something that lay
very urgently on his mind; but he always finished merely by repeating
the pastor's last few words with a nod to emphasize them, as for instance:
" Ay, ay, Herr Pastor, sorely tried parents."

Then Joachim had to leave for Berlin. When he went to say good-bye
to his father the old man began again to march up and down. Joachim
remembered countless similar good-byes in this room which he disliked
so much, well as he knew it, with the hunt trophies on the walls, the
spittoon in the corner beside the stove, the writing equipment on the
desk, which probably had stood as it was now since his grandfather's
time, the pile of sport journals on the table, most of them uncut. He
waited for his father to stick his monocle in his eye as usual and dismiss
him with a curt: " Well, a pleasant journey, Joachim." But this time
his father said nothing, but only continued to walk up and down, his
hands behind his back, so that Joachim got up a second time. " Really,
father, I must be going now, or I'll miss my train." " Well, a pleasant
journey, Joachim," the accustomed reply came at last, " but there's
something I want to say to you. I'm afraid you'll have to come here for
good soon. The place has become empty, yes, empty . . ." he looked
round him . . . " but some people don't see that . . . of course one must
maintain one's honour . . ." he had begun his walk again, then, con-
fidentially: " And what about Elisabeth? We spoke about it before. . . ."
" Father, it's high time I was away," said Joachim, " else I'll lose my
train." The old man held out his hand, and Joachim took it unwillingly.

As he drove through the village he saw from the church clock that he
was still in ample time for the train; indeed he had known that before.
The church door chancing to be open, he ordered the coachman to
stop. He had an offence to wipe off, an offence against the church which

had been merely a pleasantly cool place to him, against the pastor to
whose well-meaning words he had not listened, against Helmuth whose
burial he had dishonoured with profane thoughts; in a word, an offence
against God. He entered and tried to recapture the feelings which as
a child had been his when every Sunday he had stood here as before
the face of God. At that time he had known a great number of hymns,
and had sung them with ardour. But it would hardly do for him to
begin singing now quite by himself, in the church. He must confine
himself to assembling his thoughts and concentrating them on God and
his own sinfulness, his littleness and wretchedness before God. But his
thoughts refused to seek God. The only thing that came into his mind
was a sentence from Isaiah which he had once heard in this place:
" The ox knoweth his owner, and the ass his master's crib: but Israel
doth not know, my people doth not consider." Yes, Bertrand was right,
they had lost their faith; and now he tried to say the Lord's Prayer
with closed eyes, being careful not to utter a single word emptily, but
to grasp the meaning of each; and when he came to the words, " as
we forgive our debtors," the tender, apprehensive and yet trustful
feelings of his childhood rose in him again; he remembered that he
had always applied this passage to his father and from it had drawn
the confidence that he would be able to forgive his father, yes, to
feel all the love towards him which it was the duty of a child to feel;
and now he remembered again that the old man had spoken of his
loneliness, of which he was visibly afraid, and which one must make
lighter for him. As Joachim left the church the words " uplifted and
strengthened " came into his mind, and they did not seem empty to
him, but full of new and encouraging meaning. He resolved to visit
Elisabeth.

In the carriage the phrase arose in his mind again, again he thought
" uplifted and strengthened," but now it was associated with the image
of a starched [1] shirt-front and the joyful expectation of seeing Ruzena
again.

II

A pedestrian was coming from the direction of Königstrasse. He was
corpulent and square-built, indeed actually squat, and everything about
him was so extraordinarily soft that one might have fancied that he was

[1] In German the same word serves for " strengthened " and " starched."

poured into his clothes every morning. He was a serious pedestrian, he
wore a grey-lustre coat over his trousers of black cloth, and his chest
was covered with a brown beard. He was obviously in a hurry, yet his
walk was not rapid and undeviating, but a sort of purposive waddle
such as suited a soft-bodied purposive man who was in a hurry. But it
was not only the beard that concealed his face; he wore eyeglasses as
well, through which he shot severe glances at the passers-by; and it was
literally impossible to picture to oneself that a man like this, waddling
with such haste in pursuit of some urgent business and shooting out
such sharp and severe glances in spite of his soft appearance, was
probably a kind and affectionate fellow in some other sphere of his
existence, and that there must be women to whom he unbent in love,
women and children to whom the beard uncovered a kindly smile,
women who might dare to seek in a kiss the rosy lips in their dark-
bearded cave.

When Joachim caught sight of this man he had mechanically followed
him. It did not matter to him in any case where he went. Since he
had learned that Bertrand had a Berlin agent for his firm, and that the
office was in one of the streets between the Alexanderplatz and the
Stock Exchange, he had sometimes felt drawn to this neighbourhood
as formerly he had felt drawn to the working-class suburb—and the fact
that he no longer had any need to look for Ruzena out there was almost
like a promotion for her. But he did not come here, all the same, on the
chance of meeting Bertrand: on the contrary he avoided the place whenever he knew Bertrand was in Berlin, nor indeed had he any interest in
Bertrand's agent. It was simply so strange to him that these should be
the surroundings in which one had to picture Bertrand's real life; and
when he walked through those streets it sometimes happened that he
not only scrutinized the fronts of the houses, as if to discover what
offices were concealed behind them, but even peeped under the hats
of the civilians as if they were women. Sometimes he wondered at
this himself, for he was unaware that he searched these faces to discover whether their existence was so totally different from his own, and
whether they could give him a clue to any qualities that Bertrand might
have adopted from them, but still kept concealed. Yes, the secrecy of
this life of theirs was so complete that they did not even need beards
to hide themselves behind. Indeed they would have looked a little more
confidential and less hypocritical to him if they had worn beards, and

this may have been one of the reasons why he sauntered in the wake
of the fat, hurrying man. Suddenly it seemed to him that the man in
front of him fitted very strangely the picture he had always had of
Bertrand's agent. It was silly, perhaps, but when several passers-by
greeted the man Joachim was quite delighted that Bertrand's agent
should enjoy so much respect. He would not have been excessively
surprised if Bertrand himself, melodramatically transformed, small and
corpulent and full-bearded, had waddled up to him: for why should
Bertrand have preserved his former external appearance, seeing that he
had slipped into a different world? And even though Joachim knew
that what he thought was without sense or sequence, yet it was as though
the apparently confused skein concealed a sequence: one had only to
disentangle the threads which bound Ruzena to these people and find
this deeper and very secret knot—and perhaps an end of one thread had
lain in his hand that time when he had divined Bertrand as Ruzena's
real lover; but now his hand was empty, and all that he had to go on
was that Bertrand had once excused himself on the plea that he had to
spend the evening with a business friend, and Joachim could not rid
himself of the idea that this man had been the business friend. Probably
they had both gone to the Jäger Casino, and the man had stuck a fifty-
mark note into Ruzena's hand.

When a man follows another in the street, even if it is only mechanically and with ostensible indifference, he will soon find himself attaching
all sorts of wishes, benevolent and malevolent, to the man he is following.
Probably he will want at least to see the man's face and wish that
he should turn round, even though since his brother's death he has
thought himself invulnerable against the temptation to seek in every
half-feared face the face of his mistress. In any case there is nothing to
explain why the sudden thought should have come to Joachim that the
erect bearing of all the people here in this street was quite unjustified,
that it was incompatible with their better knowledge, or due merely to
an abysmal unawareness that some time all their bodies would have to
stretch themselves out in death. And yet the walk of the man in front
was not in the least sharp, rapid or headlong, nor was there any fear
that he might fall and break one of his legs, for he was far too soft for
that to happen.

Now the man had stopped at the corner of Rochstrasse as if he
were waiting for something; it was possible that he was waiting to get

the fifty marks back from Joachim. And Joachim was really in honour bound to give them back, and suddenly he felt a hot rush of shame at the thought that, for fear lest people might think he kept a paid woman, or because if he stopped to reflect on it he might begin to doubt Ruzena's love, he had left her in her old hateful employment; and it was as if the scales had fallen from his eyes: he, a Prussian officer, was the secret lover of a woman who accepted money from other men. An offence against honour could be wiped out only by a pistol bullet, yet before he could think this out, with all its dreadful consequences, the know-ledge swam up, swam up like an image of Bertrand, that the man was crossing Rochstrasse and that Joachim must not let him out of sight until he . . . yes, until he . . . that was not so easy to get right. Bertrand had it easy; he belonged to this world and the other as well, and Ruzena too had a foot in each world. Was that the reason why they by rights belonged to each other? But now his thoughts jostled each other like the people in the crowd round about him, and even though he saw a goal in front of him which he wanted them to reach, it swam and wavered and was lost to view like the back of the fat man before him. If he had stolen Ruzena from her legitimate possessor, then it was perhaps fitting that he should keep her hidden now as his stolen property. He tried to maintain a stiff and erect bearing, and no longer to look at the civilians. The dense crowd around him, the hubbub, as the Baroness called it, all this commercial turmoil full of faces and backs, seemed to him a soft, gliding, dissolving mass which one could not lay hold on. What did it all lead to? And with a jerk regaining his prescribed military bearing, he suddenly thought with relief that one could love only some-one who belonged to an alien world. That was why he would never dare to love Elisabeth, and also why Ruzena had to be a Bohemian. Love meant to take refuge from one's own world in another's, and so in spite of his jealousy and shame he had left Ruzena in her world, so that her flight to him should be ever sweet and new. The garrison band was playing a little in front of him, and he held himself still more stiffly, as stiffly as when he attended church parade on Sundays. At the corner of Spandauerstrasse the man slowed down and hesitated at the edge of the thoroughfare; evidently a business man like this was afraid of the horses in the roadway. It was of course silly, the idea that he must refund money to this man; but Ruzena must be taken out of the casino, that was definite. In any case she would always remain a Bohemian, a being out of another world. But where did he fit in himself? Whither was he sliding? And Bertrand? Again Bertrand rose before him, astonishingly soft and small, glancing severely through his eyeglasses, strange to Joachim, strange to Ruzena who was a Bohemian, strange to Elisabeth who walked in a still park, strange to them all, and yet familiar when he turned round and the beard parted in a friendly smile, inciting women to kiss the dark cave where his mouth was concealed. His hand on his sword-hilt, Joachim remained standing as if the nearness of the garrison band provided him with protection and new strength against the Evil One. Bertrand's image arose, iridescent, uncanny. It emerged and vanished again: " vanished in the labyrinth of the city," the words came back to Joachim, and " labyrinth " had a diabolically underworld ring. Bertrand was concealed in all those shapes, and he had betrayed everybody: Joachim, his fellow-officers, the women, everybody. But now he noticed that Bertrand's representative had crossed Spandauerstrasse in good style at a sharp trot. Joachim thought with relief that henceforth he would keep Ruzena out of reach of them both. No, he could not be accused of stealing Ruzena; on the contrary it was his duty to protect Elisabeth as well from Bertrand. Oh, he knew, the Devil was full of wiles. But a soldier must never fly. If he fled he would deliver Elisabeth defencelessly to that man, he would himself be one of those who hid in the labyrinth of the city and were afraid of the horses' hoofs; and it would be not only an avowal of his guilt as a thief, it would mean also the renunciation for ever of his attempt to tear from that man the secret of his treachery. He must follow him farther, yet not surreptitiously like a spy, but openly as was fitting; and he would not keep Ruzena concealed either. So in the middle of the Stock Exchange quarter, though admittedly in the vicinity of the garrison band too, everything suddenly grew quiet round Joachim von Pasenow, as quiet and transparent as the clear blue sky which looked down between the two rows of buildings.

He had now a somewhat vague, yet urgent, wish to catch up the man and tell him that he was going to take Ruzena out of the casino and from now on make no secret about her; but he had taken only a few steps when he saw the other waddling hastily into the Stock Exchange. For a moment Joachim remained staring at the entrance: was this the place of metamorphosis? Would Bertrand himself come out now? He considered whether he should take Bertrand at once to meet Ruzena, and decided no: for Bertrand belonged to the world of the night clubs, and it was from that very world that he must now rescue Ruzena. But that would come all right; and how lovely it would be to forget all about it and wander with Ruzena in a still park beside a still lake. He stood still in front of the Stock Exchange. He longed for the country. The traffic roared round him; above him thundered the trains. He no longer stared at the passers-by, even though he felt that they were foreign and strange. He would avoid this neighbourhood in future. In the midst of the hubbub round the Stock Exchange Joachim von Pasenow held himself stiff and erect. He would be very good to Ruzena.

Bertrand paid him a visit of condolence, and Joachim was again not quite clear whether to regard this as considerate or presumptuous: one could take it as the one or the other. Bertrand remembered Helmuth, who had visited Culm occasionally, though seldom enough, and his memory was extraordinarily exact: "Yes, a fair, quiet youth, very reserved . . . I fancy he envied us . . . he couldn't have changed much later either . . . and he resembled you." That, now, was just a little too familiar again, almost as if Bertrand wished to exploit Helmuth's death for his own advantage; however, it was no wonder if Bertrand remembered all that had to do with his former military career with such astonishing exactitude: one liked to recall happy times that one had lost. Yet Bertrand did not speak at all in a sentimental way, but quietly and soberly, so that Helmuth's death assumed a more human and natural aspect, and in some way, under Bertrand's touch, became objective, timeless and endurable. To his brother's duel Joachim had not really devoted much thought; all the opinions that had been pronounced on it and the comments recurring again and again in the letters of condolence pointed in the same direction: that Helmuth had been tragically caught by the unalterable fatality of his sense of honour, from which there was no escape. Bertrand however began:

"The most extraordinary thing is that we live in a world of machinery and railways, and that at the same time as the railways are running and the factories working two people can stand opposite each other and shoot at each other."

Bertrand had no sense of honour left, Joachim told himself, and yet his remarks seemed natural and illuminating. But Bertrand went on:

" That may be, of course, because it's a question of sentiment."

" The sentiment of honour," said Joachim.

" Yes, honour and so forth."

Joachim looked up—was Bertrand laughing at him again? He would have liked to reply that one must not judge such things merely from the standpoint of the city man; out there in the country people's feelings were less artificial and meant more. Really Bertrand did not know anything about it. But of course one could not say such things to one's guest, and Joachim silently held out his cigar-case. But Bertrand drew his English pipe and leather tobacco-pouch from his pocket:

" It's extraordinary that it should be the most superficial and perishable things that are actually the most persistent. Physically a human being can adapt himself with incredible quickness to new conditions of life. But even his skin and the colour of his hair are more persistent than his bony structure."

Joachim regarded Bertrand's fair skin and far too wavy hair and waited to see where all this was going to lead.

Bertrand noticed at once that he had not made himself clear enough:

" Well, the most persistent things in us are, let us say, our so-called feelings. We carry an indestructible fund of conservatism about with us. I mean our feelings, or rather conventions of feeling, for actually they aren't living feelings, but atavisms."

" So you consider that conservative principles are atavistic? "

" Oh, sometimes, but not always. However, I wasn't really thinking of them. What I meant was that our feelings always lag half-a-century or a full century behind our actual lives. One's feelings are always less human than the society one lives in. Just consider that a Lessing or a Voltaire accepted without question the fact that in their time men were still broken on the wheel—a thing that to us with our feelings is unimaginable. And do you imagine that we are in a different case? "

Well, Joachim had never bothered his head over such things. Perhaps Bertrand was right. But why was he saying all this to him? He was talking like a writer for the newspapers.

Bertrand went on:

" We take it quite as a matter of course that two men, both of them honourable—for your brother would not have fought with a man who was not honourable—should of a morning stand and shoot at each other.

And the fact that we put up with such a thing, and that they do it, shows how completely imprisoned we all are in conventional feeling. But feelings are inert, and that's why they're so cruel. The world is ruled by the inertia of feeling."

The inertia of feeling! Joachim was struck by the phrase: was he not himself full of inertia, was it not a criminal inertia that had prevented him from summoning enough imagination to provide Ruzena with money in spite of her objections, and to take her out of the casino? He asked in alarm:

" Do you actually describe honour as inertia of feeling? "

" Oh, Pasenow, you ask too embarrassing questions." Bertrand had assumed again the winning smile with which he always bridged over differences of opinion. " It seems to me that honour is a very living feeling, but none the less all obsolete forms are full of inertia, and one has to be very tired oneself to give oneself over to a dead and romantic convention of feeling. One has to be in despair and see no way out before one can do that. . . ."

Yes, Helmuth had been tired. But what did Bertrand want? How was one to rid oneself of convention? With dismay Joachim saw the danger that like Bertrand one might begin to let everything slide if one began to transgress convention. Certainly in his connection with Ruzena he had already slipped through convention in the strict sense, but now he must not go any further, and honour itself demanded that he should be true to Ruzena! Perhaps Helmuth had vaguely surmised this when he warned him against returning to the estate. For then Ruzena would be lost. So he asked abruptly: " What do you think of the state of German agriculture? " almost hoping that Bertrand, who always had practical reasons for what he said, would also warn him against taking over the estate.

" Hard to say, Pasenow, especially for anyone who knows so little about agriculture as myself. . . . Of course we still have the feudal prejudice that, as we all live on God's earth, those who cultivate it have the most stable existence." Bertrand made a slightly disdainful gesture, and Joachim von Pasenow felt disappointed, yet relieved as well, at the thought that he belonged to this favoured caste, while Bertrand's insecure business existence was only, as it were, a preliminary step to a more stable life. Apparently he regretted after all that he had quitted the regiment; as an officer in the Guards he could easily have married an

estate. But that was a reflection worthy of his father himself, and Joachim
dismissed it and merely asked whether Bertrand intended to adopt a
settled life later on. No, Bertrand thought he would hardly be able to
do that now: he wasn't a man who could endure living in one place for
very long. And then they talked about Stolpin and the shooting there,
and Joachim invited Bertrand to come down for the shooting in autumn.
And suddenly the door-bell rang: Ruzena! Joachim thought, and he
looked at Bertrand almost with hostility. Bertrand had been sitting there
now for two hours, drinking tea and smoking, and his visit could no
longer, by any stretch, be called a mere visit of condolence. Yet at the
same time Joachim had to admit that it had been himself who had
pointed to the armchair and produced the cigars and induced Bertrand
to stay, although he should have known that Ruzena would be certain to
come. Of course now that the thing had happened there was no turning
back: naturally it would have been more in order if he had consulted
Ruzena first. She would probably feel put out, probably she herself
desired the secrecy which he was now preparing to infringe, perhaps in
her simple goodness she wished to avoid any chance of her disgracing
him—perhaps, indeed, she wasn't quite equal to social occasions; but
he was no longer capable of judging that, for when he tried to call up
her image all that he saw was her face and her loosened hair on the
pillow beside him. He remembered the fragrance of her body, but could
hardly tell any longer how she looked when she was dressed. Well,
after all Bertrand was a civilian, and himself wore his hair too long,
and so it could not matter very much to him. So Joachim said: " Look
here, Bertrand, I'm just having a visit from a nice girl; may I invite
you to have supper with us? " " How romantic! " replied Bertrand; of
course he would be delighted if he was not in the way.

Joachim went out to greet Ruzena and prepare her for the news.
She was visibly disconcerted to find a stranger present. But she was
amiable to Bertrand, and Bertrand was amiable to her. Joachim indeed
was displeased by the assumption of friendliness with which they treated
each other. It was decided that they should dine at home; the valet was
sent out for ham and wine, and Ruzena ran after him; he was to bring
apple-tarts and cream too. She was delighted to be allowed to preside
in the kitchen and make potato-puffs. A little later she called Joachim
out to the kitchen; he thought at first that she only wanted to show
herself in her huge white apron, the cooking-spoon in her hand, and

was preparing to appreciate this touching picture of housewifely loveli-
ness; but she was leaning against the kitchen door sobbing; it was almost
like another occasion when as a little boy he had gone to the great
kitchen to seek his mother, and one of the maids—probably she had just
been given notice—was sobbing so bitterly that he longed to cry with
her, but was restrained by a feeling of shame. " Now you not love me
no more," Ruzena sobbed on his shoulder, and although they kissed
each other more passionately than ever, she would not be comforted.
" Is finished, I know, is finished . . ." she kept on repeating, " but go
back now, must cook." She dried her tears and smiled. But he went
back unwillingly, and it was unwillingly that he thought of Bertrand in
the other room; of course it was childish of her, childish to think that
their love was finished simply because of Bertrand, yet nevertheless it
was real feminine instinct, yes, real feminine instinct, one couldn't call
it anything else, and Joachim felt suddenly dejected. For even though
Bertrand in his cynical way received him with the words, " She's
charming," and awakened in him the grateful pride of King Candaules,
the menacing thought remained unshaken: if he went back to Stolpin
Ruzena would be lost to him, and then it would all be over. If
Bertrand had only dissuaded him at least from having anything to
do with agriculture! Or did Bertrand want—and perhaps even against
his own convictions—to force him into a country life simply to get
him out of Berlin and then win Ruzena, whom in spite of everything
he probably regarded as his legitimate property? But that was
unthinkable.

Ruzena, followed by the valet, entered with the big tray. She had
taken off her apron, and sitting between the two men at the little round
table played the grand lady, and in her sing-song, staccato voice made
conversation with Bertrand, whom she encouraged to talk of his travels.
The two windows were standing open, but in spite of the dark summer
night outside, the soft paraffin lamp over the table reminded Joachim
of winter and Christmas and the security of the little living-rooms
behind the shops. How strange that he should have forgotten all about
the lace handkerchiefs which, in a fit of vague longing, he had bought
for Ruzena that evening! They were still lying in the chest of drawers,
and he would give them to her now if Bertrand were not here and if
she were not listening so intently to those stories about the cotton
plantations and the poor negroes whose fathers were still slaves—yes,

really, actual slaves whom one could sell. What? Were the girls sold too? Ruzena shuddered and Bertrand laughed, laughed easily and pleasantly: " Oh, you mustn't be afraid, little slave-girl, nothing will happen to you." Why did Bertrand say that? Was he hinting at buying Ruzena or getting her as a gift? Joachim could not but think of the resemblance between slave and Slav and reflected that all negroes were alike, so that one could hardly tell one from another, and it seemed to him again that Bertrand was trying to entangle him in a maze and to remind him that Ruzena could not be distinguished from her Italian-Slav brother. Was that why Bertrand had conjured up the picture of the black hordes? But Bertrand was only smiling at him, and he was fair, almost as fair as Helmuth, though without the beard, and his hair was wavy, far too wavy, instead of being brushed stiffly back; and for a moment everything was confused again and one did not know to whom Ruzena belonged by rights. If the bullet had found him instead of his brother, then Helmuth would have been sitting here in his place, and Helmuth would also have had the strength to protect Elisabeth. Perhaps Ruzena would have been a little beneath Helmuth; all the same he himself was nothing more than his brother's deputy. Joachim was dismayed when this became clear to him, dismayed at the thought that one individual could deputize for another, that Bertrand should have a soft little bearded deputy, and that from this standpoint even his father's ideas were excusable: for why Ruzena in particular, why himself in particular? why not Elisabeth when it came to that? it was all indifferent in some way or other, and he understood the feeling of weariness that had driven Helmuth to his death. Even if Ruzena was right and their love was nearing its end, yet now suddenly everything had receded to a great distance in which Ruzena's face and Bertrand's could scarcely be told from each other. The convention of feeling, Bertrand had called it.

Ruzena, on the other hand, seemed to have forgotten her gloomy prophecies. She had felt for Joachim's hand under the table, and when in panic good breeding, and with a side-glance at Bertrand, he had found safety for it on the open publicity of the brightly lit tablecloth, Ruzena seized it again and fondled it; and Joachim, once more happy in that possessive caress, overcame his shame with a slight effort and held her hand in his, so that it could be seen quite publicly that they belonged by right to each other. And besides they were not doing anything wrong; for in the Bible it said that when a brother died without leaving children his wife must not marry a stranger, but must take the brother of her dead husband. Yes, it had been something like that anyway, and it was absurd to think that he could betray Helmuth with a woman. But then Bertrand tapped on his glass and proposed a little toast, and once more one did not know whether he intended it seriously or whether he was joking or whether the few glasses of champagne had been already too much for him, so extraordinarily difficult to understand was his speech; in which he spoke of the German housewife, who was most charming when she was an imitation housewife, for play was the true reality of this life, for which reason art was always more beautiful than nature, peasant costume better at a ball than in a village, and the home of a German soldier complete only when, escaping from its accustomed austerity, although violated, no doubt, by the presence of a traditionless man of business, it was at the same time consecrated by the presence of the loveliest of Bohemian ladies; and so he asked the company to drink to the health of their beautiful hostess. Yes, that was all somewhat obscure and insidious, and one could not rightly tell whether all this play on the idea of *imitation* might not mean much the same as he himself had meant by deputizing; but as Bertrand continued to gaze at Ruzena very kindly in spite of the somewhat ironical expression round his lips, one knew that it was intended as a compliment to her and that one could dismiss all those puzzling thoughts; and the supper finished in a mood of general and pleasant gaiety.

Later they insisted on accompanying Bertrand to his lodgings, partly perhaps because they did not wish it to be too obvious that Ruzena was spending the night with Joachim. Ruzena in the middle, they walked through the quiet streets, all three separately, for Joachim did not dare to offer his arm to her. When Bertrand had disappeared behind the door of his lodgings they looked at each other, and Ruzena asked very seriously and humbly: " Will you see me to the casino? " He noticed the sadness and seriousness in her voice, but he felt in response only a weary indifference, and almost found himself replying as seriously in the affirmative, and could at that moment have said good-bye for ever to her; and if Bertrand had come back to lead her away Joachim could even have borne that. Nevertheless the thought of the casino was unendurable. And ashamed that he needed such a spur, yet almost glad of it too, he took her arm in silence. That night they loved each

other more passionately than ever. Nevertheless Joachim forgot this
time also to give Ruzena her lace handkerchiefs.

Every day when the little one-horse mail-van returned from the train
and drew up at the village post office, a messenger from the estate was
already leaning against the counter; true, he was only a private messenger,
yet he belonged to the post office and had himself become an official in
a sense, perhaps indeed with a superior status to the two actual officials
there, not however because of any personal qualifications, even though
he might have grown grey in service, but simply because he came from
the big house and his dignity was a prescriptive fact which had already
existed for many decades, and certainly reached back to the time when
there was not yet any State postal service, nothing but a post-chaise that
drove infrequently through the village and left the letters at the inn.
The great black post-bag whose straps had worn a diagonal stripe across
the shoulders of the servant's coat had survived many messengers, and
certainly it too must have dated from that long-dead and perhaps
happier time; for even the oldest man in the village could remember
since his earliest childhood the post-bag hanging on its hook and
the messenger leaning against the counter; and by interrogating their
memory the old people could count up all the estate messengers
who had gaily taken the road with the diagonal stripe on their jackets
and were now all resting in the churchyard. So the post-bag was
older and more venerable than the new-fashioned post office which had
been opened after 1848, that stormy year, older than the hook which,
as a mark of respect for the post-bag, or as a final act of official homage
to the people at the big house, had been hammered in there when the
post office was opened, fixed there also, perhaps, as a reminder that in
spite of the violence of progress old customs were not to be forgotten.
For in the new post office the old custom of giving preference to the
letters for the big house was still maintained, and is probably maintained
to this day. So when the coachman came in with the greyish brown
mail-bag, and with that disdainful gesture which expresses an ordinary
coachman's attitude to mail-bags threw it on the worn counter, the
postmaster, who knew better the respect due to human and official
customs, unloosed with scarcely concealed solemnity the seal and the
fastenings, and arranged the confusion of packets in little piles according to their size, so as to look through them and separate them more

expeditiously: then, all this having been accomplished in good order, the first thing that he did was always to put on one side the letters for the big house, and, before attending to anything else, to take a key from his desk and walk over to the post-bag hanging on its hook with its metal-plated mouth silently contemplating this procedure; then, inserting the key in the middle of the metal plate, he threw open the bag, which gaped at him, shamelessly showing its grey-canvas lining, and hurriedly, as if he could no longer endure the sight of that gaping canvas maw, he slipped in the letters and newspapers and also the smaller packets, gave the lower jaw of the bag a little push so that it snapped shut, turned the key again, and put it back in his desk. But now the messenger, who till then had remained a mere spectator, lifted up the heavy post-bag, slung it by its hard, worn strap over his shoulders, took the bigger parcels in his hand, and in this way brought the mail one or two hours sooner to the big house than the postman, who had to traverse the whole village first, could have done; a remarkably expeditious method which ensured that, by means of the messenger and the post-bag, an old tradition was continued, and also the practical needs of the gentry and the servants on the estate well looked after.

Joachim now received news from his home oftener than before; for the most part his father sent him curt accounts of what was happening in a sloping, running hand which reminded one so strongly of his walk that it, too, might actually be called three-legged. Joachim was informed of the visits that his parents had received, the shooting and harvest prospects, also a few particulars about the state of the crops; and generally the letters ended with the sentence: " It would be advisable for you to make preparations as soon as possible for returning here, for it is preferable that you should work yourself in sooner rather than later, and everything takes time.—Your loving Father." Joachim still felt his old dislike for this handwriting, and he read these letters with a more exacerbated inattention than usual, for each admonition that he should quit the service and return to his home was like an attempt to drag him down into a civilian and insecure existence, pretty much, indeed, as if one were to rob him of his uniform and fling him naked into the Alexanderplatz, so that all those strange and busy people could rub shoulders with him. Well, let them call it inertia of feeling;

all the same he wasn't a coward, and he would face calmly the revolver of an opponent, or march out gladly against the traditional enemy, France; but the dangers of a civilian life were of a more obscure and incomprehensible kind. Chaos and disorder everywhere, without a hierarchy, without discipline, and, yes, even without punctuality. When on his way from his flat to the barracks he passed Borsig's machine factory at the start or the finish of the day's work, and saw the workers standing before the factory gates like an exotic, dun-coloured race, much the same as the people of Bohemia, he was aware of their sinister looks, and when one or the other tugged at a black-leather cap in greeting, he never dared to respond, for he was afraid of branding the friendly workmen as turncoats, as men who had come over to his side. For he felt that those who hated him were justified, perhaps partly because he divined that they would hate Bertrand, in spite of his civilian clothes, no less than himself. There was something of that too lurking in Ruzena's aversion to Bertrand. All this was disturbing and confusing, and to Joachim it was as though his ship had sprung a leak which people were urging him to widen. But what seemed completely absurd to him was his father's demand that he should quit the service for Elisabeth's sake; for if there was one thing that could make a man worthy of her it was the distinction of being superior, in outward attire at least, to all the impurity and disorder of life; to rob him of his uniform, therefore, was to degrade Elisabeth. So he pushed aside as an importunate and dangerous exaction all thought of a civilian life or a life at home, yet to avoid flat disobedience to his father he appeared at the station with a bouquet of flowers when Elisabeth and her mother left for their summer stay at Lestow.

The conductor in front of the waiting train stood at attention when he caught sight of Joachim, and there was a silent understanding between the two men, an understanding in the eye of the trusty subordinate that he was to look after the ladies of his superior. And although it was a slight violation of good manners to leave the Baroness alone in her carriage, where she was installed with her maid and her luggage, yet when Elisabeth expressed a wish to walk along the train until the bell rang Joachim felt that it was a friendly mark of distinction. They walked up and down on the firmly trampled soil between the lines, and when they passed the open door of the carriage Joachim did not omit to glance up with a slight bow, while the Baroness smiled down at him.

Elisabeth said how much she was looking forward to being home again, and that she absolutely counted on seeing him often at Lestow during his furlough, which of course he would spend as usual—and this sad year especially—with his parents. She was wearing a short English travelling suit of light grey cloth, and the blue travelling veil which covered her little hat went well with the colour of her costume. It was almost a matter of surprise to him that a creature who always seemed so thoughtful should be able to summon the trifling interest, the frivolous taste, necessary to choose advantageous clothes, particularly as he guessed that the grey of the costume and the blue of the veil had probably been selected to suit the colour of her eyes, which alternated between a serious grey and a merry blue. But it was difficult to put this thought into words, and so Joachim was glad when the bell signalled and the conductor asked the passengers to take their places. Elisabeth put her foot on the foot-board, and by adroitly half-turning her body to continue her conversation with Joachim avoided providing the horrid spectacle of a lady bent forward clambering into her compartment; yet when she reached the top step it could no longer be helped, and she stooped resolutely through the low door. Now Joachim was standing beside the train with his face raised towards her, and the thought of his father whom he had looked up to in the same place not so long ago got entangled so strangely with his glimpse of the tails of Elisabeth's grey jacket and the marriage project which his father had hinted at in such unsavoury terms, that the very name of this girl with the grey-blue eyes and the grey jacket, though he saw her physically above him in the carriage-door, suddenly seemed irrelevant and, as it were, effaced from his memory, submerged horribly and surprisingly in his amazed indignation that there should be men like his father who in their depravity had the brazenness to apportion a pure creature like this for her lifetime to some man who would both humiliate and desecrate her. But clearly as he had recognized her as a woman at the moment of her resolute entry into the carriage, he painfully recognized at the same moment that he could not expect from her the sweetness of his nights with Ruzena, neither their glowing passion, nor their twilight dreaminess, but a serious, perhaps religious submission, unimaginable to him not only because it had to happen without either travelling costume or uniform, but also because the comparison with Ruzena, whom he had rescued from men's degrading lusts, seemed almost a blasphemy. But already the bell had rung a third time, and while he stood on the platform saluting them the ladies fluttered their lace handkerchiefs, until at last only two white dots could be seen, and a thread of tender longing detached itself from Joachim's heart and stretched and span its way to the white dots at the very last moment, before they vanished in the distance.

Saluted stiffly by the porter and the staff, he left the station and stepped out into the Küstrinerplatz. The square looked empty and a little unkempt, gloomy too, although it was still penetrated by the sun, a kind of borrowed sun, while the real one was shining outside on the golden fields. And if this reminded him, in a way very difficult to understand, of Ruzena, yet it was true that Ruzena, full as she was of the sun, yet dark and a little unkempt, was as closely akin to Berlin as Elisabeth was to the fields through which she was travelling now, and to her father's house standing in its park. There was an orderly satisfaction in coming to this conclusion. Nevertheless he was glad that he had rescued Ruzena from her obscure occupation with its false glitter, glad that he was about to free her from the tangle of threads which stretched over this whole city, from this net which he felt everywhere, in the Alexanderplatz and in the dingy machine factory and in the suburb with the little greengrocer's shop, an impenetrable, incomprehensible net of civilian values which was invisible and yet darkened everything. He must deliver Ruzena from these entanglements, for here too he had to prove himself worthy of Elisabeth. But this was only a very vague thought, a thought which moreover he had no wish to make clear, probably because it would have seemed absurd even to himself.

Eduard von Bertrand, who found himself in a position to extend his industrial commitments in Bohemia, suddenly remembered Ruzena in Prague, felt a sort of homesickness for her, and wished he could say something kind to comfort her. And as he did not know her address he wrote to Pasenow, saying that in grateful recollection of their last meeting he hoped to meet him again when he stopped at Berlin on his way back to Hamburg, and added his kindest regards to Ruzena, praising up her beautiful country. Then he took a stroll through the town.

After the evening when Bertrand and Ruzena had met, Pasenow had expected something unexpected and solemn, something perhaps even dreadful, to happen; for example that Bertrand might repay in the same coin the privilege and confidence into which he had been admitted that evening, though an abduction of Ruzena also did not lie beyond the sphere of possibility; for business men were conscienceless. But when neither the one thing nor the other happened, and Bertrand simply departed according to programme, not even sending a line, Joachim actually felt hurt. Then quite unexpectedly came the letter from Prague; he showed it to Ruzena and said hesitatingly: " You seem to have made an impression on Bertrand." Ruzena made a grimace: " Not care. Not like your friend; he's ugly man." Joachim defended Bertrand, saying that he wasn't ugly. " Not know: not like him: says such things," Ruzena decided, " mustn't come again." Joachim was very well pleased by her words, though he felt urgently in need of Bertrand's help, especially when she added: " To-morrow I go to dramatic school." He knew that she would not go unless he conducted her, for of course she couldn't very well, but how could he conduct her there? How did one set about such a thing? Ruzena was quite resolved to " work," and the planning of an occupation for her provided a new subject of conversation with the unusual charm of seriousness, although Joachim felt quite helpless in front of all the questions it threw up. Perhaps he felt that an ordinary vocation would rob her of the exotic grace with which she hovered between two worlds, and cast her back into her native barbarism; and it was indeed for this reason that his imagination stopped at the idea of a part as an actress, an idea with which Ruzena concurred enthusiastically: " You see how famous will I be! You love me then." But the prospect was a distant one, and nothing happened. Bertrand had once spoken of the vegetative indolence in which most people lived; probably it was much the same as that inertia of feeling he had talked about. Yes, if Bertrand were only here: with his knowledge of the world and his practical experience, perhaps he might be of some help. And so when Bertrand reached Berlin he found an urgent invitation from Pasenow awaiting him in reply to his friendly note.

It could be managed, Bertrand said, to the great astonishment of both of them, it could be managed, though they mustn't imagine that the stage provided either an easy career or one with a particularly brilliant future. Of course he had better connections in Hamburg, but he would be glad to do what he could here. And then things developed far more quickly than they had hoped for; in a few days Ruzena was summoned to a voice test which she stood not too badly, and shortly after that she was engaged as a chorus girl. Joachim's suspicion that his friend's sudden readiness to oblige sprang from his designs on Ruzena could not hold out against Bertrand's benevolently indifferent, one might almost say clinical, attitude. It would all have been much clearer if Bertrand had made his efforts on Ruzena's behalf a pretext for openly declaring his love for her. In his heart Joachim was now seriously offended with Bertrand, who had indeed spent three evenings in his and Ruzena's company talking in his usual irrepressible way, but had showed nothing except the old friendly reserve of which Joachim was already sick, and still remained a stranger though he had done more for Ruzena than Joachim himself with his mooning, romantic fancies. All this was very painful. What was this fellow Bertrand after? Now that he was going away, and, as was only fitting, declined all thanks from or on behalf of Ruzena, he was expressing once more the hope that he would soon see Joachim again. Wasn't it hypocritical? And Joachim, astonished at himself, replied: " I'm afraid, Bertrand, that you won't find me in Berlin when you come next, for I'll have to go to Stolpin for a few weeks after the manœuvres. But if you would really like to visit me there I should be awfully glad to see you." And Bertrand accepted.

It had always been a custom of Herr von Pasenow to await the arrival of the post in his study. From time immemorial a place had been kept free on the table beside the pile of sports journals, and on this place the messenger had duly to deposit his bag. And although on most days the contents of the bag were disappointing, often consisting of nothing but two or three journals, yet Herr von Pasenow always took down the key from the antler-rack, where he used to hang it, and opened the lock in the yellow brass plate with the same avid eagerness. And while the messenger, cap in hand, waited in silence, gazing at the floor, Herr von Pasenow took out the letters and packets, sat down with them at his desk, set aside first those for himself and his family, and after carefully scrutinizing the addresses on the others handed them to the messenger to take to the servants they were destined for. Sometimes he had to put a curb upon himself to refrain from opening this or the other letter addressed to one of the maids, for this seemed to him an obvious right, a variation of the *jus primæ noctis* of the master; and the fact that the secrecy of the post should protect menials was a new-fangled notion that went against the grain. Nevertheless there were a few among the servants who actually complained about his external scrutiny of their

envelopes, especially as the master did not scruple to inquire afterwards
into the contents of the letters and to quiz the maids. This had led
already to violent scenes, which had ended however with dismissals,
and the rebels no longer objected openly, but either fetched their letters
from the post office themselves, or gave secret instructions to the postmaster to have them delivered by the postman. Yes, for some time even
the deceased young master had been seen daily dismounting from his
horse at the post office so as to collect his correspondence; it may have
been that he was expecting letters from some lady which he did not
want the old man to see, or that he was engaged on business which
must remain secret; but the postmaster, who usually was free enough
with his information, could not confirm either of those suppositions,
as the few letters which Helmuth von Pasenow received gave no clue.
Nevertheless the obstinate rumour persisted that, through some machina-
tions or other with the post office, the old man had ruined a project of
marriage and the happiness of his son. The women on the estate and
in the village stuck to this with particular obstinacy, and perhaps they
were not so very far wrong, for Helmuth had become more and more
indifferent and melancholy, had soon discontinued his rides to the
village, and had let his letters be brought again in the great post-bag
to the estate and his father's writing-table.

Herr von Pasenow had always had this passion for the post, and so
it was not a matter for surprise that as time went on it should become
more intense. Now he often so arranged his morning ride or walk as
to meet the messenger, and then it was seen that, instead of leaving
the key hanging on the antler-rack, he now carried it in his pocket so
that he might unlock the bag under the open sky. There he would busily
look through the letters but then put them back in the bag again so
as not to disturb the household ritual, which was still gone through in
the usual way. One morning, however, he actually got as far as the
post office where the messenger was still leaning against the counter,
and waited until the mail-bag was emptied on the worn table, and then,
together with the postmaster, arranged and sorted the letters. When the
messenger related this extraordinary incident at the big house the house-
maid Agnes, known everywhere for her sharp tongue, remarked: " Now
he's beginning to suspect himself." That was of course a saying without
any sense in it, and the unshakable obstinacy with which she, more
than any of the others, maintained that the master was responsible for

his son's death may perhaps be put down as a belated outcome of the resentment which she had nursed for years at being quizzed by the old man about her correspondence while she was still young and buxom.

Yes, Herr von Pasenow had always been queer about the post, and so his behaviour now was nothing to be surprised at. Nor was it a surprising thing that the pastor was invited to supper more often, nor that in his walks Herr von Pasenow now and then actually presented himself at the parsonage. No, there was nothing strange in that, and the pastor regarded it as the fruit of the spiritual comfort he had expended. Only Herr von Pasenow himself knew that it was an inexplicable and mysterious impulse which drove him to the pastor although he could not endure the man, an undefined hope that the voice which was uplifted in the church must needs reveal to him something for which he was waiting, something which, in spite of his fear that it would never be vouchsafed, he was not able even to name to himself. When the pastor brought the conversation round to Helmuth, often Herr von Pasenow would say: " It doesn't matter," and to his own astonishment would change the subject as if he were afraid of the Unknown he was yet longing for. But sometimes there were days when he suffered the Unknown to draw near, and then it was like a game which he had played as a child: someone hid a ring where it could be seen, hanging it perhaps on a chandelier or a key, and when the seeker moved away from it the others shouted " Cold," and when he drew near they said " Warm," or " Hot." And so it was quite natural that once when the pastor began to speak of Helmuth, Herr von Pasenow should say, suddenly and clearly, " Hot, hot! " and almost clap his hands. The pastor agreed politely that it had indeed been very warm that day, and Herr von Pasenow found himself back in his surroundings again. Yet it was strange how close things were to each other: one thought one was in the middle of a childish game, and yet death was already taking a hand. So " Yes, yes, it's warm," said Herr von Pasenow, though he looked as if he were freezing, " yes, in these hot nights the barns easily take fire."

The thought of the heat did not leave him even at supper: " In Berlin it must be terribly hot these days. Joachim hasn't said anything about it, though . . . but then he says so little in his letters in any case." The pastor touched on the strenuous duties of the service. " Service! What service? " asked Herr von Pasenow so sharply that in his confusion the pastor could not think of an answer. The pastor meant of course, Frau von Pasenow put in, that the service did not give Joachim much leisure for writing, especially now when the manœuvres were on. " Well then, he should leave the service," growled Herr von Pasenow. Then he drank several glasses of wine rapidly one after another and declared that he felt better. He filled the pastor's glass: " Drink up, Pastor, drinking warms you, and when you see double you feel less lonely." " The man who has God with him is never lonely, Herr von Pasenow," replied the pastor, and Herr von Pasenow found the reproof tactless. Hadn't he always rendered to God what was God's and to the Emperor, or more correctly the King, what was his due? One son was serving the King and did not write, and the other God had taken to Himself, and the world was empty and cold. Yes, it was easy for the pastor to talk so loftily; his house was full, too full for his circumstances, and now there was another on the way again. It wasn't so difficult to have God with one in these circumstances: he would have liked to tell the pastor that, but he dared not fall out with him, for who would be left then, when nobody wanted to visit him now except . . . then, just when It was becoming visible, the thought broke off and hid itself, and Herr von Pasenow said softly and dreamily: " It must be warm in the byre." Frau von Pasenow looked in dismay at her husband: had he been drinking his wine too fast? But Herr von Pasenow had got up and stood listening near the window; the lamp lighted up only the table, else she must have seen the expression of terrified expectation on his face, which vanished however when the crunching tread of the night watchman became audible on the gravel outside. Herr von Pasenow went to the window, leant out and called: " Jürgen." And when Jürgen's heavy footsteps halted before the window Herr von Pasenow ordered him to keep an eye on the barns. " It's just twelve years since the big barn on the home farm was burned down on a warm night like this." And when Jürgen dutifully remembered and said: " No fear, sir," for Frau von Pasenow too the incident passed again into the accustomed and the ordinary, so that she thought no more of it when Herr von Pasenow said good-night, adding that he had still a letter to write which must go by the morning post. At the door he turned round again: " Tell me, Herr Pastor, why do we have children? You should know: you've had plenty of practice." And he scuttled away tittering, but a little like a dog hobbling on three legs.

Alone with the pastor, Frau von Pasenow said: " I'm glad to see him in better spirits again. Since the departure of our poor Helmuth he's been very downcast."

As August drew towards its end the doors of the theatre opened again. Ruzena now had visiting-cards on which she was designated as an actress, and Joachim would soon have to depart to Upper Franconia for the manœuvres. He was annoyed at Bertrand for having established Ruzena in a profession which in reality was no less disreputable than her work in the Jäger Casino. Of course one could not but put some of the blame on Ruzena herself for allowing herself to be implicated in such a profession, though perhaps still more on her mother for not having brought up her daughter better. But all that he had intended to do to remedy that had been ruined now through Bertrand. Perhaps indeed things were actually worse than before. For in the casino you knew where you were, and everything was plain sailing: the stage, on the other hand, had its own peculiar atmosphere, an atmosphere of homage and bouquets; and nowhere else was it so difficult for a young girl to remain respectable. That was generally admitted. Yes, it only meant a deeper and deeper descent, and Ruzena refused to see this, but instead was actually proud of her new profession and her visiting-cards. With an air of great consequence she recounted green-room gossip and all the scandal of the boards which he had no wish to listen to, and into the twilight of their life together reflections from the glare of the footlights were now perpetually breaking. How could he have ever imagined that he would find his way to her or that she had really belonged to him, she who had been lost from the beginning? He still sought her, but the stage had arisen before him like a menace, and when she eagerly recounted the love affairs of her colleagues, he saw in this a challenge and the firm intention of her awakened ambition to do what they did, saw too that this would mean a return to her former life, which had probably been spent not so very differently: for human beings were always drawn back inevitably to their starting-point. He regretted the shattered bliss of his twilit passion, the lost sweetness of longing which still filled his heart, it was true, and brought tears to his eyes, yet bore within it the presage of an eternal parting.

And now too emerged once more a fancy of which he had thought himself rid for good, and if he felt no compulsion now to seek in Ruzena's face for that of her Italian brother, yet it was engraved there in a perhaps more baffling form, engraved as the indelible countenance of that life from which he had not been able to deliver her. And again his suspicions awoke that it was Bertrand who had suggested this fancy to him, who had engineered it all, and who like Mephistopheles wished to destroy everything, not even sparing Ruzena. And on the top of this the manœuvres were approaching: how would he find Ruzena on his return? Would he ever, indeed, find her again? They promised each other that they would write often, daily; but Ruzena had all sorts of difficulties with her German, and as moreover she was proud of her visiting-cards, and he was unwilling to destroy her childish pleasure, the post often brought him nothing but one of those cards with the hateful inscription " Actress " and the words " Send lots of luv," a word which seemed to desecrate the sweetness of her kisses. Nevertheless he was greatly disturbed when for a few days he received no word from her, although he had to tell himself that his rapid movements during the manœuvres made a delay of the post quite explicable; and he was delighted when presently one of the horrid little cards arrived. And suddenly and without warning, like a memory, there came the thought that Bertrand too was a sort of actor.

Ruzena really longed for Joachim. His letters contained descriptions of his camp life and the evenings in the little villages, where he would feel really happy only " if you, dear, sweet little Ruzena, were beside me." And when he requested her to look at the moon at nine o'clock in the evening precisely, so that their glances might meet up there, she ran to the stage door during the interval, and though the interval did not come until half-past nine she gazed up dutifully at the sky. To her it seemed that that early spring afternoon in the rain still held her fast and paralysed something in her; the flood-tide which had submerged her then was only gradually receding, and although the girl's will was not strong enough and she had besides no resources out of which to erect dams to hold the waters, yet the air which she breathed in and out was still permeated with a soft humidity. True, she envied those colleagues who received bouquets at their dressing-room doors, but she envied them simply for Joachim's sake, since he ought to have had a celebrated diva as a lover. And although a woman in love often carries about with her that suggestion of the erotic which to many men is so delicately attractive, the men who laid their homage before the actresses were of a different type, and not likely to recognize such gentle indications.

So it happened that Ruzena was more inviolate than ever when she received Joachim on his return to Berlin after the manœuvres, and she looked on this as a victory, a victory on which, she nevertheless knew, defeat would follow; but she did not want to acknowledge this and stifled the knowledge under embraces.

Ever since the train had left the station and she had waved good-bye with her lace handkerchief, Elisabeth had been trying to make clear to herself whether she loved Joachim. It was an almost joyful ground for reassurance that the feeling which she hopefully designated as love should have such a very unassuming and civilized appearance; one had actually to search one's mind to discern it, for it was so faint and thin that only against a background of silvery ennui did it become visible. But now that she drew nearer and nearer to her home, and her ennui was changed into mounting impatience, the soft contours of the image faded; and when the Baron met them at the station with the new pair of horses, and also when they reached Lestow, and the green tree-tops of the peaceful park appeared, enclosed by the quiet massiveness of the gate—the first surprise, for to right and left two new lodges had been erected, so that the ladies uttered cries of lively astonishment, which were but the prelude, however, to the many they would utter in the next few days—it was only too comprehensible that Elisabeth should no longer think of love at all. For the Baron had once more employed the absence of his two ladies, or as he sometimes called them to Elisabeth's gratified pride, his two wives, to carry out countless improvements and embellishments to the house, alterations which delighted them and gained for him many words of praise and tender gratitude. They had indeed every cause to be proud of their artistic papa; although he had no exaggerated respect for the existing order and had already adorned the old manor-house with all sorts of additions, he yet had an eye for more than mere architecture; for he never forgot that there was always a free space on a wall where a new picture would look well, a corner which could be set off by a massive vase, or a sideboard which could be furnished with a gold-embroidered velvet cloth: and he was the man to carry out his ideas. Since their marriage the Baron and the Baroness had become collectors, and the continual further perfecting of their home had grown for them into a sort of perpetuation of their first engagement, and had remained so even after the arrival of their daughter. As time went on Elisabeth indeed became conscious that her parents' passion for emphasizing the various family festivals of the year, for celebrating the birthdays and continually thinking out new surprises, had a deeper significance and was connected in a profound way, difficult to fathom, with their delight, indeed one might almost call it their greed, in surrounding themselves continuously with new things. Certainly Elisabeth did not know that every collector hopes with the never-attained, never-attainable and yet inexorably striven-for absolute completeness of his collection to pass beyond the assembled things themselves, to pass over into infinity, and, entirely subsumed in his collection, to attain his own consummation and the suspension of death. Elisabeth did not know this, but surrounded by all those beautiful dead things gathered together and piled up around her, surrounded by all those beautiful pictures, she divined nevertheless that the pictures were hung up as though to strengthen the walls, and that all those dead things were put there to cover, perhaps also to conceal and guard, something intensely living; something with which she herself was so intimately bound that she could not but feel at times when a new picture was brought in that it was a little brother or sister; something which begged to be cherished and was cherished by her parents as though their common life together depended upon it. She divined the fear behind all this, fear that sought to drown in festivals the monotony of every day which is the outward sign of growing old, fear that was always reassuring itself—by perpetual fresh surprises—that they were all alive and in the flesh and definitively together, and that their circle was closed for ever. And just as the Baron was always adding new stretches of his property to the park, whose dark and thickly grown copses were now surrounded on almost every side by wide borders of tender light-green young wood, so it seemed to Elisabeth that with almost feminine solicitude he wished to turn all their life into an ever more spacious enclosed park full of pleasant resting-places, and that he would reach his goal and be free of all apprehension only when the park had spread over the whole earth, attaining its object of becoming a park in which Elisabeth might walk about for ever. It is true that occasionally something in her rebelled against this gentle and inescapable compulsion, but as her resistance was hardly ever very definite, it dissolved into the sunny contours of the hills that lay in the distance beyond the seclusion of the park.

" Oh! " cried the Baroness as they stood admiring the new pergola in

the rosarium. " Oh, how pretty! It might have been set up for a bride."
She smiled at Elisabeth, and the Baron smiled too, but in their eyes
could be read their fear of the ineluctable menace, their helplessness,
their fore-knowledge of a coming infidelity and treachery which nevertheless they forgave in advance, for they too had sinned. How terrible
it was that the mere thought of her future marriage should seem already
to oppress her parents. And Elisabeth put all thoughts of marriage
completely out of her mind, so completely indeed that it almost seemed
to her that she could listen without compunction to her parents when,
as a sort of concession to her presumable destiny to fall in love and at
the same time as a sort of act of recognition which raised her to their
own level, giving her almost the status of a sister, they talked of a possible
match. Perhaps that was why, when her mother pressed a tender kiss
on her cheek, Elisabeth could not help thinking of her Aunt Brigitte's
wedding day, could not help feeling that this kiss too was a kiss of
farewell: for just so had her mother kissed Aunt Brigitte, kissed her with
tears, with tears although she had declared that she was very happy
and was delighted with her new young brother-in-law. But of course
that was all long past now; it was childish to muse on it, and going
between her parents Elisabeth put her arms round their shoulders and
walked with them to the pergola, where they sat down. The rose-beds,
threaded with narrow, symmetrically winding paths, blazed with all their
hues and were full of fragrance, yet all the shadows were not yet dis-
persed, and the Baron said, pointing sadly towards one bed: " I've tried
to set some Manettis there, but I'm afraid our climate is too rough for
them," and as if he wished to bribe his daughter with the promise, he
added: " but if it succeeds and they grow all right, then they'll belong
to Elisabeth." Elisabeth felt the pressure of his hand, and it was almost
like an intimation that there was something that could never be clutched
firmly enough, something that might almost be time itself, something
compressed and twisted like a watch-spring and that was threatening
to uncoil, to wind out between their fingers, becoming longer and longer,
an alarming, long, thin white band which presently would begin to
creep, seeking to twine round her like an evil snake, until she became
fat and old and hideous. Perhaps her mother too was feeling this, for
she said: " When the child leaves us one day we'll sit out here by ourselves." And, conscious of her guilt, Elisabeth said: " But I'm going to
stay with you always," said it with a feeling of shame, for she did not

believe it herself, and yet it sounded like the renewal of an old vow.
" In any case, I can't see why she shouldn't stay here with her husband
when that happens," the Baroness went on. But her father warded the
subject off: " It's a long time still before that can happen." And Elisabeth
could not help once more thinking of Aunt Brigitte, who passed her days
in Würbendorf, and had grown fat, and squabbled with her children,
and had now so little in common with the beloved figure of former days
that one could not imagine she had ever existed and was almost ashamed
of the happiness that she had once given one. And yet Würbendorf
was a gayer and friendlier place than Stolpin, and everybody had been
delighted to get a new young relation in Uncle Albert. It may have been
that it was not really Aunt Brigitte whom she had loved so much, and
that it was simply the admission of a new relation into the circle that
had roused such exciting and dear emotions. For if one were related to
everybody the world would be like a well-kept park, and to acquire a
new relation would be like planting a new variety of rose in the garden.
Infidelity and treachery would then turn to lighter offences; she had
surely divined that already at the time when she had been so glad about
Uncle Albert; and in the ocean of injustice surrounding them it was
perhaps on this little islet of forgiveness that her parents now sought
refuge when they spoke of her possible marriage as of an auspicious fate.
But the Baroness had not yet given up her idea; and as life consists of
compromises she said: " Besides, our little house in the west end will
always be ready for them." But Elisabeth's hand still lay in her father's
and felt its pressure, and Elisabeth would not hear of compromise.
"No; I'll stay with you," she repeated almost defiantly, and she remembered how bitterly she had resented as a child being banished from her
parents' bedroom and not being allowed to watch over their breathing;
still, though the Baroness had always had a weakness for talking about
death, which she said often came upon people in their sleep, and though
she had alarmed Elisabeth and her husband with such sayings, yet there
had been the morning's joyful surprise that the night had not parted
them for ever, a surprise which grew into a daily renewed wild longing
that they should take one another by the hand and hold on so fast that
they could never be torn asunder. So they sat now in the pergola, which
was filled with the roses' scent; Elisabeth's little dog came scampering
up and greeted her as though he had found her for eternity, and put
his paws on her knees. The stems of the rose-trees stood up stiff and

hard against the green wall of the garden and the clear blue sky. Never would she be able to greet a stranger, no matter how nearly related he was to her, with the same intense joy in the morning; never would she think of his birthday with such passionate and almost pious devotion as of that of her father; never would she surround him with that incomprehensible and yet sublime anxiety which was love. And having recognized this she now smiled affectionately at her parents and stroked the head of her little dog Bello, which with apprehensively loving eyes gazed up devotedly at her.

Later she began to feel bored, and the faint feeling of resistance too returned once more. Then it was not unpleasant to think of Joachim, and she remembered his slim figure as he had stood bowing slightly, in his long angular officer's coat, on the platform. But his image got strangely and inextricably entangled with that of her young Aunt Brigitte, and by this time she could not make out whether it was Joachim who was going to marry Brigitte, or she herself who was going to wed the young Uncle Albert of her childhood. And although she knew that love was not what it was represented to be in operas and romances, yet this much was certain, that she could think of Joachim without apprehension; indeed, even when she tried to picture to herself that the departing train might have caught his sword and flung him under the wheels, the picture filled her with horror certainly, but not with that sweet sorrow and dread, that trembling anxiety, which bound her to the lives of her parents. When she recognized this it was as though she had renounced something, and yet there was a sort of melancholy relief in it. Nevertheless she resolved to ask Joachim some time what was his birthday.

Joachim had returned to Stolpin. While he was still on his way from the station, just after he had passed through the village and reached the first fields on the estate, a new feeling had unexpectedly risen in him: he tried to find words for it and found them: my property. When he got down at the manor-house he was furnished with a new sentiment of home.

Now he was with his father and mother, and if their company had been restricted to the breakfast-hour it would have been very tolerable; it was a pleasure to sit out under the great lime-trees, the cool sunny garden stretching before him; and the rich yellow butter, the honey and the big basket of fruit, were all in pleasing contrast to his hurried break-fasts in the army. But already the midday and evening meals were an affliction; the more the day advanced the more their companionship weighed on all three, and if in the mornings the old people felt happy at the reappearance of their absent son, and, it may be, daily expected something beautiful and life-giving from him, yet the day—punctuated by the meals—turned stage by stage into a disappointment, and towards late afternoon Joachim's presence had grown almost into an intensifica-tion of their mutual unendurable loneliness; indeed even the prospect of the post, the one ray of light in the monotony of the day, was made poorer by their son's presence, and if the old man in spite of this still went out every morning to meet the messenger, it was almost an act of despair, was almost like a veiled appeal to Joachim to go away for heaven's sake and send a few letters. And yet Herr von Pasenow himself seemed to know he was awaiting something quite different from Joachim's letters, and that the messenger for whom he was looking was not the messenger with the letter-bag.

Joachim made a few faint attempts to become more intimate with his parents. He went to see his father in the room decorated with the antlers, and inquired about the harvest and the shooting, and hoped perhaps that the old man might be gratified by this indirect attempt to follow his request to " work himself in." But either his father had for-gotten his request, or did not himself know very much about what was happening on the estate; for he gave only reluctant or evasive responses and once actually said: " You needn't trouble yourself about that so early in the day," and Joachim, though relieved from a burdensome obligation, could not help thinking again of the time when he had been sent to the cadet school and robbed for the first time of his home. But now he had returned and was awaiting a guest of his own. It was a pleasant sensation, and though it hid within it a good deal of hostility towards his father, Joachim was not aware of this; indeed he hoped that his parents would be delighted with this interruption of their growing boredom and look forward with the same impatience as himself to Bertrand's arrival. He submitted to his father's going through his corre-spondence, and when finally the old man handed it over to him with the words: " Unfortunately there still seems to be no news of your friend, that is, if he's coming at all," Joachim refused to read anything but regret into the sentence, although it had a malicious ring. His irritation did not come to a head until once he saw a letter from Ruzena in his father's hands. Yet the old man made no comment, but only stuck his monocle in his eye and observed: " Really, you must pay the Baddensens a visit soon; it's high time you did." Well, that might be taken as sarcasm, or it might not: but in any case it was sufficient to spoil so completely Joachim's pleasure at the prospect of seeing Elisabeth that he kept putting off the visit again and again; and though her image and her fluttering handkerchief had faithfully accompanied him till now, he felt himself filled more and more urgently with the wish, which he pictured in his imagination, that Eduard von Bertrand should be sitting beside him on the seat of the carriage when he drew up before the front door at Lestow.

But that did not happen, at least to begin with, for one day Elisabeth and her mother paid a belated visit of condolence to Herr and Frau von Pasenow. Elisabeth felt disappointed, and yet in some way relieved, that Joachim was not there when they arrived; she felt also a little offended. They sat in the smaller drawing-room, and the ladies learned from Herr von Pasenow that Helmuth had died for the honour of his name. Elisabeth involuntarily remembered that perhaps in no very long time she too would bear this name for which someone had fallen, and with an access of pride and pleased astonishment she realized that Herr and Frau von Pasenow would then become new relations. They talked about the melancholy occurrence, and Herr von Pasenow said: " That's how it is when one has sons; they die for honour or for their king and country—it's stupid having sons," he added sharply and challengingly. " Oh, but daughters get married, and before you know they're away," responded the Baroness with an almost meaning smile, " and we old people are always left behind alone." Herr von Pasenow did not reply, as would have been polite, that the Baroness could not by any means be regarded as old, but became quite still, staring fixedly in front of him, and after a short silence said: " Yes, we're left behind alone, left behind alone," and after he had reflected a little longer with obvious concentration, " and we die alone." " But, Herr von Pasenow, we have no need to think of dying yet! " the Baroness brought out in a dutifully cheerful voice. " Oh, we needn't think of that for a long time yet: the rain brings sunshine, my dear Herr von Pasenow; you must always try to remember that." Herr von Pasenow found his way back to reality and became again the cavalier: " Provided that the sunshine comes to us in your person, Baroness," he said, and without waiting for the Baroness's flattered response he went on: " yet how strange things are now . . . the house is empty, and even the post brings nothing. I've written Joachim, but I don't hear much from him; he's at the manœuvres." Frau von Pasenow turned in dismay to her husband: " But . . . but, you know Joachim is here." A venomous glance was her punishment for this correction. " Well, did he write, yes or no? And where is he now? " and there would have been a mild squabble if the canary in its cage had not released its quiver of golden notes. They gathered round it as round a fountain and for a few moments forgot everything else: it was as though this slender golden thread of sound, rising and falling, were winding itself round them and linking them in that unity on which the comfort of their living and dying was established; it was as though this thread which wavered up and filled their being, and yet curved and wound back again to its soürce, suspended their speech, perhaps because it was a thin, golden ornament in space, perhaps because it brought to their minds for a few moments that they belonged to each other, and lifted them out of the dreadful stillness whose reverberations rise like an impenetrable wall of deafening silence between human being and human being, a wall through which the human voice cannot penetrate, so that it has to falter and die. But now that the canary was singing not even Herr von Pasenow himself could hear that dreadful stillness, and they all had a feeling of warmth when Frau von Pasenow said: " But now we must have some coffee." And when they went through the big drawing-room, whose curtains were drawn to keep out the afternoon sun, none of them remembered that Helmuth had lain there on his bier.

Then Joachim arrived and Elisabeth had a second disappointment, for her memory held an image in uniform, and now he was dressed in hunting kit. They were distant and embarrassed towards each other, and even when with the others they had returned to the drawing-room, and Elisabeth was standing before the canary's cage amusing herself by pushing a finger through the wires and seeing the little creature pecking wrathfully at it, even while she was deciding that in her own drawing-room—if she ever should marry—she would always have a little yellow bird such as this one, even then she could no longer associate Joachim with the idea of marriage. Yet that was actually rather pleasant and reassuring and made it easier for her as she said good-bye to arrange that they should at an early date go out riding together. Before that, of course, he must pay them a call.

Bertrand had at last found time to comply with Pasenow's invitation, and on the way down stepped out of the evening train for a two days' stay in Berlin. Naturally enough he wanted to have news of Ruzena; so he made straight for the theatre and sent his name, along with a bouquet of flowers, to her dressing-room. Ruzena was delighted when she got his card, delighted too with the flowers, and it flattered her that Bertrand should be waiting for her at the stage door at the end of the performance: " Well, little Ruzena, how are you getting on? " And Ruzena replied in one breath that she was getting on splendidly, splendidly, oh, really very badly, because she longed so much for Joachim; but now of course she felt all right because she was so delighted that Bertrand had called for her, for he was such an intimate friend of Joachim's. But when they were sitting opposite each other in the restaurant, having talked a great deal about Joachim, Ruzena, as often happened with her, became suddenly sad: " Now you go to Joachim and I have stay here: world is unjust." " Of course world is unjust, and far worse than you have any conception of, little Ruzena "—it seemed to both of them natural that he should address her as " du "—" and it was partly my anxiety about you that brought me here." " What you mean by that? " " Well, I don't like your being in this stage business." " Why? It very nice." " I was too hasty in giving in to you both . . . just because you were romantic and had formed God knows what picture of the stage." " I not understand what you mean." " Well, never mind, but it's out of the question for you to stay in it. What can it lead to finally? What is to become of you, child? Someone must look after you, and that can't be done with romantic notions." Ruzena replied stiffly and on her dignity that she could quite well look after herself, and Joachim could just go if he wanted to be rid of her, he could just go, " and you bad man, to come here just to speak ill of friend "; then she cried and gave Bertrand hostile looks through her tears. He found it difficult to reassure her, for she persisted that he was a bad man and a bad friend who wanted to spoil her happy evening. And all at once she grew very pale and fixed terrified eyes upon him: " He sent you to say he finish with me: all over! " " But, Ruzena! " " No, you can say ten time no, I know it; oh, you bad, both two of you. You brought me here, so to shame me."

Bertrand saw that by rational means nothing could be done; yet in her untutored suspicions there was perhaps a divination of the real state of affairs and its hopelessness. She looked as desperate as a little animal that does not know where to turn. And yet perhaps it would be good for her to regard the future more soberly. So he merely shook his head and replied: " Tell me, child, couldn't you go back to your own home and stay there while Joachim is away? " All that she could draw from this was that she was going to be sent away. " But, Ruzena, who wants to send you away? Only it would be much better for you to be with your people than alone here in Berlin in this silly stage life. . . ." She would not let him finish: " I have nobody, all bad to me . . . I have nobody, and you want send me away." " But be reasonable, Ruzena: when Pasenow is in Berlin again you can come back too." Ruzena would not listen any more to him and said she was going. But he did not want to let her go like that, and considered how he could turn her thoughts in a happier direction; at last he hit upon the idea that they should write Joachim a letter between them. Ruzena agreed at once; so he had notepaper brought and wrote: " In warm remembrance of a happy evening with you, kindest greetings from Bertrand," and she added: " And lots of luv from Ruzena." She pressed a kiss on the letter, but she could not restrain her tears. " All over," she repeated again and asked him to take her home. Bertrand gave in. But so that he might not have to leave her too soon to her melancholy fancies he suggested that they should go on foot. To calm her—for words were useless —he took her hand like a kind and skilful doctor; she snuggled close to him gratefully and as if seeking support and with a faint pressure left her hand in his. She's just a little animal, thought Bertrand, and hoping to cheer her he said: " Yes, Ruzena, am I not a bad friend and an enemy of yours? " But she did not reply. A slight but tender irritation at her confused thinking arose in him and extended to take in Joachim too, whom he held responsible for Ruzena and her fate, and who yet seemed no less confused than the girl herself. It may have been because he could feel the warmth of her body that, at any rate for the space of a moment, he had the malicious thought that Joachim deserved to be betrayed with Ruzena: but he did not entertain this seriously and soon found again the affectionate good will which he had always cherished for Joachim. To him Joachim and Ruzena seemed creatures who lived only with a small fraction of their being in the time to which they

belonged, the age to which their years entitled them; and the greater
part of them was somewhere else, perhaps on another star or in another
century, or perhaps simply in their childhood. Bertrand was struck by
the fact that the world was full of people belonging to different centuries,
who had to live together, and were even contemporaries; that accounted
perhaps for their instability and their difficulty in understanding one
another rationally; the extraordinary thing was that, nevertheless, there
was a kind of human solidarity and an understanding that bridged the
years. Probably Joachim, too, only needed to have his hand stroked.
What should and what could he talk to him about? What object was
there really in this visit to Stolpin? Bertrand felt irritated, but then he
remembered that he would have to talk to Joachim of Ruzena's future;
that gave a rational meaning to the journey and the waste of time,
and once more restored to good spirits he squeezed Ruzena's hand.

They said good-night before her door; then they stood facing each
other dumbly for a few moments, and it looked as though Ruzena were
still expecting something. Bertrand smiled and before she could give him
her mouth kissed her somewhat avuncularly on the cheek. She touched
his hand lightly and was about to slip away, but he kept her for a moment
in the doorway: " Well, Ruzena, I'm leaving to-morrow morning. What
message am I to give to Joachim? " " Nothing," she replied quickly
and crossly, but then she reflected: " You bad, but I come to station."
" Good-night, Ruzena," said Bertrand, and again the slight feeling of
exasperation rose in him, but as he could still feel on his lips the downy
softness of her cheek he continued walking to and fro in the dark street,
gazing up at the block and waiting for a light to appear behind one
of the windows. But either her light had been burning before or her room
looked out on the back yard—Joachim might surely have got her better
lodgings—at any rate Bertrand waited in vain, and after he had regarded
the block for some time, he decided that he had done quite enough for
the cause of romanticism, lit a cigar and went home.

While the reception-rooms were provided with parquet-flooring, the
guest-rooms on the first floor had merely polished boards, huge planks
of soft white wood separated from each other by somewhat darker
connecting boards. The trunks from which those planks were once cut
must have been gigantic ones, and although the wood was rather soft,
yet their size and uniformity witnessed to the opulence of the man who

had had them laid here. The joinings between the planks and the boards were closely fitted, and where they had widened on account of the shrinking of the wood they were so neatly plugged with chips that one scarcely noticed it. The furniture had obviously been made by the village carpenter and probably dated from the time when Napoleon's armies had passed through the vicinity; at least it forced one to think of that time, remotely reminding one of that style which is usually called Empire; however, it may have belonged to a slightly earlier or later period, for it diverged with all sorts of bulging lines from the severity of that norm. Here, for instance, was a wardrobe whose mirrored front was violently divided in two by a vertical strip of wood, and there were chests of drawers which, by possessing too many or too few shelves, offended against the laws of pure symmetry. Yet even although these furnishings were ranged against the walls almost without plan, even although the bed was stationed in the most inconvenient way between two doors, and the great white-tiled stove in the corner was squeezed between two cupboards, yet the spacious room had a comfortable and easy look, very pleasant when the sun shone through the white curtains, and the window, with its cross-bars, was mirrored on the glittering polish of the furniture. At such moments, indeed, it could actually happen that the great crucifix which hung on the wall over the bed no longer seemed a mere ornament or a customary article of furniture, but became once more what it had originally been when it was brought here: an admonition and reminder to the guest, warning him that he was in a Christian household, in a house which, it was true, provided in hosts of ways for his bodily comfort and from which he could ride out to the hunt in a merry company and return to devote himself to a hearty supper with abundance of strong wines, a house too where the roughest of practical jokes was permitted him, and where, at the time when the furniture in this room was joinered, an eye was closed if he should take a fancy to one of the maids; but a house nevertheless where it was considered inevitable that the guest, no matter how heavy he might feel after his wine, would have on retiring a desire to remember his soul and to repent of his sins. And it was in accordance with this essentially austere way of thought that over the sofa covered with green repp should be hung a sober and austere steel-engraving which in many of the guests' minds awakened thoughts of Queen Luise, for it represented a stately lady in antique robes—*La Mère des Gracches* was the title of the picture

—and not only did this costume remind them of the Queen, but the altar towards which she was lifting her arms also suggested the altar of the Fatherland. Certainly the majority of the huntsmen who had slept in this room had led a worldly life, seizing advantage and enjoyment wherever they offered, not scrupling to screw from the dealers the most they could for their grain and their pigs, devoted to a savage pastime in which God's creatures were shot down barbarously in heaps, many of them, too, filled with lust for women; but insolently as they claimed the arrogant and sinful life they led as an obvious right and privilege granted by Heaven, they were prepared to sacrifice it at any moment for the honour of the Fatherland or the glory of God, and even if the opportunity should never arise, yet this readiness to regard life as something secondary and scarcely worth considering was so potent that its sinfulness hardly counted for anything in the balance. And they did not feel that they were sinful when in the morning mist they strode through the faintly crackling undergrowth, or when at evening they climbed a steep, narrow ladder to a look-out perch, and gazed across bush and clearing, where the midges still wove their dances, to the edge of the wood. Then when the moist fragrance of grass and tree rose up to them and along the dry bulwark of the perch an ant came running and vanished in the bark, then sometimes in their souls, though they were pragmatic fellows with their feet firmly planted on the earth, something awoke that rang like music, and the lives they had lived and had still to live were concentrated so intensely into one moment that they could still feel the touch of their mother's hand on their hair as if for eternity, while another shape already stood before them, separated from them no longer by any span of time, any span of space, the shape which they did not fear: Death. Then all the woods around might turn for them into the wood of the Cross, for nowhere do the magical and the earthly lie closer together than in the heart of the hunter, and when the buck appears on the border of the clearing, then the illumination is bodily present and life seems to be timeless, evanescent and eternal, held in one's closed hand, so that the shot which kills a strange life is like a symbol of the need to save one's own life in the arms of grace. Always the hunter goes out to find the Cross in the antlers of the deer, and for that illumination the price even of death seems to him not too high. And so, too, when after his abundant supper, he returns to his room, he can presume to lift his eyes again to the crucifix, and, though from afar off, to think of the eternity in which his life is embedded. And perhaps in front of that eternity even the cleanliness of his body weighs no more in the balance than the sinfulness of his earthly life: on the wash-table stands a basin whose smallness is in ludicrous contrast to the size of the hunter and the customary dimensions of his life, and the jug, too, holds far less water than the wine he is accustomed to drink. Even the small commode beside the bed, which in the guise of a cupboard gives hospitality to a night-vessel, merely ratifies the inadequate proportions of the rest. The hunter employs it and flings himself on the groaning bed.

In this chamber, admirably suited to the needs of hunters for generations past, Bertrand was installed during his stay at Stolpin.

Among the remarkable memories which Bertrand brought back with him from his stay at Stolpin his picture of old Herr von Pasenow was not the least strange. On his very first day, immediately after breakfast, he was invited by the old gentleman to accompany him on his walk and be shown over the estate. It was a dull, thundery morning; the air was motionless, but the stillness was broken by the muffled thud of the flails coming from the direction of the two threshing-floors. Herr von Pasenow seemed to find pleasure in the rhythm; several times he remained standing and kept time with his stick. Then he asked: " Would you like to see the byres? " and set off towards the long, low sheds; but in the middle of the yard he stopped, shaking his head: " No use, the cows are out grazing." Bertrand inquired politely what breeds they were; Herr von Pasenow first gazed at him as though he did not understand the question, then said with a shrug of the shoulders " It doesn't matter," and led his guest out through the gate: all round the little hollow in which lay the farm hills broadened in field after field, and everywhere the harvest work was in progress. " It all belongs to the estate," said Herr von Pasenow, making a proud circular sweep with his stick; then his uplifted arm with the stick remained motionlessly fixed in one direction; Bertrand followed it with his eyes and saw the village church tower rising behind a hill. " That's where the post office is," Herr von Pasenow confided to him, making straight for the village. The heat was oppressive; the dull thudding of the flails fell gradually into silence behind them, and only the hissing of the scythes, the sound of blades being sharpened, and the rustling of the falling grain

still hung in the air. Herr von Pasenow came to a stop: " Are you
sometimes afraid too? " Bertrand was startled, but felt sympathetically
touched by this very human question: " Me? Oh, often! " Herr von
Pasenow grew interested and came nearer: " When are you afraid?
When everything is still? " Bertrand saw that there was something
wrong here: " No, stillness is sometimes wonderful: I simply love this
stillness over the fields." Herr von Pasenow seemed put out and annoyed:
" You don't understand. . . ." After a pause he began again: " Have
you any children? " " To the best of my knowledge, no, Herr von
Pasenow." " Well, then." Herr von Pasenow looked at his watch and
peered into the distance; he shook his head: " Incomprehensible," he
said to himself, then to Bertrand: " Well, then *when* are you afraid? "—
yet he did not wait for an answer, but looked again at his watch: " But
he should have been here by now." Then he looked Bertrand full
in the face: " Will you write to me sometimes when you're on your
travels? " Bertrand said yes; he would be glad to do so, and Herr von
Pasenow seemed greatly pleased. " Yes, do write to me, I'm interested,
I'm interested in lots of things . . . write and tell me too when you're
afraid . . . but he isn't here yet; you see nobody writes to me, not even
my sons. . . ." Then far away a man with a black bag became visible.
" There he is! " Herr von Pasenow set off at a brisk pace, stick and
legs going together, and as soon as the man was within hearing distance
he screamed at him: " Where have you been idling all this time? This
is the last time that you'll go for the post . . . you're dismissed, do
you hear? you're dismissed! " He had grown red and waved his stick
in the man's face; while the latter, obviously used to such encounters,
calmly took the bag from his shoulder and handed it to his master,
who almost docilely drew the key from his waistcoat-pocket and with
trembling fingers turned it in the lock. With a trembling hand he dived
into the post-bag, but when he drew out only a few journals it looked
as if his fit of rage were about to repeat itself, for he held his mail speech-
lessly under the messenger's nose. But thereupon he evidently recollected
the presence of his guest, for he showed the journals to Bertrand:
" Here, you can see for yourself," he grumbled and put them back
in the bag, locked it, and said as they walked on again: " I'll have to
go and live in the town this year, I'm afraid: it's too quiet for me here."
    They had just reached the village when the first drops of the thunder
shower fell, and Herr von Pasenow proposed that they should seek

refuge in the pastor's house until it passed over. " You'll have to meet him in any case," he added. He was furious on learning that the pastor was not at home, and when the lady of the house said that her husband was at the school he broke out: " You seem to think too that you can tell an old man any story you like, but I'm not so old as not to know that this is the school holidays." Yes, but she hadn't meant that the pastor was teaching in the school, and besides he would be back in a minute. " Taradiddles," grumbled Herr von Pasenow, but the lady refused to be daunted and asked the gentlemen to sit down and she would get them a glass of wine. When she had left the room Herr von Pasenow leant over to Bertrand: " He always tries to avoid me, for he knows that I see through him." " See through what, Herr von Pasenow ?" " Why, that he's a thoroughly ignorant and incapable pastor, of course. But unfortunately I must keep on good terms with him all the same. Here in the country you're thrown on the mercy of everyone and . . ." he hesitated, and added more softly: " and besides, he's in charge of the graves." The pastor came in and Bertrand was introduced to him as a friend of Joachim's. " Yes, one comes and the other goes," said Herr von Pasenow dreamily, and they did not know whether this indirect reference to poor Helmuth was intended as a compliment or an insult to Bertrand. " Yes, and this is our theologian," he went on with his introduction, while the theologian smiled awkwardly. The Frau Pastor brought in the wine and a few slices of cold ham, and Herr von Pasenow emptied his glass hastily. While the others were still sitting round the table he went and stood at the window, tapped on the panes the rhythm of the threshing flails, and stared at the clouds as though he were impatient to get away. Into the halting phrases of the conversation he threw from the window: " Tell me, Herr von Bertrand, have you ever in your life met a learned theologian who knew nothing about the next world ? " " Herr von Pasenow is pleased to have his joke with me," said the abashed pastor. " Be so good then as to tell me yourself in what respect the priest of God is distinguished from us ordinary people if he has no connection with the next world ? " Herr von Pasenow had turned round and now stared angrily and sharply through his monocle at the pastor. " And if he has learned anything about it, which I permit myself to doubt, what right has he to conceal it from us ? . . . to conceal it from me ? " He became somewhat more placable, " from me . . . on his own admission a sorely tried father." The pastor replied softly:

" God alone can send you a message, Herr von Pasenow; please believe me when I say that." Herr von Pasenow shrugged his shoulders: " Oh, I believe it . . . I believe it, take my word for that." After a pause, turning to the window with another shrug he said: " It doesn't matter," and glanced, once more drumming on the panes, along the street. The rain was falling more slowly, and Herr von Pasenow gave the word: " Now we can go." As he left he shook the pastor's hand: " And don't forget to call on us . . . for supper to-night, what? Our young friend will be there too." Then they went. There were pools in the village street, but on the fields the soil was almost dry again, the rain had hardly served to efface the cracks in the ground. The sky was still covered by a faint white veil, but the scorching sun, which would soon break through, could already be felt. Herr von Pasenow was silent and did not make any response to Bertrand's conversation. But once he stopped and said solemnly with his stick uplifted: " You must be very much on your guard with these learned divines. Keep that in mind."

On the following days these morning walks were repeated, and occasionally Joachim joined in them. But when Joachim was there the old man was morose and silent and even gave up his attempts to discover what Bertrand's fears were. Indirectly and tentatively as he usually framed his questions, he now remained completely silent about them. But Joachim too was silent. For he too did not dare to ask Bertrand the questions he wished to have answered, and Bertrand remained obstinately in possession of his revelations. In this way the three of them wandered over the fields, and both father and son took it ill of Bertrand that he should disappoint their eager expectations. But Bertrand had the greatest difficulty in keeping a conversation going.

If at first Joachim had postponed his visit to Lestow because he had a fixed picture of arriving there with Bertrand, so now the slight annoyance which he felt against Bertrand was perhaps to blame for the fact that he postponed it still further: a vague hope had risen in him that if Bertrand would only speak out now, everything would fall into its place so smoothly and easily that without further ado he would be able straightway to take him to Lestow. But as in spite of this inducement, of which besides he knew nothing, Bertrand in the most disappointing manner persevered in his silence, Joachim was finally driven to make a decision and went alone. One afternoon he drove over to Lestow in the gig, his legs smoothly and decorously wrapped in the carriage rug, the whip held at the correct angle before him, and the reins running easily in his brown-gloved hand. When he left his father had said: " At last," and now Joachim was filled with distaste for this fantastic marriage project.

In front arose the church spire of the neighbouring village; a Catholic church, and it reminded him of Ruzena's Roman Catholic creed: Bertrand had told him about Ruzena. Wouldn't the most honest thing be to break off his silly stay here, and simply go back to her? Every-thing here was beginning to disgust him: the dust on the road, the dusty, wilting leaves of the trees beside it announcing the approach of autumn; he loathed it all. Since Bertrand's arrival he had been longing again for his uniform; two men in the same uniform, that was some-thing impersonal, the King's badge; two men in the same kind of civilian clothes, that was shameless, it was like two brothers; and he felt that the short civilian jacket which left visible one's legs and the opening of one's trousers was in some way shameless. Elisabeth, who was con-demned to seeing men in short jackets and unconcealed trousers, was to be pitied—strange that he had never had such regrets where Ruzena was concerned—but at least for this visit he should have put on his uniform. The broad white cravat with the horseshoe tie-pin concealed the opening of his waistcoat; that was good. He put up his hand and made certain that it was properly in place. It was not for nothing that they laid a cloth over the lower parts of the dead lying on their biers. Helmuth too had driven along this road to Lestow, had called on Elisabeth and her mother, and dust like this had been poured on him in his grave. Had his brother really left Elisabeth to him as a legacy? Or Ruzena? Or perhaps even Bertrand? They should have given Bertrand Helmuth's room, instead of putting him in the solitary guest-chamber; but that would not have been right either. It was all like a sort of inevitable clockwork which yet in some way depended on his own will and simply for that reason seemed inevitable and self-evident, certainly more inevitable than the clockwork routine of the service. But he could not follow out any further these thoughts, behind which lay probably something terrible, for now he was driving into the village and must keep a look-out for the children playing on the road; just beyond the village he turned into the park through the gate flanked right and left by the two lodges.

" I'm delighted to see you here again at last, Herr von Pasenow," said the Baron, meeting him in the hall, and when Joachim mentioned the guest because of whom his visit had been postponed the Baron reproached him for not having brought Bertrand along with him. Joachim himself could not understand now why he had not done so; certainly it would have given no offence; but when Elisabeth entered he thought after all that it was better that he should have come alone. He found her very beautiful, even Bertrand would not be able to resist the charm of such beauty, that was certain, and as certainly he would never dare in her presence to maintain that far too unconstrained tone which was customary with him. Nevertheless Joachim could almost have wished to see him doing so, somewhat as one wishes to hear a coarse word spoken in a church or even to be present at an execution.

They had tea on the terrace, and Joachim, who sat beside Elisabeth, had the sensation that he had been in the same position not so very long ago. But when could it have been? Almost three years had passed since his last visit to Lestow, and then it had been late autumn and it would not have been possible to sit out on the terrace. But while he was still brooding over this, and it seemed to him that during that visit they had had to light the lights in the house, a fantastic association led his thoughts quite into the absurd, and the confusion became almost inextricable, for his accomplice Bertrand—it repelled him a little that the word accomplice should occur to him—for the accomplice and witness of his intimacy with Ruzena was evidently expected to keep him company beside Elisabeth too! How on earth could he have ever thought of introducing him to his parents? The fatalistic feeling that through Bertrand's agency he had slipped from the straight path came back again, and suddenly the idea that after his tea he would have to stand up in his civilian clothes became painful to him; he would have liked to leave his serviette lying on his knees, but already they were proposing a walk through the park. When the farm buildings came in sight the Baron observed that now of course his guest would soon be coming back to live in the country; at least his father had hinted at it. Joachim, filled with renewed antagonism to his father's attempt to determine his life, would have liked to reply that he had no intention of returning to his parents' house; of course one could not say such things, it would not be quite in accordance with the truth nor with his newly found attachment to his home and his property; and so he merely said that it wasn't an easy matter to leave the service, all the more as he would soon be given a captaincy. And one could not give up a profession one had grown fond of so easily as all that, even on grounds of sentiment; he had seen that most clearly in the case of his friend, Herr von Bertrand, who in spite of his many striking successes in business still probably longed in secret to be back with his regiment. And as though against his will he began to speak of Bertrand's world-wide business dealings and long journeys, and he surrounded him, almost with a boy's fantasy, with the nimbus of the explorer, until the ladies could not help expressing their delight over their approaching acquaintance with such an interesting man. All the same Pasenow had the impression that they were all afraid, if not of Bertrand, yet of the life which he led, for Elisabeth became almost subdued and remarked that she was quite incapable of thinking of a brother, say, or some other near relation, being so far away that one could never tell with certainty what part of the world he was in. And the Baron agreed that only a man without a family could lead such a life. A sailor's life, he added. But Joachim, not wishing to be outshone too much by his friend, and feeling, indeed, that here he was nothing less than his friend's deputy, now related that Bertrand had encouraged him to report for the colonial service, and the Baroness said with severity: " You can't do that and leave your parents alone." " No," said the Baron, " your place is in your father's fields," and Joachim was rather pleased to hear it. Then they turned back and, led by Elisabeth's dog, reached again the wide clearing in front of the house. The moist and dewy fragrance of the grass was already rising, and the lights in the house were being lit, for the evenings were beginning to draw in.

When Joachim drove away darkness was falling. The last he saw of Elisabeth was her silhouette on the terrace; she had taken off her garden hat and in the twilight of the fading day she stood against the clear sky which was ribbed with reddish bars of cloud. Joachim could see distinctly the heavy knot of hair at the nape of her neck, and he asked himself why it was that he thought this girl so beautiful, so beautiful that Ruzena's sweetness seemed to vanish from his memory when he saw her. And yet it was for Ruzena that he longed, and not for Elisabeth's purity. Why was Elisabeth beautiful? The trees beside the road rose darkly and the dust smelt cool, as it would smell probably in a cave or a cellar. But in the west a reddish strip still hung in the darkening sky over the rolling landscape.

On the same afternoon that Joachim paid his visit to Lestow, and just after he had driven away, Herr von Pasenow climbed the stairs to the first floor and knocked at Bertrand's door: " I must pay you a visit too . . ." and then as if in secret understanding " I've got rid of him, . . . it wasn't an easy business! " Bertrand murmured a few polite words: he would have been delighted to come down. " No," said Herr von Pasenow, " good form must be preserved. But after tea we'll go for a little walk. I've some things I want to talk to you about." He sat down for a little to preserve the form of his visit, but with his accustomed restlessness presently left the room, to return before the door was closed after him and say: " I only want to see that you have everything you need. In this house you can't depend on anybody." He walked round the room, regarded *La Mère des Gracches*, examined the floor, and then said genially: " Well then, till tea-time."—

Having lighted their cigars they strolled through the park, crossed the kitchen gardens, on whose trees the fruit was already ripening, and at last reached the fields. Herr von Pasenow was obviously in a good humour. A group of women harvest workers came towards them. So as to make place for the gentlemen they formed up in single file at the side of the path, and one after another curtsied as they passed. Herr von Pasenow peered at each one under her head-cloth, and when the single file had passed he said: " Stalwart wenches." " Poles? " asked Bertrand. " Of course, that is, the most of them . . . well, they're an unreliable pack." It was lovely here, Bertrand went on, and he sincerely envied the life of a country gentleman. Herr von Pasenow clapped him on the shoulder: " You could lead it if you liked." Bertrand shook his head: that wasn't such a simple matter, and besides one had to be brought up to it. " I'll see to that," Herr von Pasenow replied with a confidential smile. Then he became silent and Bertrand waited. But Herr von Pasenow seemed to have forgotten what he had wanted to say, for after a long pause he gave utterance to the outcome of his thoughts: " Of course you must write me . . . often, yes." Then: " If you'll come and live here we need have no more fears: both of us need have no more fears . . . what? " He had put his hand on Bertrand's arm, and gazed at him anxiously. " But, Herr von Pasenow, why should we have

any fears?" Herr von Pasenow seemed astonished: "But you said . . ."
he stared in front of him. "Well, it doesn't matter . . ." He remained
standing, then turned round, and it looked as though he were about to
turn back again. But he recollected himself and went on. After a while
he asked: "Have you been to see him yet?" "Him?" "Well, to see
the grave." Bertrand felt a little ashamed; but in the atmosphere of
this house there had really been no fitting opportunity to express a
wish to visit the grave. As he was preparing to answer the question as
diplomatically as possible in the negative, Herr von Pasenow laughed
and said with satisfaction: "Well, then we have still something to do,"
and as another pleasant surprise for his guest pointed with his stick
at the wall of the cemetery, which lay before them. "You go in, I'll
wait for you here," he commanded, and when Bertrand hesitated for a
little he added impatiently and sharply: "No, I'm not coming with
you," and he led Bertrand as far as the gate, over which in golden letters
glittered the inscription: "Rest in Peace." Bertrand entered and after
he had remained for a due period by the grave returned again. Herr von
Pasenow was marching backwards and forwards along the wall with
visible impatience: "Were you with him? . . . well . . .?" Bertrand
pressed his hand, but Herr von Pasenow apparently desired no sympathy
and was waiting for him to say something; he even made a gesture as
of encouragement, and when in spite of this nothing followed, he sighed:
"He died for the honour of his name . . . yes, and meanwhile Joachim
pays visits." Once more he pointed with his stick, this time in the
direction of Lestow. Later with a titter he supplemented his thought:
"I've sent him a-courting," and as though this reminded him that he
had something he wished to discuss with Bertrand: "Right! I'm told
you're good at business matters." Well, yes, but only in his special
branch, replied Bertrand. "Well, for our business that will do well
enough. You see, my dear fellow, I'm naturally in need of advice
now that he's dead." He paused for a little and then said importantly:
"Question of inheritance." Bertrand replied that Herr von Pasenow
must surely have a confidential legal adviser who would guide him, but
Herr von Pasenow paid no attention: "Joachim will be provided for
through his marriage; he could be disinherited"; and he laughed again.
Bertrand tried to turn the conversation and pointed to a hare: "They'll
soon be out with the guns again, Herr von Pasenow." "Yes, yes, he can
come to the shooting if he likes; he's all right for things like that. . . .

we'll invite him, what? and of course he must write to us; we'll soon bring him up to the scratch there, what? " As Herr von Pasenow laughed, Bertrand smiled too, though he felt very uncomfortable. He was a little annoyed at Joachim for delivering him up to this man; but how incapable the fellow showed himself even here to have allowed this old dotard to get into such a mood! Had the clumsy creature invited him here too, to straighten out his affairs? So he said: " Yes, yes, Herr von Pasenow, we'll soon lick him into shape." And this appeared to be the tone that the old man wished him to adopt. He leant on Bertrand's arm, carefully suiting his step to that of his companion, and did not remove his arm again even when they reached the house. Though darkness had fallen they walked up and down the yard until Joachim drove up. When Joachim jumped down from the gig Herr von Pasenow said: " Let me introduce my friend, Herr von Bertrand," and with a somewhat casual wave of the hand: " and this is my son . . . just back from his courting," he added facetiously. The smell of the byres came across on the wind, and Herr von Pasenow felt in good spirits.

" She isn't really beautiful," Bertrand told himself as he regarded Elisabeth sitting at the piano; " her mouth is too large and her lips are of a curiously soft and almost evil sensuality. But when she smiles she's charming."

It was to a " musical tea " that Joachim and Bertrand had been invited. Elisabeth's accompanists in Spohr's trio were an old friend from a neighbouring estate and the indigent local teacher, and when the silvery crystalline drops of the piano fell into the brown stream of the two stringed instruments it seemed to Joachim that it was all due to Elisabeth. He loved music, although he did not understand much about it, but now he thought he had caught its meaning; it was pure and clear and hovered high above everything as on a silvery cloud, and from its celestial height let fall its cold and pure drops on the earth. And perhaps only to Elisabeth did it manifest itself, even though Bertrand, as he remembered from the days in Culm, could play a little on the violin. No, it did not look as if Bertrand would try to conquer Elisabeth from the musical side. When asked about his violin-playing he had replied evasively, with a deprecatory wave of the hand; and it may have been pure hypocrisy—for it had sounded cynical enough—when on the way back he had found nothing better to say than: " If she would only play something else than that horribly boring Spohr! "—

They had arranged to go riding: Joachim and Bertrand called for Elisabeth. Joachim rode Helmuth's horse, which had now once more become his property. They galloped over the stubble-fields where the shocks were still standing, and then at a sharp trot turned into a narrow forest-path. Joachim let his friend ride in front with Elisabeth, and while he followed it seemed to him that in her long black riding-habit she looked still taller and slenderer than usual. He would have liked to turn away his eyes, but she did not sit quite faultlessly on her horse and it disturbed him; she bent a little too far forward as she sat, and as she rose and sank, touching the saddle and then rebounding again, up and down, he could not but recall the day when he had said good-bye to her in the station, and the despicable wish that he could desire her as a woman rose up again, doubly despicable since his father, and before Bertrand too, had spoken of his courting. But almost more loathsome was the thought that Elisabeth's parents too, yes, her very mother, might regard him as an object of desire for their daughter, hold him up to her as an attraction, both of them persuaded that they might reckon upon this desire, that it would appear and that it would not fail their expectations. Yet something more essential, more profound, remained still concealed behind all this, an indefinite idea of which Joachim desired to remain ignorant, although he felt his mouth becoming dry and his face hot; it was indefinite, and yet it made him angry that they should dare to consider Elisabeth capable of such things; he felt ashamed before her and ashamed for her. Let Bertrand have her if he wanted to, he thought, forgetting that in doing so he was committing the self-same offence which he had just rejected with such indignation. But suddenly that did not matter, suddenly it seemed to him that Bertrand did not come into the question: with his wavy hair he was so feminine, in some way sisterly, with a sisterly solicitude to which perhaps Elisabeth could be safely confided. That was not quite true, of course, yet for a moment it was reassuring. Besides, what was it really that made her beautiful? And he contemplated her body bobbing up and down and her hips returning to the saddle again and again. And doing this he discovered that it was not beauty, but far more truly the opposite of beauty, that awakened desire; but he pushed the thought aside, and the picture of Elisabeth clambering into her carriage still in his mind, his thoughts flew to Ruzena, whose countless imperfections made her so charming. He let his horse fall into a walk to increase the distance between him and the couple in front, and drew Ruzena's last letter from his breast-pocket. The notepaper smelt of the perfume which he had given her, and he breathed again the air of their illicit intimacy. Yes, that was where he belonged, that was where he wanted to be, and he felt he was a voluntary exile from society, and yet an outcast; he felt unworthy of Elisabeth. Bertrand was his accomplice, true, but Bertrand had the cleaner hands, and when Joachim recognized this he saw too why Bertrand had always treated him and Ruzena with a touch of superiority, of the avuncular, as a doctor might treat one, and had kept his own secrets hidden. A father's secrets should never be uncovered; that was as it should be, and yet because of it that fellow in front of him was in a position, was at liberty, to ride by Elisabeth's side, though he too was unworthy, yet better than Joachim himself. He thought of Helmuth. And as though he wanted Helmuth's horse at least to be beside them, he set it to a trot. Its hoofs thudded softly on the leafy ground, and when they encountered a twig he could hear the sharp cracking of the wood. The leather of the saddle creaked pleasantly, and from the darkness of the leafage came a cool wind.

He overtook them at the border of a long clearing which rose gently. The coolness of the woods was as if cut off here, and one could smell the sun's heat rising from the grass. With the lash of her riding-whip Elisabeth flicked at the horse-flies that had fixed themselves to her mount, and the horse, which knew the way, was impatient, awaiting its usual gallop over the clearing. Joachim felt superior to Bertrand; no matter how wide his business interests might be, at a desk one did not acquire the practice necessary to leap over obstacles. Elisabeth pointed out the hurdles, a hedge which she was accustomed to take, a fallen tree-trunk, and a ditch. They were not difficult. The groom was left behind at the edge of the clearing: Elisabeth took the lead, and Joachim again came last, not merely out of politeness, but because he wanted to see how Bertrand would take the jumps. The grass had not yet been mown, and it rustled lightly and sharply against the legs of the horses. Elisabeth rode first towards the ditch; it was a mere trifle, and it was only to be expected that Bertrand would take it. But when the hedge too was taken by Bertrand in good style Joachim felt really annoyed; the tree-trunk was far too easy, his last hope was gone. Joachim's horse, which was trying to overhaul the others, was pulling hard at the curb, and Joachim had to hold it back to preserve his distance. Now came the tree-trunk; Elisabeth and Bertrand had negotiated it easily, almost elegantly; and Joachim gave his horse a free head for the leap. But when it was gathering itself for the jump he checked it suddenly, why he was never able to tell; the horse stumbled on the trunk, came down sideways and rolled over him on the grass. This of course happened very quickly, and when the other two turned round he and the horse were quietly standing together in front of the trunk, the bridle still in his hands. " What's happened? " Happened? He didn't know himself: he examined his horse's legs, it was lame in one forefoot; it would have to be taken home. The finger of God, thought Joachim; it was not Bertrand but himself who had fallen, and now it was only right and just that he must go away and leave Elisabeth with that fellow. When Elisabeth suggested that he should take her groom's mount and send him back with the lame horse, he declined morosely, for he still saw in the incident a judgment from God. And after all it was Helmuth's horse and it could not be entrusted to anyone. He started for home at a walking pace and resolved to return to Berlin as soon as possible.

They rode side by side along the forest-path. Although the groom followed at a short distance Elisabeth had the feeling that she was deserted by Joachim, a feeling which acutely depressed her. Perhaps she felt Bertrand's glance hovering round her face. " Her mouth is strange," Bertrand told himself, " and her eyes have that clearness which I love so much. She would be an easily wounded and provoking and really difficult mistress. Her hands are too big for a woman, thin and slender. She's a sensual boy, that's what she is. But she's charming." To escape from her depression Elisabeth tried to start a conversation, although a little time before she had already made the remark with which she began:

" Herr von Pasenow has told us a lot about you and your great travels."

" Yes? He has told me a lot about your great beauty."

Elisabeth did not reply.

" Doesn't that please you? "

" I have no wish to hear anything about my alleged beauty."

" You are very beautiful."

Elisabeth said a little uncertainly: " I didn't think that you were one of the lady-killers."

She's cleverer than I imagined, thought Bertrand, and he replied: " I couldn't bring myself even to utter that awful term, not even if I wanted to be insulting. But I'm not being a lady-killer; you know well enough how beautiful you are."

" Then why do you tell me? "

" Because I'll never see you again."

Elisabeth looked at him in surprise.

" Of course you don't like anyone to talk to you of your beauty, for behind the compliment you suspect the wooer. But if I go away and never see you again, then logically I can't be trying to court you and am justified in telling you the nicest things I can."

Elisabeth had to laugh.

" Dreadful that one can listen to nice things only from a complete stranger."

" At least one can believe them only from a complete stranger. Intimacy contains necessarily the seeds of dishonesty and falsehood."

" If that were true it would be really frightful."

" Of course it is true, but that doesn't make it at all frightful. Intimacy is the slyest and really meanest kind of courting. Instead of simply saying that one desires a woman because she's beautiful, one insinuates oneself into her confidence, so as to catch her off her guard."

Elisabeth reflected for a little, then she said: " Isn't there something outrageous behind your words? "

" No, for I'm going away . . . a stranger can afford to speak the truth."

" I'm afraid of everything strange."

" Because you're attracted by it. You're beautiful, Elisabeth. May I call you that for this one day? "

They rode in silence side by side. Then she said, finding the right words: " What do you really want? "

" Nothing."

" But then there's no meaning in all this."

" I want the same thing as everybody else who courts you and tells you for that reason that you're beautiful; but I'm more honest."

" I don't want anyone to court me."

" Perhaps what you hate is simply the dishonest form it takes."

" Aren't you really more dishonest than the others? "

" I'm going away."

" What does that prove? "

" Among other things, well, my modesty."

" How? "

" To court a woman means to offer oneself to her as the living biped that one is, and that's indecent. And it's quite possible, indeed quite probable, that that's why you hate any kind of courting."

" I cannot say."

" Love is an absolute thing, Elisabeth, and when the absolute tries to express itself in earthly terms, then it always turns into pathos, simply because it can't be demonstrated. And as the whole thing then becomes so horribly earthly, the pathos is always very funny, represented by the gentleman who goes down on his knees to get you to accede to all his wishes; and if one loves you one must avoid that."

Was his intention in saying this to intimate that he loved her? As he became silent she looked at him questioningly. He appeared to understand:

" There is a true pathos, and we call it eternity. And as there is no positive eternity for human beings it must be a negative one and can be put in the words ' never-to-meet-again.' If I go away now, eternity is here; then you will be eternally remote from me and I can say that I love you."

" Don't say such dreadful things."

" Perhaps it's the absolute clearness of my feelings that makes me talk like this to you. But perhaps there's a little hate and resentment too in my forcing you to listen to my monologue, jealousy perhaps, because you'll stay here and live on."

" Real jealousy? "

" Yes, jealousy, and a little pride as well. For there's the wish in it to let a stone fall into the well of your soul, so that it may rest there for ever."

" So you want to intrude yourself into my intimacy too? "

" It may be. But still stronger is the wish that the stone may turn into a talisman for you."

" When? "

" When the man will kneel before you whom I'm jealous of at this moment, the man who will offer you with that antiquated gesture his physical proximity: then the memory of, let us say, an aseptic form of love may help to remind you that behind every pseudo-æsthetic gesture in love there is hidden a still grosser reality."

" Do you say that to all the women you run away from ? "

" One should say it to them all, but I generally run away before it comes to that."

Elisabeth stared reflectively at her horse's mane. Then she said: " I don't know, but all this sounds strangely unnatural and beside the point to me."

" If you're thinking of the propagation of the human race, then of course it's unnatural. But do you find it more natural that some man or other, who lives somewhere at present, eating and drinking and looking after his affairs, will meet you some time by a stupid chance, and take a suitable opportunity of telling you how beautiful you are, getting down on one knee before you, so that afterwards, having gone through certain formalities, the two of you might produce children. Do you find that quite natural ? "

" Be silent! That's dreadful! . . . That's horrible! "

" Yes, it is dreadful, but not because I speak of it as it is; for it's a still more dreadful thing to think that you're certainly destined, and very soon, to experience it and not merely to hear about it."

Elisabeth fought down her tears; she said with an effort: " But why, in Heaven's name, should I hear about it ? . . . please, please, be silent."

" What are you afraid of, Elisabeth ? "

She replied softly: " I'm afraid enough as it is."

" Of what ? "

" Of everything unknown, of others, of what's to come . . . I can't express it. I have a desperate hope that what is still to come will be as familiar to me as everything that's familiar now. My father and mother belong to each other after all. But you want to take away my hope from me."

" And you refuse to see the danger because you're afraid of it. Isn't it one's duty to shake you awake so that you mightn't let your life run away, or dry to dust, or shrink to nothing, or something like that, out of mere indifference, or conventional notions, or ignorance ? . . . Elisabeth, I mean very well by you."

Once more Elisabeth found the right words when she said softly, hesitatingly, against her will: " Then why don't you stay ? "

" I've only been flung in your way by mere chance. And if I remained it would be as much an assault on your feelings as those I've been trying to warn you against; a somewhat aseptic assault, but still an assault."

" What should I do? "

" That can be answered only negatively: nothing that isn't approved by every fibre of you. No one can come to fulfilment except by submitting freely and absolutely to the law of his feelings and his nature —forgive the pathos."

" Nobody ever helps me."

" No, you are alone, as alone as you will be on your deathbed."

" It isn't true. It isn't true, what you say. I've never been alone, nor are my father and mother alone. You talk like that because you want to be alone . . . or perhaps because it gives you pleasure to torment me? "

" Elisabeth, you are so beautiful that perhaps your fulfilment and completion lie simply in your beauty. Why should I torment you? But all I've said is true, and I've not said the worst either."

" Don't torment me."

" Somewhere in everybody there's an insane hope that the little scrap of love that is given us will fling that bridge over the void. Be on your guard against the pathos of love."

" What are you warning me against now? "

" All pathos comes to this, that it promises us a mystery and tries to redeem its promise by a cliché. I should like to see you safeguarded against that kind of love."

" You're a poor creature."

" Because I show my empty pockets? Be on your guard against anyone who doesn't show them."

" No, not that. I feel that you're more to be pitied than the others, even than those others you talked about. . . ."

" I must warn you again. Never pity anyone in this business. A love born of pity is no better than a love that's bought."

" Oh! "

" Yes, you won't admit that, Elisabeth. Well, put it this way then: the woman who sins out of pity presents afterwards the most pitiless reckoning."

Elisabeth looked at him almost with hostility: " I have no pity for you."

" But you shouldn't look at me so angrily, all the same, although it's almost honester that you should."

" Why honester? "

Bertrand was silent. Then after a while he said: " Listen, Elisabeth, one must carry even honesty to the bitter end. I don't like to say such things. But I love you. I state that with all the seriousness and all the honesty that one can be capable of in these matters of feeling. And I know, too, that you could come to love me——"

" For Heaven's sake, be silent . . ."

" Why? I don't overestimate these vague emotional states in the least, and I won't try to be pathetic. Yet no man can quench the insane hope that some time he'll find that mystical bridge of love. But just because of that I must go away. There is only one real kind of pathos, the pathos of separation, of pain . . . if one wants to make the bridge capable of holding, then one must stretch it so far that no weight can be put on it. If after that——"

" Oh, be silent."

" If after that necessity is still stronger than all that one has voluntarily set against it, if the tension of an indescribable longing becomes so sharp that it threatens to cut the world in two, then the proven hope may arise that the weak individual destiny of two human beings is lifted above the chaos of chance, above a stale and sentimental melancholy, above a mechanical and fortuitous intimacy."

And as though he were talking to himself and no longer to Elisabeth, he continued: " I believe, and this is my deepest belief, that only by a dreadful intensification of itself, only when in a sense it becomes infinite, can the strangeness parting two human beings be transformed into its opposite, into absolute recognition, and let that thing come to life which hovers in front of love as its unattainable goal, and yet is its condition: the mystery of oneness. The gradual accustoming of oneself to another, the gradual deepening of intimacy, evokes no mystery whatever."

Elisabeth was crying.

He went on softly: " I should like you never to know and suffer from love except in that final and unattainable form. And even if I should not be the one, I would not be jealous of anybody then. But I suffer and feel jealous and impotent when I think that you will put up with something cheaper. Are you crying because perfection is unattainable? Then you are right to cry. Oh, I love you, I long to sink in your strangeness, I long that you might be the final and predestined woman for me. . . ."

Now once more they rode on in silence side by side; they emerged from the forest and came to a field-path leading down to the main road which they had to take to get back. When he caught sight of the dusty road, which lay white under the sunlight and the pale sky, he drew up his horse so that in the shadow of the trees he might say again, very softly, and as in farewell: " I love you . . . love you, it's fantastic." But that they should ride together after this on the dry, sunny road seemed to both of them impossible, and she felt grateful to him when he stopped and said: " I'll try to overtake our unlucky friend, I think," and then, very softly: " Farewell." She gave him her hand. He bowed over it and she heard once more: " Farewell." She said nothing, but when he had turned to go she cried: " Herr von Bertrand! " He came back; she hesitated for a little, then she said: " Till we meet again." She would have liked to say " Farewell," but it seemed out of place and theatrical. When after a little he looked round, he could hardly distinguish any longer which of the two figures was Elisabeth and which the groom; they were already too far away and the sun blinded his eyes.

Peter the serving-man stood on the terrace at Lestow and struck the gong. The Baroness had initiated this manner of announcing meals after a visit to England with her husband, and it had since become a custom. And although Peter the serving-man had been striking the gong for several years, he still remained a little ashamed of causing such a childish din, especially as the sound carried as far as the village street and had once gained him the nickname of " The Drummer." Consequently he struck the gong discreetly, eliciting from it only a few deep tones that reverberated roundly in the silence of the park, and the rest of his performance was a flat, unmusical, brazen something that thinly died away.

Riding at a slow footpace through the noonday village street, Elisabeth heard the serving-man softly beating the gong and admonishing her that the time had come to change her dress. Nevertheless she did not hasten her horse's pace, and if she had not been so lost in thought it might have struck her that to-day, perhaps for the first time in her life, she felt a sort of repugnance for the family gathering at the lunch-table, indeed that her return to the beautiful, quiet park, her entry through the gate with the two lodges, weighed on her with a feeling of heavy oppression. A disturbing longing for distant things had risen up in her and along with this longing an absurd idea, doubly absurd in this midday heat, that Bertrand could not thrive in this cold climate, and that consequently he had always to flee and always to be saying good-bye. The echoes of the gong had died away. She dismounted in the yard, the groom holding her horse by the bridle; she hurried into the house, the tail of her riding-habit over her arm; she went up the steps, went the familiar way, yet as if in a waking dream. A mild fit of courage came over her, a somewhat melancholy pleasure at the thought of going wherever she pleased, of taking her destiny in her own hands and directing it; but her thoughts did not go very far and remained held up by the question what her parents would say if she appeared at the lunch-table in her riding-habit. Joachim von Pasenow too was one of those who could be shocked by such offences. Her little dog Bello tumbled down the stairs barking, mechanically she gave him her riding-whip; but she did not smile at the pride with which he carried it to her boudoir, and artfully as he laid himself at her feet, devoutly gazing up at her as though he found in her beauty fulfilment and consummation, Elisabeth did not stroke his head, but went up to the mirror and gazed into it for a long time without recognizing herself, seeing only the slender black silhouette; and it was as though the figure in the mirror and she herself were receding from each other in an immobility which slowly dissolved only when the maid entered, according to the daily custom, to help her to take off her riding-habit. But while the girl knelt before her to pull off her riding-boots, while her outstretched feet slipped with a light, cool sensation from the long boots and lay, small now in their black silken stockings, on the maid's knee, she sought anew in the mirror that receding image, receding, as it were, in flight to someone or other who lived somewhere or other and perhaps would some day go on his knees before her. Her riding-whip was still lying on the carpet. Elisabeth tried to recall Bertrand at the railway station in his long, angular service coat, his sword by his side, and imagined that the departing train had caught him and was dragging him with it. There was a certain malicious pleasure in the fancy, but also a stifling fear such as she had never felt before. She sat with her head bent back, her hands at her temples, as though in this posture she could free herself from the power of an unexpected compulsion. " Still, nothing has happened," something said within her, and she could not understand her vague feeling of excitement, which yet seemed so strangely definite that it could almost be expressed in words: cut the world in two. It was not quite definite, certainly, yet a frontier line had been drawn, and what had once been indivisible, this closed world of hers, now fell asunder, and her parents stood at the other side of the frontier line. Behind all this was fear, the fear from which her parents wished to guard her as though their very life depended upon it; but the thing they feared had now broken in, strangely moving and exciting, and yet not in the least fearful. One could say " Du " to a stranger: that was all. And it was so little that Elisabeth became almost sad. She got up resolutely; no, she would not resign herself to a stale and sentimental melancholy. She went up to the mirror and patted her hair straight.

At the foot of the great staircase on an ebony frame hung the dull, yellow, bronze gong, decorated with flat Chinese designs. A genuine piece which the Baron had purchased in London. Peter the serving-man held the baton with the soft, grey leather head in one hand, while he gazed at his watch and waited. Fourteen minutes had elapsed since his first announcement, and when the watch-hand reached the fifteenth Peter would deliver three discreet taps on the bronze plate.

III

On the following day Bertrand excused himself from breakfasting with the family, then waylaid Joachim and told him that to his sincere regret he had been called away on business, and must leave the very next morning. Joachim's first feeling was one of relief. " I'll come with you," he said, looking gratefully at Bertrand, who had, it was obvious, given Elisabeth up. And to show him that he too would renounce her he added kindly: " I don't know of anything to keep me here."

Joachim went to impart this decision to his father. But when Herr von Pasenow started in surprise and asked suspiciously, with his usual indiscretion: " How is that possible? He hasn't had any letters since the day before yesterday," Joachim too was startled: how, indeed, was that possible? What could have moved Bertrand to the renunciation? And along with a feeling of shame at becoming his father's accomplice in indiscretion by posing these questions, the vision arose of a friendly triumph: it was because Elisabeth loved him, Joachim von Pasenow, that she had rebuffed Bertrand. Of course it was quite incredible that anyone should have had the face to propose to a lady so hastily, almost in the twinkling of an eye. But anything was possible to a business man who thought he had the chance of a rich heiress. Joachim was not able to pursue these reflections, for he was startled by the sudden change in his father's appearance; he was huddled up in the chair by the writing-table and with a vacant stare was muttering: " The scoundrel, the scoundrel . . . he has broken his promise." Then he looked at Joachim and screamed: " Out you get, you and your fine friend . . . you're in the plot too! " " But, Father! " " Out you go, both of you; get out! " He had sprung to his feet, and advanced upon his retreating son, driving him in short rushes towards the door. And at every pause he thrust forward his head and spat at him: " Get out! " When Joachim was in the corridor the old man slammed the door, but opened it again immediately and stuck his head out: " And tell him not to dare to write to me. Tell him I've no further interest in him." The door crashed to and Joachim heard the key being turned.

He found his mother in the garden; she showed no great consternation: " He's not one to say much, but for some days he has seemed angry with you. I think he can't forgive you for not giving up the army. Still, it is queer." When they turned towards the house she added: " Perhaps he was offended, too, because you brought your friend down here so soon; I think it might be better for me to see him first alone." Joachim escorted her upstairs; the door giving on the corridor was locked, and there was no answer to her knocking. It was a little uncanny, and so they went round to the large drawing-room, since it was just possible that he might have left his study by the other door. Through the chain of empty rooms they reached the study and found it unlocked. Frau von Pasenow opened the door and Joachim saw his father sitting motionless at the writing-table, a quill in his hand. He did not move even when Frau von Pasenow advanced and bent over him. He had pressed so heavily on the quill-point that it was splintered; and on the paper stood the words: " I disinherit for dishonourable conduct my . . ." and then came the splutter of ink made by the broken quill. " In the name of God, what has happened? " But he made no answer. Helplessly his wife regarded him; when she noticed that the inkpot too had been upset she hastily seized the blotting-pad and tried to mop up the mess. He thrust her away with his elbow and then caught sight

of Joachim in the doorway, grinned malignantly, and attempted to go
on writing with the broken quill. When it caught again in the paper
and tore a hole in it he groaned aloud, pointed his forefinger at his son
and cried: " Out with him! " At the same time he tried to rise, but
apparently found it impossible, for he collapsed again in a huddle, dis-
regarding the flowing ink, and sank forward over the writing-table with
his face on his arms like a crying child. Joachim whispered to his
mother: " I'll call the doctor," and ran downstairs to send a messenger
to the village.

The doctor came and sent Herr von Pasenow to bed. He administered
bromide and spoke of a cold-water cure; it was simply a nervous break-
down following on the death of his son. Yes, yes, that was the doctor's
banal explanation. But it was no explanation. There was more in it than
that, and it could not be mere coincidence; the accident to Helmuth's
horse had been a kind of preliminary warning, and now when, in spite
of everything, Joachim was about to triumph over Bertrand, now when
Elisabeth for his sake had rebuffed Bertrand and he was making ready
to play Bertrand false and to play Ruzena false, ostensibly in obedience
to his father, now was the hour for fate to strike. An accomplice who
betrayed his fellow-accomplices; accused, and rightly accused, by his
father of plotting with Bertrand! Must not the whole web now fall to
pieces, and treachery cancel treachery? And Bertrand must appropriate
Ruzena again to convince the father that he was no longer the son's
accomplice and to avenge himself for Elisabeth's refusal! In all the foul
and hateful suspicion with which Joachim now regarded Bertrand's
departure to Berlin, he saw only his own departure postponed indefinitely,
and that tormented him more than his anxiety about his afflicted father.
The tangled web unravelled itself only to be knotted in fresh tangles.
Was this what his father had in mind when he had pressed him to visit
Lestow? And besides, it was impossible to discover what had happened
between his father and Bertrand. Perhaps it might have been cleared
up if he could have mentioned to Bertrand the old man's dark insinua-
tions, but he had to confine himself to announcing his sudden illness.
He begged Bertrand to explain the situation to Ruzena; in any case he
would himself come to Berlin soon for a few days, to get his leave
extended and see to other things. Well, said Bertrand, as Joachim
escorted him to the station, well, and what was to become of Ruzena
now? Of course it was to be hoped that Herr von Pasenow would soon

recover, but Joachim's presence in Stolpin would none the less become more and more indispensable. " She ought to be provided with some regular occupation," he observed; " something she enjoys doing; that would help her over the difficult times ahead." Joachim was offended, for after all that was his own affair; he said hesitatingly: " But the theatre you got her into, she enjoys herself there." Bertrand dismissed this statement with a wave of the hand, and Joachim stared at him uncomprehendingly. " But don't you worry, Pasenow, we'll find something or other." And although it was a worry that had not previously occurred to Joachim, he was now sincerely glad to have it so lightly taken off his shoulders by Bertrand.

Since the old man's illness, which still kept him in bed the greater part of the day, life had become curiously simplified. Joachim could now reflect more quietly on many things, and some of the riddles appeared less obscure, or at least more approachable. But now an almost insoluble problem confronted him, and it was no use trying to decipher it in Elisabeth's face, for her face itself constituted the problem. Lying back in her chair she was gazing at the autumn landscape, and her up-tilted face, thrown back almost at a right angle to the taut line of the throat, was like an irregular roof set upon the pillar of her neck. One could perhaps say just as well that it rested like a leaf on the calyx of the throat, or that it was a lid covering the throat, for it was really no longer a face, merely a continuation of the throat, an extension from the throat, with a far-off resemblance to the head of a serpent. Joachim followed the line of her throat; the chin jutted out like a hill, behind which lay the landscape of her face. Softly rounded the rim of the crater which was her mouth, dark the cavern of the nose, divided by a white pillar. Like a miniature beard sprouted the hedge of the eyebrows, and beyond the clearing of the forehead, cut by finely ploughed furrows, was the edge of the forest. Joachim was again forced to ask the question why a woman can be desirable, but nothing gave him an answer; it remained insoluble and perplexing. He shut his eyelids a little and peered through the slits at the landscape of that extended face. It blended at once with the real landscape, the woodland verge of the hair bordered the yellowing leaves of the forest, and the glass balls that decorated the rose-beds in the garden glittered with the same light as the jewel that in the shadow of the cheek—ah, was it still a cheek?—shone as an ear-ring.

This was both startling and comforting, and when the eye combined these separate things into a unity so strange, past all disjoining, one was curiously reminded of something, transposed into some mode that lay beyond convention far back in childhood, and the unsolved riddle was like a sign that had emerged from the sea of memory.

They were sitting in the shady front garden of the little inn; their horses were in the yard behind with the groom. From the rustling of the leaves above them one could tell that it was September. For it was no longer the clear, soft purling of spring leafage, nor yet the full note of summer: in summer the trees simply rustle without much variation, but in the early days of autumn a sharper, silvery metallic tone is already perceptible, as if the broad harmony in the flowing sap were breaking up. When autumn begins the midday hours are quite motionless; the sun still shines with summer warmth, and when a lighter, cooler breeze comes wandering through the branches there is, as it were, a streak of spring in the air. The leaves that drop from the trees on to the rough inn table are not yet yellowed, but dry and brittle for all their greenness, and the summer-like sunshine seems then doubly precious. With its bow pointing upstream the fisherman's boat lies in the channel; the water glides past smoothly, as if moving in broad planes. These autumn days have none of the drowsiness of summer noons; a soft and watchful serenity lies over everything.

Elisabeth said: " Why do we live here? In the south there would be days like this all the year round." Joachim recalled the southern face of the Italian with the black moustache. But in Elisabeth's features it was impossible now to descry those of an Italian, or even of a brother, so removed were they from humanity, so akin to the landscape. He tried to find in them again their ordinary shape, and when it suddenly reappeared, when the nose became a nose again, the mouth a mouth, the eye an eye, the transformation was once more startling, and he was comforted only by the smoothness of her hair, which was not too insistently waved. " Why? Don't you like the winter? " " Your friend's right; one ought to travel," was her answer. " He wants to go to India," said Joachim, and thought of its olive-skinned races and of Ruzena. Why had he never once thought of travelling abroad with Ruzena? He was aware of Elisabeth's eyes on his face, felt caught, and turned aside. But if anyone was to blame for this fever for travel it was Bertrand. His need to compensate himself for the lack of an ordered life and to deaden his regrets by business deals and exotic journeys was infectious, and if Elisabeth was yearning for the south it was perhaps because she regretted—even though she had refused Bertrand—that she was not travelling by his side. He heard Elisabeth's voice: " How long have we known each other? " He cast it up; it wasn't so easy to determine; when he was a twelve-year-old boy home for the holidays he had often visited Lestow with his parents. And at that time Elisabeth was only a few weeks old. " So I've known you always, all my life," decided Elisabeth, " and yet I've never really been aware of you; I've always counted you among the grown-ups." Joachim said nothing. " And I suppose you've never been aware of me either," she went on. Oh yes, he said, he had, one day when she suddenly blossomed out as a young lady, all at once and most surprisingly. Elisabeth said: " But now we're almost contemporaries. . . . When is your birthday, by the way? " And without waiting for an answer she added: " Can you still remember what I looked like as a child? " Joachim had to think back; in the Baroness's drawing-room there hung a portrait of Elisabeth as a child that obstinately displaced the actual memory. " It's queer," he said; " I know very well what you looked like, and yet . . ." He wanted to say that he could not find the child's face in .hers, although of course it must be there, but as he looked at her once more her face ceased to be a face at all, and was simply hill and valley again, covered with something called skin. As if she wanted to challenge his thoughts she said: " With a little effort I can see what you looked like as a boy, in spite of the moustache." She laughed. " That's really funny; I must try to do it with my father too." " Can you see me as an old man as well? " Elisabeth eyed him keenly: " That's queer; no, I can't . . . but wait a minute, yes, I can: you'll be still more like your mother, with a nice, round face, and your moustache will be white and bushy. . . . But what about me as an old woman? Shall I create a very dignified impression? " Joachim declared himself incapable of imagining it. " Oh, don't be gallant, do tell me." " Excuse me, I'd rather not. There's something unpleasant in suddenly looking like one's parents or one's brother or anything else than oneself . . . it makes so many things meaningless." " Is that your friend Bertrand's opinion too? " " No, not so far as I know: why should you think so? " " Oh, only that it would be like him." " I don't know, but Bertrand seems to me so much concerned with the external details of his busy life that he simply never thinks of things like that. He is never fully himself."

Elisabeth smiled. " You mean that he always sees things from a great distance? Through the eyes of a stranger, as it were? " What was she thinking of? What was she hinting at? He despised himself for his curiosity, he felt that he was unchivalrous, and at the same time realized anew that it was an unchivalrous proceeding to let a woman fall into another man's hands instead of shielding her, shielding her from everybody. Yet he was really pledged to marry Elisabeth. But Elisabeth looked far from unhappy as she said: " It has been lovely; but now we must go home for lunch, they're expecting us."

They rode homewards, and the tower of Lestow was already in sight when she said, as if she had been reflecting on their conversation: " It's queer, all the same, how closely intimacy and strangeness are knit together. Perhaps you are right in not wanting to think of growing old." Joachim, preoccupied with thoughts of Ruzena, did not understand her in the least, but this time he did not concern himself about it.

If there was one thing that contributed to Herr von Pasenow's recovery it was the mail-bag. One morning while he was still in bed the thought struck him: " Who's looking after the post-bag? Joachim, I suppose." No, Joachim wasn't bothering about it. He grumbled that Joachim never bothered about anything, but seemed relieved, insisted on getting up, and slowly went to his study. When the messenger appeared the usual ritual was gone through, and it was rehearsed as usual from that day on. And if Frau von Pasenow happened to be in the room she had to listen to the usual complaint that nobody wrote to him. He asked often enough if Joachim was about the place, but he refused to see him. And when he heard that Joachim had to go for a few days to Berlin he said: " Inform him that I forbid it." Sometimes he forgot this, and complained that not even his own children wrote to him; and this put the idea into his wife's head of getting Joachim to write a letter of reconciliation to his father. Joachim remembered the congratulations that he and his brother had had to inscribe on rose-bordered paper whenever his parents had a birthday; it had been a frightful torment to him. He declined to submit to it again and announced that he was going away. They could conceal it from his father if they liked.

He set off without enthusiasm; if he had once objected to having a marriage prescribed for him, he now rebelled in the same way against the fact that his three days' sojourn in Berlin plighted him to three

nights with Ruzena. He found it degrading for Ruzena too. He would
have preferred to put off their meeting as long as possible, and to prevent
her at least from coming to the station he had omitted to mention the
time of his arrival. In the train it occurred to him that he ought to bring
her a present of some kind; but since neither partridges nor other game
would have been suitable, the only thing he could do was to buy her
something in Berlin; so it was a good thing she would not be at the
station. He tried to think of a suitable gift for her, but his imagination
lagged; he could not hit upon anything and wavered back and forward
between perfume and gloves; oh, well, in Berlin he would find something
or other.

When he reached his flat the first thing he did was to write a note to
Bertrand, who would certainly be glad to have at last an opportunity
of discussing with him the weird events of his last day at Stolpin. He
wrote to Ruzena also, and sent both notes by a messenger with instructions to wait for an answer. He felt pleasantly at home in his flat. The
warmth of summer still brooded captive behind the shuttered windows.
Joachim opened a shutter and basked in the stillness of the street; it
was late afternoon, rain might fall before night, there was a grey wall
of cloud in the western sky. The vines on the fences of the front gardens
were red, yellow chestnut leaves lay on the pavement, and the horses
in the shafts of the four cabs at the corner of the street stood with
their forelegs bent in peaceful resignation. Joachim leaned out of the
window and watched his valet open the others; if the man had leaned
out too Joachim would have smiled and nodded to him along the house-
front. And while his bags were being unpacked he stayed there at the
window, gazing at the quiet, darkening street. Then he drew his head
in; the rooms had become cooler, only here and there a stray patch of
summer still lingered in the air, filling him with a sweet melancholy.
But it did him good to feel his uniform on him again; he walked about
among his private belongings, surveying them and his books. Yes, he
would do more reading this winter. Then he winced; in three days'
time he was due to leave all this again. He sat down as if to show that
he was a settled occupant, ordered the windows to be shut, and asked
for tea. Some time later the messenger, whom he had forgotten, came
back: Herr von Bertrand was not in Berlin, but was expected in the
next few days, and the lady had given no answer except simply that she
was coming at once. To Joachim it was as if some slight hope had finally

vanished; he could almost have wished that the messages were reversed and that it was Bertrand who was to come at once. Besides, he had intended to go out and buy a present. In a few minutes, however, the door-bell rang; Ruzena was there.

When he was a cadet and learning to swim he had balked at jumping in, until one day he was summarily thrown into the water by the swimming instructor; and after all it was simply pleasant in the water, and he had laughed. Ruzena came in like a whirlwind and flew to embrace him. It was pleasant in the water, and they sat hand in hand, exchanging kisses, and Ruzena babbled on about things that seemed irrelevant. None of his uneasiness remained, and his happiness would have been almost cloudless had not his vexation at forgetting Ruzena's present suddenly obtruded itself with renewed force. But since God had arranged everything for good, if not for the best, He led Joachim to the cupboard in which the lace handkerchiefs had been lying unremembered for months. And while Ruzena, as usual, made ready their supper, Joachim found tissue-paper and a light blue ribbon and slipped the package under Ruzena's plate. And before they knew where they were they had gone to bed.

It was not until next day that Joachim recollected how soon he must depart again. Hesitatingly he broke the news to Ruzena. But the outbreak of misery or anger that he had expected did not follow. Ruzena merely made the simple statement: " Can't go; stay here." Joachim was struck; she was right after all, why shouldn't he stay? What spell could it have been that made him stray aimlessly about the yard at home and keep out of his father's way? Moreover, it seemed imperatively necessary to wait in Berlin for Bertrand. Perhaps this was a breach of good form, a kind of civilian irregularity, into which Ruzena was enticing him, but it gave him a slight sense of freedom. He decided to sleep on the matter, and since he did so in Ruzena's company he wrote next day to his mother saying that his military duties would keep him longer in Berlin than he had anticipated; a duplicate of the letter, which he enclosed, was for her to give to his father should she think it expedient. Later he reflected that there wasn't much sense in doing that, since his father opened all the letters anyhow; but by that time it was too late; the letter was posted .

He had reported himself for duty, and was standing in the riding-school. The riding-masters were a sergeant-major and a corporal, each

with a long whip, and along the walls was ranged a restive chain of
horses mounted by recruits in coarse linen tunics. The place smelt
like a vault, and the soft sand in which one's feet sank reminded him
with a faint nostalgia of Helmuth and the dust he had strewn upon him.
The sergeant-major cracked his whip and ordered a trot. Rhythmically
the linen-clad figures by the wall began to bob up and down. Elisabeth
would soon be coming to Berlin for the autumn season. But that was not
quite true: they never came until October, nor could the house possibly
be ready for them yet. And indeed it wasn't really Elisabeth he was
waiting for, but Bertrand; of course it was Bertrand he meant. He saw
Bertrand and Elisabeth riding before him at a trot, both rising and
sinking in their stirrups. It was amazing how Elisabeth's face had melted
into the landscape and how he had strained to recapture it again. He
wondered if the same could have happened to Bertrand's face; he tried
to imagine that one of the figures along the wall was Bertrand rising
and sinking in his stirrups, but he abandoned the attempt; it was somehow blasphemous, and he was glad that Helmuth's face had been hidden
from him. Now the sergeant-major ordered a walking pace, and the
white jumping-posts and hurdles were brought out. He was involuntarily reminded of clowns, and suddenly he understood a saying of
Bertrand's, that the Fatherland was defended by a set of circus clowns.
It was still incomprehensible to him how he had managed to come a
cropper over that tree.

He drove once more past Borsig's engineering works. Once more
there were workmen standing about. He had really had enough of that
kind of thing. It wasn't his world, and he had no need to barricade
himself from it behind a gay uniform. True, Bertrand belonged to it,
perhaps reluctantly, but still he was acclimatized; well, he had had
enough of Bertrand too: the best thing after all would be to return to
Stolpin. In spite of that, however, he stopped his carriage at Bertrand's
door, and was delighted to hear that Herr von Bertrand was expected
that evening. Good; he would look in anyhow for a few minutes, and
he left a note to that effect.

They went together to the theatre, where Ruzena displayed her
mechanical gestures as a chorus girl. During the interval Bertrand said:
" That's no job for her; we'll have to find her something else," and
Joachim once more had a feeling of security. When they were at supper
Bertrand turned to Ruzena: " Tell me, Ruzena, you're going to become

a famous and marvellous actress now, aren't you?" Of course she was, wasn't that just what she was going to do! "Ah, but what if you should think better of it and change your mind? We've gone to a lot of trouble to give you the chance of becoming famous, and what if you should suddenly leave us in the lurch and make us look silly? What shall we do with you then?" Ruzena became reflective and suggested: "Well, there's the Jäger Casino." "No, no, Ruzena, one should never turn back when one has begun to climb. It must be something better than the theatre." Ruzena began to cry: "There's nothing at all for poor girl like me. He is bad friend, Joachim." Joachim said: "Bertrand's only joking, Ruzena." But he himself was uncomfortable and thought that Bertrand was overstepping the limits of tact. Bertrand, however, laughed: "There's no need to cry just because we're considering how to make you rich and famous, Ruzena. You'll have to keep all of us then." Joachim was shocked; one could see how commercial life vulgarized a man.

Later he said to Bertrand: "Why do you torment her?" Bertrand answered: "Well, we have to prepare her, and one can operate only on a healthy body. Now's the time." He spoke like a surgeon.

What Joachim had half feared had now happened. His letter had fallen into his father's hands, and the old man had obviously begun to rave again, for his mother wrote that there had been a fresh stroke. Joachim was amazed by his own indifference. He felt no obligation to go home, there was still plenty of time for that. Helmuth had charged him to stand by his mother, but it was little that one could do to help her; she would have to bear alone the fate she had taken upon herself. He wrote that he would come as soon as he could and stayed where he was, leaving things to take their own course, performing his duties, taking no steps whatever to make a change, and with an inexplicable fear thrusting aside every thought that suggested change. For it often required an actual effort to hold things firmly in their proper shapes, an effort so difficult that many a time all those people who bustled about as if all was in order seemed to him limited, blind and almost crazy. At first he had not thought much about it, but when for a second time he saw the military spectacle in terms of a circus he decided that Bertrand was to blame for everything. Why, even his uniform refused to sit upon him as well as formerly: the epaulets on his shoulders suddenly worried

him, and the cuffs of his shirt, and one morning before the glass he
asked himself why it should be on the left side that he had to wear his
sword. He took refuge in thoughts of Ruzena, telling himself that his
love for her, her love for him, was something exempt from all ambiguous
conventions. And then, when he gazed long into her eyes and stroked
her eyelids with a gently caressing finger, and she took it to be love, he
was often merely losing himself in an agonizing game, letting her face
grow dimmer and more indefinite, until it touched the boundary at
which it threatened to lose its human character, and the face became
no face at all. Things were elusive as a melody that one thinks one
cannot forget and yet loses the thread of, only to be compelled to seek
it again and again in anguish. It was an uncanny and hopeless game to
play, and with angry irritation he wished that Bertrand could be saddled
with the blame for that queer state of mind as well. Had he not, indeed,
spoken of his demon? Ruzena divined Joachim's irritation, and her
suspicion of Bertrand, which had rankled in her since that last evening,
flared out after a long, sullen silence with clumsy abruptness: " You
not love me any more . . . or have to ask friend's permission . . . or
has Bertrand already forbidden? " And although they were angry and
wounding words, Joachim was glad of them, for they came as a relief,
confirming his own suspicion that the demonic root of all his afflictions
was in Bertrand. And it even seemed to him like the final emanation of
such an evil, Mephistophelian and treacherous influence that the aversion
Ruzena shared with him should bring her no nearer, but rather, by
provoking rude and uncontrolled outbursts, should put her more on a
level with Bertrand and his equally offensive jokes; between his mistress
and his friend, both unstable, between these two civilians, he felt as if
caught and helplessly ground between two millstones of tactlessness.
He felt the smell of bad company, and often could not tell whether
Bertrand had led him to Ruzena, or Ruzena had been the means
of bringing him to Bertrand, until in alarm he realized that he
was no longer capable of grasping the evanescent, dissolving mass
of life, and that he was slipping more and more quickly, more and
more profoundly, into brain-sick confusion, and that everything had
become unsure. But when he thought of finding in religion some
way out of this chaos, the abyss opened afresh that parted him from
the civilians, for it was on the other side of the abyss that there
stood the civilian Bertrand, a Freethinker, and the Catholic Ruzena,

both beyond his reach, and it almost looked as if they exulted in his isolation.

He was glad that he was due for church parade on Sunday. But even into this military rite he was dogged by civilian values. For the faces of the rank and file who had marched, as enjoined, in two parallel columns into the House of God, were the everyday faces of the drill-ground and the riding-school; not one of them was devout, not one was solemn. The men must have been recruited from Borsig's engineering works; real peasants' sons from the country would not have stood there so indifferently. Except for the non-commissioned officers, standing piously at attention, not one of them was listening to the sermon. The temptation to label this ritual, too, a circus came affrightingly near. Joachim shut his eyes and tried to pray, as he had tried to pray in the village church. Perhaps he was not praying, but when the soldiers joined in the anthem, his voice raised itself among the others, although he did not know it, for with the hymn that he had sung as a child there rose also the memory of a picture, the memory of a small, brightly coloured holy picture, and once the picture was clearly imaged he remembered, too, that it was the black-haired Polish cook who had brought it to him: he heard her deep, sing-song voice and saw her seamed finger, with its chapped tip, tracing its way over all that brightness, pointing out that here was the earth on which men lived, and up above it, not too remotely above it, the Holy Family sat peacefully together on a silvery rain-cloud portrayed in the brightest of colours, and the gold that adorned their garments rivalled in splendour their golden haloes. Even now he did not dare to recall how blissful it had been to imagine oneself as a member of that Catholic Holy Family, reposing on that silver cloud in the arms of the virgin Mother of God or in the lap of the black-haired Pole . . . that was a point he could not now decide, but he was sure that the rapture was permeated by fear at its blasphemous presumption and at the heresy in a born Protestant's yielding to such a wish and such imagined bliss, and that he had not dared to make room for the wrathful Father in that picture; he did not want Him there at all. And while he strained his attention and bent his will to realize the picture more closely, it was as if the silver cloud floated up a little higher, as if it even began to evaporate upwards, and with it the figures that rested upon it; they seemed lightly to dissolve and float away on the melody of the anthem, a soft effluence that in no way effaced the remembered imagery, but

rather illumined and defined it, so that for a moment he was even
inclined to believe that it was the needful resolution into evangelical
truth of a Catholic holy picture: the Virgin's hair, too, seemed no longer
dusky, and she was less like the Polish woman, nor was she Ruzena,
but her locks brightened and became more golden, and might almost
have been the maiden tresses of Elisabeth. All that was a little peculiar
and yet a deliverance, a ray of light and the promise of coming grace in
the midst of obscurity; for was it not an act of grace that permitted a
Catholic picture to resolve itself into evangelical truth? And the fluidity
of the figures, a fluidity as gracious as the murmuring of rain or the
mist on a drizzling spring evening, made him aware that the dissolution
he so feared of the human face into a blankness of mobile heights and
hollows might be the first step towards its new and more radiant integra-
tion within the blissful company in the cloud, no mere rough copy of
earthly features but an initiation into the pure image, the crystalline
drop that falls singing from the cloud. And even if this more exalted
countenance wore no earthly beauty or familiarity, but was at first alien
and alarming, perhaps still more alarming than the blending of a face
with a landscape, yet it was the first step upwards, the presentiment of
an awful divinity, but also the surety for that divine life in which all
earthly life is resolved, dissolving like the face of Ruzena and the face
of Elisabeth, perhaps even dissolving like the shape of Bertrand. So it
was no longer the childish picture of old, with an actual father and
mother, that now displayed itself: true, it hovered still on the same spot,
floating in the midst of the same silver cloud, and he himself still
sat in the same way at the feet of the figures as once he had sat at his
mother's feet, himself a boyish Jesus; but the picture had grown in
meaning, no longer the imagined wish of a boy, but the assurance of
an attainable end, and he knew that he had taken the first painful step
towards that end, that he had entered upon his probation, although
only on the threshold of what was to come. His feeling was one almost
of pride. But then the blissful picture faded; it vanished like an imperceptibly ceasing rain, and that Elisabeth was part of it came as a final
drop of realization from the veiling mist. Perhaps that was a sign from
God. He opened his eyes; the anthem was closing, and Joachim thought
that he saw many of the young men gazing up to heaven with the same
trust and resolute ardour as himself.

In the afternoon he met Ruzena. He said: " Bertrand is right; the theatre is no fit place for you. Would you not like to have a shop and sell pretty things, lace, for instance, and fine embroidery?" And in his mind's eye he saw a glass door with a homely lamp burning behind it. But Ruzena looked at him quietly, and, as now often occurred, tears rose into her dark eyes. " Bad men you are," she said, and held his hand.

In view of his patient's fresh relapse the doctor had asked for a consultation, and it fell to Joachim, as a matter of course, to escort the nerve specialist to Stolpin. He regarded it as a part of the penance he was to undergo, and was more strongly confirmed in this belief when the doctor, with an amiable detachment, set to questioning him about the nature of the illness, the course it had previously run, and the general family situation. For these questions appeared to Joachim an inquisition, courteous enough, but none the less a keen and probing inquisition, and he expected the inquisitor suddenly to give him a severe look through his eyeglasses and to point an outstretched finger at him; already he heard the accusing damning sound of the frightful word: murderer. Yet the amiable old gentleman with the spectacles showed no disposition to utter that frightful but emancipating word, remarking merely that the shock of his son's death had certainly occasioned the deplorable symptoms that were now afflicting Herr von Pasenow, although the original roots of the malady might lie deeper. Joachim began to regard the specialist with mistrust and yet with a certain satisfaction, being convinced that a man who expressed such opinions was incapable of helping the sufferer.

Then conversation died away, and Joachim saw the familiar fields and trees gliding past. The rhythm of the train had set the specialist nodding drowsily, his chin between the points of his stiff collar, and his white beard spread over his shirt-front. It was unimaginable to Joachim that he also might be as old as that one day, unimaginable too that the other had once been young and that a woman might have looked for kisses in his beard; surely some trace of that would still have been perceptible in the beard, like a feather or a straw. He drew his hand over his own face; it was an imposture on Elisabeth that of the kisses which Ruzena had given him in farewell not a trace remained: God was merciful to mankind in drawing a veil over the future, but pitiless in that He removed all traces of the past; would it not be merciful to brand a man's deeds on him? But God seared the brand only on a man's conscience, and not even a nerve specialist could discover it. Helmuth had been branded, and that was why he could not be looked at in his coffin. But his father too was branded; anyone who behaved as he did could not but look furtive.

Herr von Pasenow was out of bed, but in a state of complete apathy; nevertheless Joachim's presence was concealed from him in case he should have a fresh outbreak of rage. He met the strange doctor with indifference, but presently took him for a notary and broached the subject of making a new will. Joachim was to be disinherited for dishonourable conduct, yes, but he wasn't a hard father, he only wanted Joachim to beget him a grandson on Elisabeth. The child must thereupon be brought into the house and become the heir. After some reflection he added that Joachim must not be permitted to see the child, or it would be disinherited too. His mother hesitatingly informed Joachim of this, and, contrary to her custom, fell into lamentation: where was all this going to lead to! Joachim shrugged his shoulders; he merely felt again what a disgrace it was to have a parent who dared to mention the possibility of children by himself and Elisabeth.

The nerve specialist too had shrugged his shoulders; there was no need to give up hope, he said; Herr von Pasenow was still extraordinarily vigorous, but for the present there was nothing to do but await developments; only the patient should not be allowed to stay too much in bed, for that might lower his vitality, considering his years. Frau von Pasenow objected that her husband was very desirous of staying in bed, for he always felt cold, and it seemed, too, that he was tormented by some secret fear that abated only when he was in his bedroom. Well, of course, one must act according to the patient's condition, observed the nerve specialist; all he could say was that in the care of his colleague— here the local doctor bowed his thanks—Herr von Pasenow was in the very best of hands.

It had grown late, the pastor had turned up, and the evening meal was served. Suddenly Herr von Pasenow appeared in the doorway: " So, there are supper-parties here without my knowledge; apparently because the new master of the house has arrived." Joachim made to leave the room. " Stay where you are and keep your seat," commanded Herr von Pasenow, setting himself down at the head of the table in the big chair that was left vacant for him even in his absence; obviously he was somewhat conciliated by this discovery. He insisted on having the courses served to him again: " Things need setting in order here. Herr Notary, have you been properly looked after? Have you been offered your choice of red or white wine? I see nothing but red wine. Why is there no champagne? A will should have a bottle of champagne cracked upon it." He laughed to himself. " Well, what about that champagne? " he hectored the parlourmaid. " Must I go foraging myself? " The nerve specialist was the first to regain his composure, and to save the situation said he would gladly accept a glass of champagne. Triumphantly Herr von Pasenow surveyed the table: " Yes, things need setting in order again. Nobody has any sense of honour . . ." then in a low voice to the specialist, " Helmuth, you know, died for honour. But he never writes to me. Perhaps he's still resentful . . ." he thought it over, " or this pastor here intercepts the letters. Wants to keep his own secrets, doesn't want laymen to get a peep behind the scenes. But as soon as there's any disorder in the churchyard he'll take to his heels, the man of God. That I'll go bail for." " But, Herr von Pasenow, the church-yard is in the best of order." " Apparently, Herr Notary, apparently, but it's nothing but eyewash, only it's not so easy for us to discover it because we don't understand their language; they're quite obviously hiding from us. We others only hear how silent they are, and yet they're complaining to us all the time. That's why everybody's so afraid, and when a guest comes I have to take him out myself, old as I am," he, darted a hostile look at Joachim, " a man without honour of course can't screw up his courage to it and sneaks out of sight in the byre." " Well, Herr von Pasenow, you must yourself have to see often enough that everything's all right and inspect the fields; you must in any case go out." " I like doing it, Herr Notary, and I do it too. But as soon as one sets foot outside the door they often block the road completely, the air's so full of them, so full that not a sound can find its way past them." He shuddered, seized the physician's glass, and before anyone could hinder him emptied it at a gulp. " You must visit me often, Herr Notary, we'll make wills together. And meanwhile won't you write to me? " he implored. " Or will you disappoint me too," he looked suspiciously at him, " and perhaps conspire with the others? . . . he has tricked me already with someone, that creature there. . . ." He had sprung to his feet, and his finger pointed at Joachim. Then he seized a plate, and, shutting one eye as if he were taking aim, screamed:

" I've ordered him to get married. . . ." But the specialist was already beside him and laid a hand on his arm: " Come with me, Herr von Pasenow; we'll go to your room and talk there for a little longer." Herr von Pasenow gazed at him blankly; the other met his eye steadily: " Come along, we'll have a little talk all by ourselves." " All by ourselves, really? And I shan't be afraid any more. . . ." He smiled helplessly and patted the doctor's cheek. " Yes, we'll let them see." He made a contemptuous gesture towards the company and suffered himself to be led away.

Joachim had buried his face in his hands. Yes, his father had branded him; the blow had fallen now, and yet he rebelled against it. The pastor came up to him, and as if from afar he heard the banal words of comfort; his father was right in that, too: this minister of the Church was a poor makeshift, or else he would have known that the curse of a father lies irremediably upon his children; he would have known that it is the voice of God Himself that speaks through one's father's mouth and proclaims the hour of trial. Oh, that was why his father's wits were clouded now, for no man could be God's mouthpiece and not suffer for it. And of course the pastor must be a commonplace creature; for if he were really an instrument of God on earth he too would mouth strange sayings. Yet God had pointed the way to His grace without the media-tion of priests; there was no getting away from that, one must win that grace alone and in suffering. Joachim said: " I thank you for your kindly words, Pastor; we shall certainly be often in need of your consolation." Then the doctor returned; Herr von Pasenow had been given an injection and was now asleep.

The nerve specialist stayed in the house for two more days. And when shortly afterwards a profoundly disquieting telegram of Bertrand's arrived from Berlin, and the invalid's condition remained obviously unchanged, Joachim too was enabled to depart.

Bertrand had come back to Berlin. In the afternoon he went to visit Joachim, but found only Ruzena in the flat. She was tidying up the bed-room, and when Bertrand appeared she said: " I not speak to you." " Hallo, Ruzena, you're very amiable." " I not speak to you, know what you are." " Am I a bad friend again, my little Ruzena? " " Not your little Ruzena." " Very well, then, what's the matter? " " What's matter! . . . know it all, you send him away. I spit on your lace-shop." " All right, a lace-shop I may have, I don't mind, but that's no reason for not speaking to me. What's the matter with my lace-shop? " In silence Ruzena went on putting underlinen into the chest of drawers; Bertrand drew up a chair and waited with amusement for what was to come. " If it was my flat, throw you out, not let you sit." " Look here, Ruzena, in all seriousness what's gone wrong? Has the old man been taken bad again, so that Pasenow had to go off? " " Not pretend you not know; I not so stupid." " I'm afraid you are, little one." She turned her back on him and went on with her task. " Not let you laugh over me . . . not let anybody laugh over me." Bertrand went up to her and took her head between his hands to look into her face. She tore herself away. " Not touch me. First you send him away and then laugh over me." Bertrand understood it all, except for the reference to the lace-shop. " Well, Ruzena, so you don't believe that old Herr von Pasenow is ill? " " Believe nothing, you all against me." Bertrand grew a little impatient. " Apparently if the old man dies it will be just to spite the little Ruzena." " If you kill him he die." Bertrand would have liked to help her, but it was not easy; he knew that there was not much to be done with her in that mood, and he rose to go. " You should be killed," said Ruzena in conclusion. Bertrand was amused. " All right," he remarked, " I have no objection, but will that make things any better? " " So you have no objection, no objection? " Ruzena hunted excitedly in a drawer, " but make mock at me, yes? " . . . she went on hunting, " . . . no objection . . ." and found what she was looking for. Bristling with hostility, Joachim's army revolver in her hand, she faced up to Bertrand. This is too silly, thought Bertrand. " Ruzena, put that down at once." " You have no objection." A touch of anger and even of shame prevented Bertrand from simply quitting the room; he took a step towards Ruzena with the idea of seizing the weapon, and all at once a shot rang out, followed by a second when the revolver that she had let fall hit the floor. " That's really too stupid," said Bertrand, and bent down to pick it up. The valet came rushing in, but Bertrand explained that the thing had fallen on the floor and gone off. " Tell the Lieutenant that he shouldn't keep pistols lying about loaded." The valet went out again. " Well, Ruzena, are you a silly goose or not? " Ruzena stood white and petrified, pointed to Bertrand and said: " There! " Blood was dripping from his sleeve. " Let me locked up," she stammered. Bertrand took off his coat and undid the shirt-sleeve; he had felt nothing; his arm seemed only grazed, but it would be necessary to see a doctor about it. He ordered the valet to call a cab. With some linen of Joachim's he made a provisional bandage and bade Ruzena wash away the blood, but she was so upset and confused that he had to help her. " So, Ruzena; and you'd better come with me, for now I can't let you stay here alone. You won't be locked up if you'll admit that you are a silly goose." She followed him mechanically. At his doctor's door he enjoined her to wait for him in the cab.

He told the doctor that by a clumsy accident he had had his arm grazed by a bullet. " Well, you've been lucky, but don't treat the matter too lightly; you'd better lie up for a day or two in hospital." Bertrand thought that this was exaggerated caution, but as he went down the steps he became aware that he felt dizzy. To his amazement he found no trace of Ruzena in the cab. Not very nice of her, he thought.

He drove home first and collected everything that a practical man of some standing needs for a sojourn in hospital, and after being admitted to a ward he sent a note to Ruzena with the request that she should come and visit him. The messenger returned with the news that the lady hadn't come home yet. That was strange and almost disquieting; but he was not in the mood to take any fresh step that day. Next morning he sent another message; she had still not come home, nor had she been seen in Joachim's flat. That decided him to send a wire to Stolpin, and two days later Joachim arrived.

Bertrand felt no call to give Joachim a truthful account of what had happened; the tale of an accident caused by Ruzena's clumsiness sounded plausible enough. He ended up: " Since then she's vanished completely. That might mean nothing at all, but a girl in such an excited state might easily do something foolish." Joachim thought: what has he been doing to her? But he was suddenly horrified to remember that often enough, sometimes in jest, but sometimes in deadly earnest, Ruzena had threatened to throw herself into the water. He saw the grey willows on the banks of the Havel, the tree under which they had once sheltered; yes, she must be lying there in the river. For the space of a heart-beat he felt flattered by this romantic situation. But then the horror of it flooded over him again. Inevitable fate, inescapable discipline of God! And if he had prayed in the church, while still full of hope before his visit to Stolpin, that his father's illness might not be a penance laid upon him, the son, but merely one of the chances of life, the finger of God now showed him that even that prayer had been sinful. One dared not question God's discipline; there was no such thing as chance; for Bertrand, although he had parted in apparent enmity from Herr von Pasenow and was now depreciating the revolver incident as a stupid accident, was only trying to disguise the fact that he was an emissary of evil, deliberately chosen by God and by Herr von Pasenow to discipline the penitent, to lure him into temptation, to lead him into snares, so that in his extremity he might learn that the tempted is as much to blame as the tempter, and with the same fatality, now and always, brings ruin on those nearest him, and that no effort of his can avail to cheat the Tempter of his victims. When a man has come to such knowledge, is it not better for him to destroy himself? How much better it would have been if the bullet had killed him instead of Helmuth! But now it was too late, now Ruzena was lying at the bottom of the river, staring with glazed eyes at the fishes darting over her in the grey water. Quite unexpectedly her drowned image blended again with that of the Italian at the opera; but that too vanished when Joachim discovered that the man under the water was really himself. Yes, in his own blue eyes was the unlucky evil glance that the Italians believed in, and it would serve those eyes right if the fishes were darting over them. Bertrand said: " Have you any idea where she might be? Let's hope that she has simply gone back to her home. I suppose she would have enough money for that? " Joachim felt annoyed by this question; it had a touch of the inquisitorial detachment of a doctor. What was Bertrand hinting at? Of course she had money on her. Bertrand did not remark his annoyance. " All the same, we'd better inform the police; it's not impossible that she may be wandering about." Of course they must inform the police; Bertrand was right, yet Joachim shrank from doing so; he would be questioned about his connection with Ruzena, and even though he told himself that it was unimportant, yet he feared that vague and mysterious consequences might follow. His connection with Ruzena had been all too long sinfully concealed; perhaps God had planned to have it brought to His notice by means of the police; perhaps this was another of the penances he must do, made still harder by the fact that the police office was situated in the Alexanderplatz, which he shrank more than ever from entering. Yet he rose to his feet. " I shall drive round to the police." " No, Pasenow, I'll arrange that for you; you're still too upset, and anyhow they'll suspect melodrama." Joachim was sincerely grateful. " Yes, but your arm . . ." " Oh, that doesn't matter;

they're just going to discharge me here." " But I'll come with you." " All
right, then, and I hope I'll still find *you* in the cab when I get into it
again." Bertrand was once more gay, and Joachim felt secure. In the cab
he begged Bertrand to tell the police to search the banks of the Havel.
" Very well, Pasenow, but in my opinion Ruzena's long since back in
Bohemia; a pity you don't know the name of her village, but we'll
soon unearth it." Joachim himself was now surprised that he did not
know the name of Ruzena's native village, scarcely, indeed, her family
name. She had often in fun tried to make him pronounce these names,
but he could never get his tongue round the foreign words and could
not remember them. It occurred to him now that he had never really
wanted to know them or to keep them in his memory; yes, almost as if
he had been a little afraid of those harmless names.

He accompanied Bertrand through the corridors of the police building;
he had to wait outside the door of an office. Bertrand soon came back.
" They know it all right," and on a piece of paper he showed the name
of a Czech village. " Did you direct them to the banks of the Havel? "
Of course Bertrand had done so. " But, my dear Pasenow, there's something unpleasant for you to do this evening, for I can't do it because
of my arm. You must get into mufti and hunt through all the cafés and
cabarets. I didn't want to suggest that to the police; we can always do
that later. They might pounce on poor Ruzena and arrest her in the
middle of some dancing-floor." Joachim had not thought of such a vulgar
and repulsive possibility. Bertrand was indeed a disgusting cynic. He
looked at Bertrand. Did the man know more? Mephisto alone understood what Margaret had to do penance for. But Bertrand's face
betrayed nothing. There was nothing for it but to submit and accept
the task Bertrand had laid upon him as a further discipline.

He had entered upon his degrading pilgrimage, asking questions of
waiters and barmaids, and was relieved to be told in the Jäger Casino
that nothing had been seen of Ruzena. But on the staircase he met one
of the plump dancing partners. " Looking for your sweetheart, I suppose,
dearie; has she given you the slip? Well, come along, you can easily get
another." What did the woman know of his connection with Ruzena?
It was possible, of course, that she had met Ruzena somewhere, but the
thought of asking her sickened him, and he hurried past her and into the
next café. Yes, Ruzena had been there, said the woman at the buffet,

yesterday or the day before, that was all she could tell him; perhaps the attendant in the ladies' toilet could give him more information. He had to continue his sorrowful quest, again and again overwhelmed with shame as he interrogated barmaids and lavatory attendants, and learned that she had been seen or had not been seen, that she had had a wash, that she had gone away once with a gentleman, that she had looked quite down-at-heels. " We all tried to persuade her to go home, for a girl in a state like that is no credit to any café, but she just sat and said nothing." Many of these people simply addressed him at once as " Herr Lieutenant," so that the suspicion awoke in him that Ruzena had taken them all into her confidence, and had betrayed his love to all these people. It was the lavatory attendants to whom he was always referred.

And it was in a toilet-room that he found her. She sat sleeping in the corner under a burning gas-jet; her hand, with the ring that he had given her, lay limp on the wet marble of the washstand. She had undone her boots, and over one foot, which showed beneath her skirt, the shape-less, unbuttoned top of the boot hung down, showing its grey lining. Her hat had slipped to the back of her head, dragging her hair with it by the hatpins. Joachim would have preferred to turn and go; she looked like a drunk woman. He touched her hand; Ruzena wearily opened her eyes; when she recognized him she shut them again. " Ruzena, we must go." She shook her head, keeping her eyes shut. He stood helplessly before her. " Give her a good kiss," the attendant encouraged him. " No! " shrieked Ruzena in terror, springing up and making for the door. She stumbled over her unbuttoned boots and Joachim caught hold of her. " But you can't go into the street with your boots and your hair like that," said the attendant; " the Herr Lieutenant isn't going to do you any harm." " Let go; let me go out, I say," panted Ruzena, and into Joachim's face: " All over, you know it, all over." Her breath smelt foul and stale. But Joachim still barred her way, so Ruzena turned round, tore open a lavatory door and locked herself in. " All over! " she screamed from behind the door. " Tell him must go away, all over." Joachim had sunk on to a chair beside the wash-basin; his mind could grasp nothing, he knew only that this too was one of the trials sent by God, and he stared at the half-open brown drawer of the toilet-table, in which the attendant's few possessions—handkerchiefs, a corkscrew, a clothes-brush—were bestowed higgledy-piggledy. " Is he gone? " he heard Ruzena's voice. " Ruzena, come

out," he begged. " Fräulein, dearie, come out," begged the attendant,
" this is the ladies' toilet and the Herr Lieutenant can't stay here." " He
must go away," was Ruzena's answer. " Ruzena, please, do come out,"
implored Joachim once more, but behind her bolted door Ruzena
was mute. The attendant drew him by the sleeve into the passage and
whispered: " She'll come out when she thinks the Herr Lieutenant has
gone. The Herr Lieutenant can wait for her downstairs." Joachim
accepted her suggestion, and in the shadow of a neighbouring house he
waited for a full hour. Then Ruzena appeared; beside her waddled a fat,
bearded, soft-fleshed man. She peered cautiously round with a curiously
fixed, malicious smile, and then the man hailed a cab and they drove
away. Joachim had to fight against an inclination to vomit; he dragged
himself home, scarcely knowing how he got there, and perhaps his
worst torture was his inability to rid himself of the thought that the fat
man should really be pitied, because Ruzena was unwashed and had a
stale smell. The revolver was still lying on the chest of drawers; he
examined it, two shots were missing. With the weapon in his clasped
hands he began to pray: " God, take me to Thee like my brother; to
him Thou wert merciful, be merciful also to me." But then he bethought
himself that he still had to make his will; and he dared not leave Ruzena
unprovided for, or else she would be justified in all she had done to
him, incomprehensible as it was. He looked for pen and ink. Dawn
found him fast asleep over an almost blank sheet of paper.

He concealed his misadventure with Ruzena, being ashamed before
Bertrand and unwilling to grant him the satisfaction of having been
right, and although the lie disgusted him he reported that he had found
her in her own room. " That's all right," said Bertrand; " have you
notified the police? If not, she might get into trouble with them." Of
course Joachim had not thought of that, and Bertrand sent a messenger
with the requisite information to the police. " Where has she been, then,
for these three days? " " She won't say." " That's all right." Bertrand's
dry indifference irritated him; he had nearly put a bullet through himself and the fellow merely said: " That's all right." But he had refrained
from suicide because he had to provide for Ruzena, and for that he
needed Bertrand's advice: " Listen, Bertrand, I expect I'll have to take
over the estate now; but Ruzena needs some means of livelihood and
an occupation, and I thought first of buying her a shop or something

of that kind . . ." (" Aha," said Bertrand) " but she won't hear of it. So I'd like to settle some money on her. How does one do that? " " You must make it over to her. It would be better, though, to allow her an income for a certain time; otherwise she would go through all the money at once." " Yes, but how does one do that? " " Well, of course I'd be glad to arrange it for you, but it would be better to put my lawyer on to it. I'll fix up an appointment with him for to-morrow or next day. But, my dear chap, you're looking wretched." That didn't matter, remarked Joachim. " Well, what is it that's pulling you down? You really don't need to take this affair so much to heart," said Bertrand with light good-humour. His ironical indiscretion and that flicker of irony about his mouth are hateful, thought Joachim, and from afar the suspicion again began to steal upon him that behind Ruzena's inexplicable behaviour and her instability were hidden Bertrand's intrigues, and that Ruzena had been driven into this folly by her connection with Bertrand. It was a minor satisfaction that, in a sense, she had betrayed Bertrand too with the fat man. The sick disgust that had overwhelmed him on the previous evening began to rise again. Into what a morass had he fallen. Outside the autumn rain was pouring down the window-panes. Borsig's factory buildings must now be black with running soot and water, the paving-stones must be black, and the courtyard, that one could see through the gateway, a sea of black, gleaming slime. He could smell the smoke driven down by the rain from the blackened top of the long red chimney-stack: it smelt foul, stale, sulphurous. That was the morass; that was the natural setting for Ruzena and the fat man and Bertrand; it was akin to the night haunts with their gas-jets and their lavatories. The day had turned into night, as the night into day. The word night-spirit occurred to him, a word, indeed, that conveyed no clear meaning. Were there also light-spirits? He could hear the phrase, " virginal shape of light." Ah, that was the opposite of night-spirit. And he had a vision of Elisabeth, who was different from all the others, hovering on a silver cloud high above the morass. Perhaps he had already divined this when he first saw the white clouds of lace in Elisabeth's room and had longed to watch over her slumbers. She would soon be coming now with her mother, moving into the new house. Extraordinary that there must be lavatories there too; he felt it was blasphemy to think of this. But not less blasphemous was the fact that Bertrand was lying here with his golden hair waved, lying in a white room like a young girl. Thus darkness obscures its real nature and keeps its mystery intact. Bertrand, however, went on to say with friendly concern: " You are looking so wretched, Pasenow, that you ought to be sent on holiday, and a little travel would do you good, too. It would put other thoughts into your mind." He wants to get rid of me, thought Joachim; he has had his way with Ruzena and now he wants to ruin Elisabeth too. " No," he said, " I can't go just now. . . ." Bertrand was silent for a while, and then it was as though he had divined Joachim's thoughts and was himself forced to betray his evil designs on Elisabeth, for he asked: " Are the Baddensens in Berlin yet? " Bertrand was still smiling sympathetic-ally, almost frankly, but Joachim, with a gruffness unusual to him, answered curtly: " They'll probably remain at Lestow for some time to come." And now he knew that he must go on living, that chivalry demanded it of him, lest another destiny should be ruined by his fault and fall a prey to Bertrand; but Bertrand only gave him a gay good-bye, saying: " Well, I'll arrange things with my lawyer . . . and when Ruzena's affairs are settled you should take a holiday. You really need it." Joachim said nothing more; his decision was made, and he went off full of heavy thoughts. It was always Bertrand who aroused such thoughts in him. And with the slight straightening of the shoulders, almost as if at the word of command, by which Joachim von Pasenow sought to shake off his thoughts, suddenly it was as if Helmuth had taken his hand, as if Helmuth wanted to show him the way again, to lead him back into convention and order, to open his eyes again. That Bertrand, whose expedition the previous day to the police headquarters had certainly done him no good, was again fevered, Joachim von Pasenow did not observe in the least.

The news from his father's sick-bed remained persistently bad. The old man no longer recognized anyone: he was sinking into a lethargy. Joachim caught himself entertaining the hateful-pleasant thought that now one could, in all security, send any letter to Stolpin, and pictured the messenger with the post-bag entering the bedroom and the old man incomprehendingly dropping letter after letter, incomprehendingly letting them fall, though there might be a betrothal announcement among them. And that was a kind of relief, and a vague hope for the future.

The possibility of seeing Ruzena again filled him with dread, although many a time when he came off duty it seemed inconceivable that he should not find her in his rooms. In any case he was daily expecting to hear from her, for he had settled the matter of her income with Bertrand's lawyer, and could not but presume that she had been informed. Instead of a message from her, he got a letter from the lawyer to say that the money had been refused. This would never do; he set out for Ruzena's flat; the building, the staircase and the flat filled him with profound uneasiness, indeed with an almost anguished yearning. He feared that he would have to stand again before a locked door, perhaps even be turned away by some charwoman or other, and much as he shrank from forcing his way into a lady's room, he merely asked if she were at home, knocked at her door and walked in. The room and Ruzena were alike in a state of dirt and disorder, neglected and barbaric. She was lying on the sofa and made a defensive, weary gesture, as if she had known that he would come. Haltingly she said: " Not take nothing from you. The ring I keep, souvenir." Joachim could feel no sympathy rising within him; if on the very staircase he had still intended to point out that he literally did not understand what she had against him, he was now merely embittered; he could see nothing in her attitude but obstinacy. Yet he said: " Ruzena, I don't know what has really happened . . ." She laughed contemptuously, and his resentment of her obstinacy and instability, which had injured him and done him injustice, reasserted itself. No, there was no sense in trying to persuade her, and so he merely said that he could not bear the thought that she was not even half provided for, and that he would have done it long ago whether they had stuck to each other or not, only he could do it more easily now because—and he added this deliberately—he had to take over the estate and so had more money at his disposal. " You are good man," said Ruzena, " only you have bad friend." That was ultimately what Joachim believed at the bottom of his heart, but since he did not want to admit it he only said: " Why do you think that Bertrand is a bad friend? " " Wicked words," replied Ruzena. It was tempting to think of making common cause with Ruzena against Bertrand, but was it not just another temptation of the Devil's, another intrigue of Bertrand's? Obviously Ruzena felt so too, for she said: " Must beware him." Joachim answered: " I know his faults." She had raised herself up on the sofa, and they now sat side by side. " You are poor, good soul, can't know how bad peoples are." Joachim assured her that he knew it very well, and that he was not so easily deceived. And so they spoke for a while about Bertrand without mentioning his name, and since they did not want to stop speaking, they pursued the theme until the brackish melancholy that flowed behind their words rose higher and higher, and the words were drowned in it and blended with Ruzena's tears into a stream that broadened and slackened more and more. Joachim, too, had tears in his eyes. Both were helplessly delivered to the senselessness of Fate, now they were aware that they could no longer find comfort in each other. They did not dare to look at each other, and finally Joachim's woebegone voice said: " Please, Ruzena, please take the money at least." She made no reply, but she had grasped his hand. When he bent over her to kiss her she bowed her head, so that the kiss landed among her hairpins. " Go now," she said, " quick go," and Joachim silently left the room, in which it was already dusk.

He informed the lawyer, so that the deed of settlement could be drawn up again; this time Ruzena would surely accept it. But the kindness with which Ruzena and he had taken leave of each other depressed him more than the helpless resentment he had previously felt at her incomprehensible behaviour. It was indeed still as incomprehensible and dreadful as ever. His thoughts of Ruzena were full of sad yearning, full of that reluctant homesickness with which, in his cadet days, his mind had turned to his father's house and his mother. Was the fat man by her side now? He had to think of the jesting insult his father had put upon Ruzena, and here too he recognized the curse of his father, who, himself sick and helpless, had sent a deputy in his stead. Yes, God was fulfilling his father's curse, and all he could do was to submit.

Sometimes he made a feeble attempt to find Ruzena again; but whenever he was a few streets away from her flat he always turned back or took a side-street, landing in the slum quarter or in the turmoil of the Alexanderplatz, and once even going as far as the Küstriner Station. He was entangled all over again in the toils, and had lost hold of all the threads. His one firm certainty was that at least Ruzena's income should be assured, and Joachim now spent much time in the office of Bertrand's lawyer, much more time than was actually needful. But the hours he wasted there were a kind of consolation, and although these dull and somewhat pointless visits could not have been very agreeable to the lawyer, and although Joachim learned nothing of what he hoped to learn from Bertrand's representative, yet the lawyer did not spare himself

in going into the semi-relevant and almost private questions raised by
his aristocratic client, applying himself to them with a professional
interest which somewhat resembled a doctor's, but none the less did
Joachim good. The lawyer, a spare man and quite beardless although
he was Bertrand's legal representative, looked like an Englishman. When,
after ample delay, Ruzena's acceptance finally came, the lawyer said:
" Well, now we've got it. But if you'll take my advice, Herr von Pasenow,
you'll allow the lady in question the option of taking the capital sum instead of the interest on it." " Yes," interposed Joachim, " but I arranged
it so with Herr von Bertrand simply because . . ." " I appreciate your
motive, Herr von Pasenow, and I know too—if you'll excuse me—
that you are not much inclined to take any bull by the horns; but what
I advise is in the best interests of both parties: for the lady it's a pretty
sum of money, which in certain circumstances might set her up better
for life than an allowance, and for you, on the other hand, it's a definite
quittance." Joachim felt a little helpless; was it really a definite quittance
he wanted? The lawyer remarked his helplessness: " If I may touch on
the private aspect of the matter, my experience has taught me that the
best kind of settlement is one which enables one to regard a past obligation as non-existent." Joachim looked up. " Yes, as non-existent, Herr
von Pasenow. Convention, after all, is the safest guide." The word
" non-existent " stuck to Joachim. Only it was strange that through the
mouth of his representative Bertrand should signify such a change in
his opinions and even acknowledge a convention of feeling. Why did
he do it? The lawyer went on to say: " So think it over from that point
of view as well, Herr von Pasenow; and, of course, for a man in your
position the loss of the capital is of no importance." Yes, a man in his
position; Joachim's sentiment for his home welled up again, warm and
comforting. He left the lawyer's office this time in an exceptionally good
mood, one might almost say uplifted and strengthened. True, he did
not yet see his way clear before him, for he still felt bewildered in the
invisible tangle that seemed to net the whole city, a tangle of invisible
forces that could not be grasped and that made his dull, persistent
yearning for Ruzena insignificant, although bringing new elements of
anguish into it, yet that bound him in such a novel and unreal relation
to Ruzena and to all the world of the city that the net of false brightness
became a net of horror winding around him, within whose tangled
confusion lurked the threat that Elisabeth too, on returning to the city,

which was not her world, might be caught in it; that she, the innocent and untouched, might be caught and entangled in these devilish and impalpable coils, entangled by his fault, entrapped because of him, because he could not free himself from the invisible embrace of the Devil, so persistently did darkness threaten to cloud what was clear, darkness invisible, perhaps, and still far off, floating, perhaps, and uncertain, but as besmirching as what his father had done to the maids in his mother's house. In spite of that, however, Joachim felt as he left the lawyer's office that he had come to a turning-point, for it was as if Bertrand had denounced his lies through the mouth of his own representative; Bertrand it had been, Bertrand, who had tried to draw him into the invisible, impalpable net, and now his own representative had had to acknowledge that the position of a Pasenow was something other, something outside this city and its swarming creatures, provided only that one was willing to regard the whole mirage as non-existent. Yes, that was Bertrand's message by his representative, and so the Devil at last was loosening his grip of his own accord; even the Devil was still subject to the will of God, Who, in the person of a father, demands the annihilation and the non-existence of whatever lies under a father's curse. The Evil One had acknowledged defeat, and even though he had not expressly renounced his claims on Elisabeth yet, he had himself advised Joachim to obey his father's wishes. And without consulting Bertrand in person Joachim resolved to empower the lawyer to pay out the capital sum.

Similarly without consulting Bertrand, Joachim put on his dress-uniform and a new pair of gloves when he was informed that the Freiherr von Baddensen and his family had arrived, and drove to visit them at an hour when he could hope to find the Baron and the Baroness at home. They wanted to show him the new house at once, but he begged the Baron first for a private interview, and after the Baron had taken him into another room Joachim straightened himself with a jerk into a correct posture, standing stiffly as before a superior officer, and asked for Elisabeth's hand. The Baron said: " Delighted and honoured, my dear, dear Pasenow," and called the Baroness in. The Baroness said: " Oh, I have been expecting it; a mother sees ever so many things," and dabbed her eyes. Yes, he would be very welcome as their dear son; they could not think of a better, and were convinced that he would do his utmost to make their daughter happy. He would do that, he returned manfully.

The Baron had taken his hand: but now, first of all, they must speak to their daughter about it; he must understand that. Joachim replied that he understood; and thereupon they spent another quarter of an hour in half-formal, half-intimate conversation, in the course of which Joachim could not refrain from mentioning Bertrand's wound; then he took his leave briefly without having seen either the new house or Elisabeth, but that mattered little now, for he had all the rest of his life to see them in.

It surprised Joachim himself that he was not more passionately impatient for Elisabeth's consent and did not feel impelled to shorten the time of waiting, and often it amazed him that he could not imagine their future life together. He could see himself, indeed, leaning on a stick with a white ivory crook-handle, standing beside Elisabeth in the middle of the stableyard, but when he tried to visualize the scene more closely the image of Bertrand always intruded. It would not be easy to tell him of their betrothal; after all it was Bertrand against whom it was directed and Bertrand from whom Elisabeth had to be shielded, and, strictly regarded, it had a look of treachery about it, since in a manner of speaking he had once surrendered Elisabeth to him. And although Bertrand deserved nothing better, yet he shrank from inflicting such a hurt upon him. Of course that was no reason for postponing the betrothal; but suddenly it began to look as if the betrothal could not take place at all unless Bertrand were previously informed of it. He was still in duty bound to keep an eye on Bertrand, and could not comprehend how he had so completely forgotten him for days together, as if he were already exempt from all obligations. Besides, Bertrand was probably still an invalid. He drove to the hospital. Bertrand was, in fact, still lying there; they had had to operate on him; Joachim was genuinely upset to discover how he had neglected the patient, and now that he set himself to inform him of the approaching event he made it at the same time a kind of excuse for such remissness. " But, my dear Bertrand, I can't always be plaguing you with my private affairs." Bertrand smiled, and there was a hint of a consultant's or a woman's solicitude in his smile. " Go ahead, Pasenow, it's not so bad as all that; I enjoy listening to you." And Joachim related how he had proposed for Elisabeth. " I don't know whether she will, I dread still more that she won't, for then I should feel that I was irretrievably floundering again in all the awful complications of the past months which you have shared with me to a great extent, while with her by my side I hope to find a way into the open." Bertrand smiled again. "Do you know, Pasenow, all that sounds very fine, yet I wouldn't care to marry you on the strength of it; but you don't need to worry. I'm convinced that you'll soon be accepting congratulations." What repulsive cynicism; the man was literally a bad friend, he was no true friend at all, even though one had to admit in extenuation that he was both jealous and disappointed. Joachim therefore ignored the cynical remark and fell back on his own train of thought, asking: "What shall I do if she says no?" And Bertrand gave him the answer he desired: "She won't say no," averring it with such conviction and certainty that Joachim once more experienced that feeling of security which Bertrand so often evoked in him. It now seemed to him almost unfair that Elisabeth should attach her preference to him, the unsure one, and renounce the sure and steady leader. And as if to justify himself a voice within him said: "Comrades in the King's uniform." And suddenly he had a vision of Bertrand as a major. But from what source did Bertrand draw his confidence? How could he be certain that Elisabeth would not refuse? Why did he smile so ironically as he said so? What did this man know? And he regretted having confided in him.—

As a matter of fact Bertrand could have found many justifications for an ironical smile, or more precisely a knowing smile; yet his smile was one of simple friendliness.

On the previous day Elisabeth had abruptly descended upon him. She had driven to the hospital and asked for him in the reception-room. In spite of his aches and pains he had gone down immediately. It was an extraordinary visit, and certainly outraged convention, but Elisabeth did not take any pains to conceal its irregularity; she was obviously in distress and went straight to the point:

"Joachim has made an offer for my hand."

"If you love him, there isn't any problem."

"I don't love him."

"Then there isn't any problem either, for I suppose you'll refuse him."

"So you won't help me?"

"I'm afraid, Elisabeth, there's nobody who can do that."

"And I thought that you could."

"I didn't want to see you again."

"Have you no friendship for me?"

"I don't know, Elisabeth."

" Joachim loves me."

" Love needs some degree of cleverness, not to say wisdom. You must allow me to be somewhat dubious of his love for you. I warned you once already."

" You are a bad friend."

" No, but there are moments when one must be absolutely honest."

" Can one be too stupid to love? "

" I have just said so."

" Perhaps, then, I too am too stupid."

" Listen to me, Elisabeth, we won't touch on questions of that kind, for these are not the motives that decide our lives."

" Perhaps I do love him . . . there was a time when I wasn't unwilling to think of marrying him."

Elisabeth sat in the large invalid-chair in the small reception-room and looked at the floor.

" Why have you come here, Elisabeth? Surely not to ask for advice that nobody can give you? "

" You don't want to help me? "

" You have come because you can't bear to have anyone run away from you."

" I am serious in this . . . you mustn't make a joke of it . . . too serious to endure your saying more of your abominable things to me. I thought I should find some understanding. . . ."

" But I must tell you the truth. That's just why I must tell you the truth. You have come because you feel that I stand posted at some point outside your world, because you think that from my outpost there might be descried a third possibility beside the banal alternatives: I love him, I don't love him."

" Perhaps that is so; I don't know any longer."

" And you have come because you know that I love you—I told you that plainly enough—and because you want to show me what my somewhat absurd conception of love leads to," he gave her a side-glance, " perhaps to discover how quickly estrangement can turn into intimacy. . . ."

" That's not true! "

" Let us be honest, Elisabeth; the question between you and me now is whether you would marry me. Or, to be more exact, whether you love me."

" Herr von Bertrand, how dare you take advantage of the situation in such a way!"

" Ah, you shouldn't have said that, for you know perfectly well that it's not true. You have a decision for life in front of you, and you can't simply take refuge in convention. Of course the only question is whether a woman can think of her man as a lover, and not whether she is willing to set up house with him. If there is one thing I can't forgive Joachim for, it's that he didn't frankly discuss this essential point with you, but went with his so-called wooing to your parents, literally degrading you. Mark my words, he'll be on his knees next."

" You're trying to torment me again. I shouldn't have come here."

" No, you shouldn't have come, because I didn't want to see you again, but, my dear, you had to come, because you l——"

She stopped her ears.

" Well, more precisely, you are on the verge of believing that you might be able to love me."

" Oh, don't torment me; have I not been tormented enough already? " With her hands pressed to her temples she lay in the easy-chair, her head thrown back, her eyes shut; that was just how she used to sit in Lestow, and this relapse into old habit made him smile and feel almost tender. He was standing behind her. The arm in the sling pained him and made him awkward. But he succeeded in bending down and touching her lips with his. She started up: " This is madness! "

" No, it's merely a farewell."

With a voice as drained of life as her face she said: " You shouldn't, you, of all people . . ."

" Who should kiss you, Elisabeth? "

" You don't love me. . . ."

Bertrand was now walking up and down the room. His arm ached and he felt feverish. She was right, it was sheer madness. Suddenly he turned round and stopped close in front of her: without his intending it his voice sounded menacing: " I don't love you? "

She stood motionless with her arms hanging, and let him bend back her head. In her very face he repeated his threatening words: " I don't love you? " And she felt that he was going to bite her lips, but it turned into a kiss. And while most incomprehensibly the rigidity of her mouth relaxed into a smile, her hands, which had been hanging limp, now came to life and raised themselves, with the outflow of her feeling, towards his shoulders to clutch them, never more to let them go. At that he said: " Take care, Elisabeth, that's where I'm wounded."

Horrified, she loosened her grasp. But then her strength forsook her: she collapsed into the easy-chair. He sat on the arm of it, drew out the pins of her hat, and caressed her blond hair. " How lovely you are, and how much I love you." She was silent; she suffered him to take her hand; she felt the fevered heat of his, felt the heat of his face as he bent close to her again. When he hoarsely repeated " I love you " she shook her head, but yielded him her lips. Then at last the tears came.

Bertrand sat on the arm of the chair stroking her hair gently. He said: " I have such a longing for you."

She answered weakly: " It isn't true."

" I have such a longing for you."

She made no reply, staring into vacancy. He did not touch her again; he had risen to his feet and said once more: " I have an unspeakable longing for you."

Now she smiled.

" And you are going away ? "

" Yes."

She looked up, questioning and incredulous; he repeated: " No, we shall never see each other again."

She was still unconvinced. Bertrand smiled: " Can you imagine me suing for you to your father? Giving the lie to everything I have said? That would make it all the most sordid comedy; the most barefaced imposition."

She grasped somehow what he meant, but yet could not understand:

" But why, then? Why . . . ? "

" I can't possibly ask you to be my mistress, to come with me . . . of course I could and you would end up by doing it too . . . perhaps out of romanticism . . . perhaps because you really care for me now . . . of course you do now . . . oh, my dear . . ." they lost themselves in a kiss . . . " but after all, I can't put you in a false position, even though it might perhaps mean more to you than . . . to put it frankly, than your marriage to Joachim."

She stared at him in amazement.

" You can still think of such a marriage ? "

" Of course; it's only "—and to escape from the unbearable tension into raillery he looked at his watch—" twenty minutes since we were both thinking of it. Either the thought must have been unendurable twenty minutes ago, or it's still endurable."

" You shouldn't make a joke of it now . . ." then in fear, " or are you in earnest? "

" I don't know . . . that's something no man knows about himself."

" You're putting me off, or else you take a delight in tormenting me. You're a cynic."

Bertrand said seriously: " Am I to deceive you? "

" Perhaps you're deceiving yourself . . . perhaps because . . . I don't know why . . . but something doesn't ring true . . . no, you don't love me."

" I'm an egoist."

" You don't love me."

" I do love you."

She looked at him directly and seriously: " Am I to marry Joachim, then? "

" I can't, in spite of everything, tell you not to."

She freed her hands from his and sat for a long time in silence. Then she stood up, picked up her hat and put in the hatpins firmly.

" Good-bye, I'm going to get married . . . perhaps that's cynical, but you can't be surprised at that . . . perhaps we are both committing the worst crime against ourselves . . . good-bye."

" Good-bye, Elisabeth; don't forget this hour; it's my sole revenge on Joachim. . . . I shall never be able to forget you."

She passed her hand over his cheek. " You're feverish," she said, and went quickly out of the room.

That was what had happened, and Bertrand had paid for it with a severe bout of fever. But that seemed to him right and fitting, for it relegated yesterday to a greater distance. And made it possible for him to regard Joachim, who now sat before him in the same building—could it be the same?—with his usual kindness. No, it would have been too grotesque. So he said: " Don't you worry, Pasenow; you'll come to anchor all right in the harbour of matrimony. And the best of luck to it." An unchivalrous and cynical fellow, Joachim could not help thinking again, and yet he felt grateful and reassured. It might have been the memory of his father, or only the sight of Bertrand, but the thought of matrimony was mingled queerly with the vision of a quiet sick-chamber through which white-clad nuns flitted. Tender and nunlike was Elisabeth, white on her silver cloud, and he recalled a picture of the Madonna, an Assumption, which he believed he had seen in Dresden. He took his cap from the hook. He felt hustled by Bertrand into this marriage, and was struck now by the bizarre idea that Bertrand only wanted to drag him back into civilian life, to strip him of his uniform and his standing in the regiment, in order to be promoted as Major in his stead; and as Bertrand gave him his hand in farewell he did not observe how hot and feverish it was. Yet he thanked Bertrand for his friendly words and took his leave, stiff and angular in his long regimental coat. Bertrand could hear the faint jingle of his spurs as he went downstairs, and could not help thinking that Joachim was now passing the door of the reception-room.

His suit was accepted. To be sure, wrote the Baron, Elisabeth did not yet want an official betrothal. She had a kind of shrinking from the final step; but Joachim was expected to supper next evening.

Even if it was not counted a definite betrothal, even if neither Elisabeth nor his future parents-in-law addressed Joachim with the familiar " Du," yes, even if the tone at the supper-table was almost formal, there was yet an unmistakable hint of festivity in the atmosphere, especially when the Baron tapped on his glass and with many fine phrases elaborated the idea that a family was an organic whole and could not easily admit a newcomer into its circle; but when by the dispensation of Providence a newcomer was admitted, then he should be admitted wholeheartedly, and the love that united the family should embrace him also. The Baroness had tears in her eyes, and took her husband's hand in her own while he was speaking of love, and Joachim had the warm feeling that he would be happy here; in the bosom of the family, he said to himself, and the Holy Family occurred to him. Bertrand would probably have smiled and made fun of the Baron's speech, but how cheap was that kind of mockery! The obscure witticisms that Bertrand used to fling about at table—how far away that was—were certainly more offensive than the deep feeling that informed the Baron's words. Then they all clinked their glasses until they rang, and the Baron cried: " To the future! "

After supper the young people were left alone to open their hearts to each other. They sat in the newly done-up music-room with its black-silk chairs on which were sewed covers of lace made by the

Baroness and Elisabeth, and while Joachim was still trying to find the
right words he heard Elisabeth say almost gaily: " So you want to marry
me, Joachim; have you thought it over carefully? " How unladylike, he
thought; it might almost have been Bertrand speaking. What was he to
do? Should he get down on one knee to follow up his suit? Fortune
was kind to him, for the tabouret on which he had set himself was so
low that when he bent towards Elisabeth his knees were in any case
almost on the floor, and his attitude, if one liked, could have been
construed as kneeling. So he remained in this somewhat constrained
posture and said: " May I venture to hope? " Elisabeth made no answer;
she had thrown her head back, and her eyes were half shut. As he now
gazed at her face he was disquieted to find that a section of landscape
could be transferred within four walls; it was the very memory he had
feared, it was that noonday under the autumn trees, it was that blending
of contours, and he almost wished that the Baron's consent had been
longer postponed. For more dreadful than a brother's apparition in a
woman's face is the landscape that luxuriates over it, landscape that
takes possession of it and absorbs the dehumanized features, so that not
even Helmuth could avail to arrest their undulating flow. She said:
" Have you taken your friend Bertrand's advice on this marriage? "
That he could deny without violating the truth. " But he knew about
it? " Yes, returned Joachim, he had mentioned the proposal to Bertrand.
" And what did he say? " He had only wished him luck. " Are you
very attached to him, Joachim? " Joachim was comforted by her voice
and her words; they brought him back to the consciousness that it was
a human being and not a landscape that he was regarding. Yet they
were disquieting. What was in her mind about Bertrand? Where was
this leading to? It was somehow unseemly to spend this hour talking
about Bertrand, although it was a relief to find any topic of conversation
at all. And since he could not abandon the topic, and since also he felt
it his duty to be absolutely honest with his future wife, he said hesitatingly: " I don't know; I always have the feeling that he is the active
element in our friendship, but very often it is I who seek him out. I don't
know whether that could be called attachment." " Does he unsettle
you? " " Yes, that's the right word . . . I am always being unsettled
by him." " He is unsettled himself, and so unsettles others," said
Elisabeth. Yes, that he was, replied Joachim, and feeling Elisabeth's
look upon him could not help wondering anew that those transparent,

rounded stars, set one on each side of a nose, could emit such a thing
as a look. What is a look? He touched his own eyes, and at once Ruzena
was there and Ruzena's eyes which he had felt with delight through
her eyelids. It was unimaginable that he would ever be able to stroke
Elisabeth's eyelids; perhaps it was true, as they said in the schools, that
there was a cold so intense that it seared; the cold of outer space occurred
to him, the cold of the stars. That was where Elisabeth hovered on a
silver cloud, intangible her effluent, dissolving face, and he felt it as an
agonizing impropriety that her father and mother had kissed her when
the meal was ended. But from what sphere did Bertrand spring, whose
slave and victim she had almost become? If Bertrand was a tempter
sent to both of them by God, it was part of the discipline laid upon him
that he should save Elisabeth from such earthly aggression. God was
enthroned in absolute coldness, and His commands were ruthless, fitting
into each other like the teeth on Borsig's cog-wheels; it was all so inevitable that Joachim felt it almost a comfort to know that there was even
a single road to salvation, the straight path of duty, although he might
be consumed in following it. " He's going to India soon," he said. " Oh
yes, India," she replied. " I hesitated for a long time," he said, " for
I can offer you only a simple country life." " We are different from
him," she returned. Joachim was touched by that " we." " Perhaps his
roots have been torn up, and he is longing to be restored." Elisabeth
said: " Every man decides for himself." " But haven't we chosen the
better part? " asked Joachim. " We can't tell," said Elisabeth. " Oh,
surely," Joachim was indignant, " for he lives for his business, and he
has to be cold and unfeeling. Think of your parents, think of what your
father has just said. But *he* calls that convention; he hasn't got real
inwardness, real Christian feeling." He fell silent: he hadn't expressed
what he wanted to say, for what he expected from God and from
Elisabeth was not a mere equivalent for Christian family life as he had
been trained to understand it; yet just because he expected more from
Elisabeth, he desired to confine his words to the neighbourhood of that
celestial sphere in which she was to manifest herself as the tenderest of
silvery, hovering Madonnas. Perhaps she would have to die before she
could speak to him in the right way, for as she sat there leaning back,
she looked like Snow-white in the glass casket and was so irradiated
by that higher beauty and heavenly essence that her face had but little
resemblance to the one he had known in life before it blended so

dreadfully and irrevocably with the landscape. The wish that Elisabeth were dead and her voice imparting angelic comfort to him from the other side grew and grew, and the extraordinary tension it engendered, or out of which itself had sprung, attained such force that Elisabeth too must have been affected by the onrush of terrifying coldness, for she said: " He doesn't need the comforting warmth of companionship as we do." Yet she disappointed Joachim by these earthly words, and even though the need for protection that echoed in them moved his heart and awakened in him the vision of Mary wandering on earth before her assumption into heaven, yet he realized that his strength was hardly equal to affording such protection, and in his twofold disappointment he wished with twofold earnestness a kind and pleasant death for both of them. And since the mask falls from the face that is confronted by death, defenceless against the breath of the Eternal, Joachim said: " He would always have been remote from you," and this seemed to both of them a great and significant truth, although they had almost forgotten that it was Bertrand of whom they were speaking. Like yellow butterflies with black spots upon their serrated yellow wings, the ring of gas-jets blazed in the wreath of the chandelier over the black-silk catafalque on which Joachim still sat motionless with his body stiffly inclined and his knees bent, and the white-lace covers on the black silk were like copies of deaths' heads. Into that frozen stillness dropped Elisabeth's words: " He is more solitary than other people," and Joachim replied: " His demon drives him out." But Elisabeth almost imperceptibly shook her head: " He hopes to find fulfilment," and then she added, as if from a fixed recollection, " fulfilment and knowledge in solitude and remoteness." Joachim was silent; it was with reluctance that he took up this thought that hung cold and bewildering between them: " He is remote . . . he thrusts us all away, for God wills us to be solitary." " He does, indeed," said Elisabeth, and it was not to be determined whether she had referred to God or to Bertrand; but that ceased to matter, since the solitude prescribed for her and Joachim now began to encompass them, and froze the room, in spite of its intimate elegance, into a more complete and dreadful immobility; as they sat motionless, both of them, it seemed as if the room widened around them; as the walls receded the air seemed to grow colder and thinner, so thin that it could barely carry a voice. And although everything was tranced in immobility, yet the chairs, the piano, on whose black-lacquered surface the wreath of gas-jets was still reflected, seemed no longer in their usual places, but infinitely remote, and even the golden dragons and butterflies on the black Chinese screen in the corner had flitted away as if drawn after the receding walls, which now looked as if hung with black curtains. The gas-lights hissed with a faint, malicious susurration, and except for their infinitesimal mechanical vivacity, that jetted fleeringly from obscenely open small slits, all life was extinguished. She will die soon now, thought Joachim, and it was almost a confirmation of it that he heard her voice saying in the emptiness: " His death will be a lonely one "; it sounded like a doom and a pledge, a pledge that he fortified: " He is sick, and may die soon; perhaps this very moment." " Yes," said Elisabeth from the other side of beyond, and the word was like a drop that turned to ice as it fell, " yes, this very moment," and in the frozen featurelessness of that second in which Death stood beside them, Joachim did not know whether it was the two of them that Death touched, or whether it was his father, or Bertrand; he could not tell whether his mother was not sitting there to watch over his death, punctual and calm, as she watched in the milking-byre or by his father's bed, and he had a sudden near intuition, strangely clear, that his father was freezing and longed for the dark warmth of the cowshed. Was it not better to die now beside Elisabeth, and to be led by her into the glassy brightness that hovered above the dark ? He said: " There will be frightful darkness around him, and no one will come to help him." But Elisabeth said in a hard voice: " No one should come," and with the same grey, toneless hardness she went on speaking in the emptiness, adding in the same breath, that yet was not a breath at all: " I will be your wife, Joachim," and was herself uncertain whether she had said it, for Joachim sat in unchanged stillness with his body inclined, and made no answer. No sign was given, and although it lasted no longer than the dulling and glazing of an eye, the tension was so charged with uncertainty and nullity that Elisabeth said again: " Yes, I'll be your wife." But Joachim did not want to hear her words, for they compelled him to turn back from that road on which there is no returning. With a great effort he tried to bend towards her; he barely succeeded, but his half-bent knee actually did touch the ground; his brow, beaded with cold sweat, inclined itself, and his lips, dry and cold as parchment, brushed her hand, which was so icy that he did not dare to touch her finger-tips, not even when the room slowly closed in again and the chairs resumed their former places.

So they remained until they heard the Baron's voice in the next room. "We must go in," said Elisabeth. Then they entered the brightly lit salon, and Elisabeth said: "We are engaged." "My child!" cried the Baroness, and with tears enfolded Elisabeth in her arms. But the Baron, whose eyes were not less wet, cried: "Let us be joyful and give thanks to God for this happy day," and Joachim loved him for those heartening words, and felt committed to his keeping.

Out of the apathetic doze into which his weariness declined amid the rattle of the droshky wheels as he drove home, the thought emerged more clearly that his father and Bertrand had died that day, and he was almost amazed to find no announcement of their death awaiting him in his flat, for that would have fitted in with the return of punctiliousness to his life. In any case one should not conceal a betrothal from even a dead friend. The thought continued to haunt him and next morning strengthened into something like certainty, if not a certainty of their death, a certainty of their non-existence at least: his father and Bertrand had departed this life, and even although he was partly to blame for their death, he remained sunk in quiet indifference and did not even once find it necessary to decide whether it was Elisabeth or Ruzena of whom he had robbed Bertrand. The task had been laid upon him to catch Bertrand from behind, to keep an eye upon him, and the path along which he was bound to pursue him had now come to an end, the mystery was annulled; all that remained was to say farewell to his dead friend. "Both good news and bad news," he said to himself. He had plenty of time; he stopped the droshky to order bouquets for his fiancée and the Baroness, and without haste proceeded to the hospital. But when he entered the hospital no one made any reference to the catastrophe; he was conducted in the usual manner to Bertrand's room as if nothing had happened: it was only when he met the Sister in the corridor that he learned that Bertrand had indeed had a bad night, but was now feeling better. Joachim repeated mechanically: "He's feeling better . . . yes, that's gratifying, very gratifying." It was as if Bertrand had betrayed and deceived him yet again, and this became a firm conviction when he was greeted by the gay words: "I take it you can be congratulated to-day." How does he know that? Joachim asked himself, and in spite of his annoyance was almost proud that his suspicions were, in a way, justified by his new character as prospective bridegroom: yes, he said, he was happy to be able to announce his engagement. Bertrand seemed, however, in a softened mood. " You know that I like you, Pasenow," he said—Joachim felt this as importunity—" and so it's with all my heart that I wish luck to you and your bride." Once more his words sounded warm and sincere, yet mocking: he—the man who always knew everything beforehand, he who had actually willed it and brought it about, although merely as the instrument of a higher power —was evading the issue, now that he saw his work accomplished, with a smooth and cordial congratulation. Joachim felt somehow exhausted; he sat down by the table in the middle of the room, looked at Bertrand, who was lying blond and almost girlish in his bed, and said gravely: " I hope that everything will turn out well," and Bertrand replied lightly with that offhand certainty which always laid its soothing and yet disquieting spell on Joachim: " Let me assure you, Pasenow, that everything will turn out for the very best . . . at least for you." Joachim repeated: " Yes, for the best . . ." but then he looked perplexed: " Why for me only? " Bertrand smiled and waved the question away with a faintly contemptuous gesture: " Oh, we . . . we're a lost generation," yet he explained himself no further, only adding abruptly: " And when's the wedding to be? " so that Joachim forgot to ask more, and at once said: well, there was still some way to go; his father's illness, above all, had to be considered. Bertrand eyed Joachim, who sat facing him with stiff propriety. " But getting married surely doesn't involve settling down on the estate at once? " he said. Joachim was shocked: apparently all his trouble had been wasted. After harping on the necessity for taking over the estate, after plunging Ruzena into despair, here was Bertrand now saying that he did not need to settle down on the estate, as if wishing to cheat him of his pride in its possession and even to deprive him of his home! With what devious cunning had Bertrand lured him on, and now he was shaking off all responsibility and actually disdaining the triumph he had scored in pulling him down to his own civilian level, repudiating him even there! It must have been sheer evil for evil's sake that Bertrand had wrought, and Joachim looked at him with indignant amazement. But Bertrand observed only the question in his eyes: " Well," he said, " you mentioned not long ago that you were just on the point of getting your captaincy, and you should stay on until you're promoted. Retired Captain sounds much better than retired Lieutenant "—now he's ashamed of himself, the Second Lieutenant, thought Joachim and straightened himself with a little jerk, as if on parade—" and during these few months your father's illness will have taken a decisive turn of some kind." Joachim would have liked to point out that married officers seemed to him an anomaly, and that he was longing for his native soil, but he did not venture to say so, remarking merely that Bertrand's suggested solution fitted in with the heartfelt desire of his future parents to see Elisabeth settled in the new west-end house. "Well, there you are, my dear Pasenow; everything turns out for the best," said Bertrand, and that was another gratuitous and abominable piece of presumption, " besides, you could certainly speed up your promotion if you were to tell your colonel that you mean to retire from the service as soon as you get your step." He was right in that, too, but it was annoying to have Bertrand interfering with even military arrangements. Joachim thoughtfully picked up Bertrand's stick from the table, scrutinized the handle, and ran his finger over the resilient black-rubber bulb at the point of it: a convalescent's stick. That the man was urging him into a headlong marriage filled him with new suspicion. What was behind it all? Yesterday evening he and Elisabeth had explained to her parents that they did not want to hurry on the marriage, and had enumerated all the obstacles; and now this Bertrand wanted simply to blow the obstacles away. " All the same, we can't precipitate the marriage," said Joachim obstinately. " Well," remarked Bertrand, " I'm only sorry that in that case I must be content with sending you a wire on the happy day, from India or somewhere. For as soon as I'm half set up again I'm going abroad. . . . This affair has pulled me down a bit." What affair? The slight wound to his arm? It was true that Bertrand looked ill, and convalescents always needed sticks, but what else had been happening? He shouldn't really let Bertrand go away until that was all cleared up, and Joachim wondered whether Helmuth, who had faced his enemy openly, hadn't been much more honourable than himself; was not the issue here the same: explanation or death? But Joachim wanted both of them, and yet neither. His father was right: he was dishonourable, as dishonourable as Bertrand, this friend of his, who could hardly be called his friend still. Yet that was almost gratifying, for it must have been in his father's mind that Bertrand should not be invited to the wedding.

None the less he listened quietly as Bertrand went on: " One thing more, Pasenow; I have the impression that the estate, except where your mother looks after it and where it runs itself, is in a fairly neglected condition. In his present state your father could possibly do it a great deal of additional harm. Excuse me for suggesting, as I feel bound to do, that you might have him declared incapable of managing it. And you should engage a good steward; he would anyhow earn his wages. I think you should discuss it with your father-in-law; after all, he's a land-owner too." Yes, Bertrand was talking like the vilest *agent provocateur*, and yet Joachim had to thank him for the advice, which he could see was just and well meant, and even had to express the hope that they would still see much of each other before Bertrand's full recovery. " Delighted," said Bertrand; " and give my humblest respects to your bride." Then he sank back exhausted on his pillow.

Two days later Joachim received a letter in which Bertrand announced that his health was much improved and that he had shifted into a hospital in Hamburg, so as to be nearer to his business. But they would certainly meet again before he started for the East. Bertrand's cool assumption that as a matter of course they would have another encounter made Joachim decide to avoid it at all costs. But he suffered from the know-ledge that from now on he would have to do without his friend's sureness and lightness of touch, and his competence in the affairs of life.

Behind the Leipzigerplatz there is a shop which externally can hardly be distinguished from its neighbours, unless it should attract attention because there are no goods displayed in its windows and the eye is prevented from seeing what is inside by opaque-glass screens, beautifully etched with Pompeian and Renaissance designs. But this peculiarity is one which the shop shares with many banking houses and brokers' offices, and even the posters affixed to the screens, although they are an unpleasant interruption of the designs, have nothing unusual about them. On these posters the word " India " occurs, and a glance at the sign above the door informs one that inside the shop the Kaiser Panorama is on view.

On entering, one advances first into a light and cosily heated room in which an elderly and obviously good-natured lady acts as a kind of cashier behind a small table, selling tickets of admission to the establish-ment. Most of the visitors, however, pause at the table only to have their books of subscription tickets stamped and to exchange a few friendly words with the old lady. When the aged attendant appears from behind the black curtains that cut off one end of the room, and with a deprecating little gesture begs one to wait a minute or two, the visitor subsides with a faint sigh into one of the cane chairs and continues his conversation, mistrustfully watching the glass door that leads into the street, and if a fresh client appears regarding him with jealous and ashamed hostility. Then there is heard the faint scraping of chairs behind the curtains, and the man who emerges blinks a little in the light, and departs with a brief salutation to the old lady, going hurriedly, nervously, and without looking at anybody, as if he too were ashamed. The waiting client, however, springs quickly to his feet lest someone should push in ahead of him, breaks off his conversation without more ado, and vanishes behind the protecting curtains. It happens but seldom that clients speak to each other, although many must get to know each other by sight in the course of years, and only one or two shameless old men bring themselves to address the other waiting clients as well as the cashier, and to praise the programme; yet even then they are answered mostly in monosyllables.

Within, however, all is darkness, and one could suppose it an ancient, oppressive darkness that has been accumulating here for years. The attendant takes you gently by the hand and leads you carefully to a seat, a round seat without arms, that is waiting for you. In front of you are two bright eyes that look at you somewhat uncannily from a black screen, and under these eyes is a mouth, a hard rectangle softened by the dull light that fills it. Gradually you realize that you are set before a polygonal construction resembling a temple, and that the screen in front of which you are sitting is a part of it; you observe, too, that to right and left of you sits a worshipper who has applied his eyes to the eyes in the screen before him, and you do the same, after taking a look at the rectangle of light and noting that it says, " Government House in Calcutta." But as soon as you peer into the open eye, Government House vanishes to the tinkle of a sweet bell and with a mechanical rattle; you can still see it sliding away while another view comes sliding after it, so that you feel almost cheated; but another bell tinkles, the view gives itself a little shake, as if to set itself off to the best advantage, and comes to rest. You see palm-trees and a well-kept path: in the background, where it is shaded, a man in a light suit is sitting on a seat; a fountain throws a congealed, whiplike jet of spray into the air, but you are not content until a glance at the softly lit rectangle informs you: " View in the Royal Park, Calcutta." Then comes another tinkle, a sliding past of palms, seats, buildings, masts, a quiver into place, a tinkle of the bell, and in bright sunlight: " View of the Harbour, Bombay." The man who has just been sitting on the seat in Calcutta Park is now standing in a sun-helmet on the hewn stones of the mole in the foreground. He is propped on a walking-stick and does not move, because he is spellbound by the taut rigging of the ships, by their funnels and cranes, spellbound by the bundles of cotton bales on the quay, and gazes at them spellbound, and his face is in shadow and cannot be recognized. Yet perhaps he will advance into the magic space, enclosed in polished brown, that lies between you and the picture, a space that is but an abstract cube and yet a long journey; perhaps he will step out freely and magically upon the wooden floor, and you will recognize that it is Bertrand, airily and yet terribly warning you that he can never more be crossed out of your life, however far away he may be. But that may be only your imagination, for God has already rung the bell for him, and without a greeting, stiff and motionless, without taking even one step, he slides away again. You peep at your left-hand neighbour to see if that is where Bertrand has gone, but his lit rectangle reports: " Government House in Calcutta," and you can almost nurse the hope that Bertrand has appeared to you alone, to greet you only. But you have no time to reflect upon it, for when you turn quickly again to your own eyepieces a delightful surprise awaits you: the " Native Mother in Ceylon " is not only lit up by soft golden sunlight but represented in her natural colours; she smiles with white teeth between red lips and may be waiting for the white Sahib who has quitted the West because he despises European women. The " Temple Buildings in Delhi " also glow in all the colours of the Orient at the far end of the brown box: there the bad Christian may learn that even subject races know how to serve God. But did he not once say himself that it would devolve upon the black races to set up the Kingdom of Christ again? You look with horror at the swarm of brown figures, and are not ill-pleased to hear the signal with which they are dismissed, to give place to the " Elephant-hunting Expedition." Here stand the colossal quadrupeds, one of them gently lifting a forefoot. The square is full of fine white sand, and when you turn your dazzled eyes away for a moment you see above the rectangular title-plate a small button, which you twirl experimentally. At once, to your delight, the picture is suffused by soft moonlight, so that you can expedite the hunters at your pleasure by day or by night.

Well, since the sun-glare no longer blinds you, you seize the opportunity of examining the hunters' faces, and if your eye does not deceive you it is Bertrand, after all, who is sitting in the howdah behind the dusky mahout, his rifle at the ready in his right hand, promising death. You change the light, and once more it is an utter stranger who smiles at you, and the mahout lays his goad behind the elephant's ear to give the signal for the prescribed start of the expedition; they slide away into the jungle, yet you hear nothing of the trampling of the herds and the trumpeting of the bulls, but with a faint tinkle and a mechanical rattle landscape after landscape advances of its own accord and vanishes, and if the passing traveller seems to be really the man you are bound to seek for ever, the man you hunger for, the man who vanishes while you are still holding his hand, then the bell tinkles, and before you know where you are you are peering anxiously at your neighbour's title-plate on the right, and discovering the inscription: " Government House in Calcutta," so that you know your hour will be over soon. Then you give a cursory look to make sure that the palms of the Royal Park are due to follow, and since they follow on ruthlessly you scrape your chair, the attendant hurries up, and blinking a little, your collar turned up, a poor creature found indulging a pleasure he has never realized, you leave with a brief salutation the room in which others are already waiting, and in which the old lady is selling books of tickets.

Into this establishment Joachim and Elisabeth strayed, accompanied by Elisabeth's companion, when they were making purchases in the city for their house and the trousseau. For although they knew that Bertrand was still in Hamburg, and although they never mentioned his name again, the word India had a magic sound for them.

The wedding at Lestow was a quiet one. The condition of Joachim's father had become stationary; he lay in a coma, no longer recognizing the outer world, and one had to be reconciled to this lasting for years. True, the Baroness said that a quiet, intimate ceremony would be far more to the taste of herself and her husband than noisy display, but Joachim already knew the importance which his parents-in-law attached to their family festivals, and he felt to blame for his father, who robbed the occasion of its splendour. And he himself would perhaps have preferred a great and brilliant social setting to emphasise the social character of this marriage, into which mere love entered so little; yet on the other hand it seemed to him more in accordance with the gravity and Christian nature of the union that Elisabeth and he should approach the altar without any thought of the world. And so it was decided not to celebrate the marriage in Berlin, even although Lestow presented various difficulties not easy to overcome, more especially as Bertrand's advice was no longer to be had. Joachim rejected the idea of leading his bride home for the wedding night: the idea of passing that night in the house of sickness filled him with repugnance, but still more impossible to him was the thought that Elisabeth should retire to rest under the eyes of the domestic staff who knew him so well; so he suggested that Elisabeth should spend the night at Lestow, and he would fetch her next day. Strangely enough this proposal encountered the opposition of the Baroness, who found such a solution unseemly: " Even if we closed our eyes to it, what would the servants think? " Finally it was decided to hold the ceremony at such an early hour that the young couple could catch the midday train. " Then you'll be able to go straight to your own comfortable house in Berlin," said the Baroness, but Joachim would not hear of that either. No, it was too far out, for they would be leaving Berlin again early in the morning, and probably they might even be able to take the night train to Munich without stopping. Yes, night travel was almost the simplest solution of the marriage problem, a safe-guard against the fear that someone might smile understandingly when he and Elisabeth had to retire for the night. Yet presently he doubted whether they really could set out for Munich straight off; after the excitement of the day could one really expect Elisabeth to undertake a night journey? And how could their day in Munich, in perpetual expectation of what was to come, be put in? It was clear that one could not have discussed such matters even with Bertrand, one had to come to a decision oneself; all the same, several things would have been appreciably simpler if Bertrand had been at hand. He considered what Bertrand would have done in such circumstances, and came to the conclusion that there was no harm in his booking rooms in the Hotel Royal in Berlin; if Elisabeth should wish it, they could still take the night train. And he was honestly proud of having found this adroit solution by himself.

It had now become quite wintry, and the closed carriages in which they drove to the church advanced only by slow stages through the snow. Joachim was in the same carriage as his mother; she sat there,

broad and complacent, and Joachim felt irritated when she reiterated:
" Father would have been delighted; well, it's a great pity." Yes, that was
all that was needed to fill his cup; Joachim was exasperated—nobody
would leave him in peace to gain that calm which was imperative at
this solemn hour, doubly imperative for him to whom this marriage
signified more than a Christian marriage, to whom it meant redemption
from the pit and the mire and a heavenly assurance that he was entering
the way of grace. In her wedding-robe Elisabeth looked more like
a Madonna than ever, looked like Snow-white, and he could not help
thinking of the legend of the bride who had fallen down dead before
the altar because she suddenly recognized in her bridegroom an incarnation of the Devil. The thought would not leave him and took such
complete possession of him that he heard neither the chant of the choir
nor the pastor's sermon: indeed he actually closed his ears to them out
of a fear that he might be compelled to interrupt them and tell those
people that a man unworthy, an outcast, stood before the altar, a man
who desecrated the holy state of matrimony; and he started in terror
when he had to pronounce the " Yes," in terror too at the thought that
the ceremony, which should have been for him the revelation of a new
life, had come to an end so quickly and almost without his being aware
of it. He found it actually comforting that Elisabeth should now be
called, without really being, his wife, but the thought that this state
would not last was appalling. During the drive back from the church
he took her hand and said: " My wife," and Elisabeth responded to
his pressure. But then everything was drowned in the tumult of good
wishes, the hurry of changing and setting out, so that only when they
reached the station did they realize what had happened.

He turned away while Elisabeth climbed into the compartment, so
as not again to fall a prey to impure thoughts. Now they were alone.
Elisabeth leant back wearily in her corner and smiled faintly at him.
" You're tired, Elisabeth," he said hopefully, glad that it was his privilege
and his duty to protect her. " Yes, I'm tired, Joachim." He did not
dare, however, to suggest that they should stop at Berlin, fearing that
she might interpret it as concupiscence. Her profile stood out sharply
against the window, beyond which stretched the grey winter afternoon,
and Joachim felt relieved that that oppressive and affrighting vision in
which her face changed into a landscape remained absent. But while
he was still regarding her he saw that the trunk, which had been placed

on the seat opposite, was outlined no less sharply against the grey sky, and he was overcome by the senselessly sharp fear that she might be a mere thing, a dead object, and not even a landscape. He got up hastily as though to do something to the trunk, but he merely opened it and took out the lunch-basket; it was a wedding present and a miniature miracle of elegance, suitable equally for train journeys and hunting expeditions: the ivory handles of the knives and forks were ornamented with decorative hunting scenes which were continued on the incised blades, and even the spirit-stove was not free from them; amid the ornamentation on each piece, however, one could recognize the inter-twined arms of Elisabeth and Joachim. The centre space of the basket served as a receptacle for food and had been solicitously filled by the Baroness. Joachim pressed Elisabeth to eat, and as they had not been able to wait for the wedding lunch she gladly acceded. " Our first married meal," said Joachim, and he poured the wine into the silver collapsible cups, and Elisabeth drank to him. In this way they passed the journey and Joachim was once more of the opinion that the train provided the best form of wedded life. He even began to understand Bertrand, who was at liberty to pass such a great part of his time in trains. " Shouldn't we go straight through to Munich this evening? " he asked; but Elisabeth replied that she felt really fatigued and would rather break the journey. So he could not but divulge to her that he had already provided for her wish and booked rooms.

He was grateful to Elisabeth for the fact that she had not lost her composure, even if it was probably only an assumed composure; for she lingered out the hour for retiring and asked for supper, and they sat for a very long time in the dining-hall; the band which played for the diners' entertainment had already put away their instruments, only a few guests were still left in the room, and grateful as any postponement of the hour was to Joachim, yet he felt again that cold, rarefied atmosphere diffusing itself through the room, that chill which on the evening of their betrothal had been like a dreadful foreboding of death. Perhaps even Elisabeth felt it, for she said that it was time now to retire.

So the moment had come. Elisabeth had parted from him with a friendly " Good-night, Joachim," and now he walked up and down his room. Should he simply go to bed? He regarded the bed, on which the sheets were folded down. Yet he had taken an oath to watch before her door, to guard her heavenly dreams, that for ever on her silvery cloud she might dream on; and now it had suddenly lost all sense and meaning, for everything seemed to point to the one conclusion, that he should make himself comfortable here. He glanced down at his clothes, and felt the long military coat as a protection; it was indecent for people to appear at weddings in frock-coats. All the same he must have a wash, and softly, as though he were committing an act of sacrilege, he pulled off his coat and poured water into the basin on the brown varnished washstand. How painful all this was, how senseless, unless it should be a link in the chain of trials laid on his shoulders; it would all have been easier if Elisabeth had locked the communicating door behind her, but out of consideration for him she had certainly not done that. Joachim vaguely remembered having been in the same position before, and now with crushing force came the memory of a locked door and a brown washstand under a gas-jet: dreadful because it was a memory of Ruzena, no less dreadful as raising the problem how, living with an angel, the thought of such a thing as a lavatory, no matter how discreetly it obtruded itself, was practically conceivable at all: in both cases a degradation of Elisabeth and a new trial. He had cleansed his face and hands gently and cautiously, so as to prevent the porcelain basin from making any sound against the marble top of the table, but now he was confronted with something quite inconceivable: for who could think of gargling in the immediate vicinity of Elisabeth? And yet he must immerse himself still more deeply in the purifying crystalline medium, must drown there, to walk forth from that utter purification as from baptism in Jordan. But how could even a bath help him here? Ruzena had recognized him for what he was and drawn the consequences. He slipped back hastily into his coat again, buttoned it up scrupulously, and walked up and down the room. There was no sound from the other room, and he felt that his presence must be an oppression to her. Why did she not scream at him to go away, as Ruzena had done behind the locked door? That time he had had the lavatory attendant at least to stand by him, but now he was alone and without support. All too prematurely he had rejected Bertrand and his easy assurance, and the fact that he had been capable of thinking it his duty to protect Elisabeth from Bertrand struck him now as hypocrisy. A terrible feeling of remorse came over him: it was not Elisabeth whom he had really wished to protect and save; he had merely hoped to save his own soul through her sacrifice. Was she kneeling on her knees in there praying that God might free her again from the fetters which she had assumed out of pity? Was it not his duty to say to her that he gave her her freedom, this very night, that if she commanded him he would drive her at once to her house in the west end, to her beautiful new house which was waiting for her? In great agitation he knocked at the communicating door and wished immediately that he had not done so. She said softly: " Joachim," and he turned the handle. She was lying in bed, a candle was burning on the commode. He remained at the door, almost as if he were standing at attention, and said hoarsely: " Elisabeth, I only wanted to tell you that I give you your freedom: I can't think of your sacrificing yourself for me." Elisabeth was astonished, but she felt relief that he did not accost her as a loving husband. " Do you think, Joachim, that I've sacrificed myself? " She smiled faintly. " Really you've thought of that a little too late." " It isn't too late yet; I thank God it isn't too late. . . . I didn't realize it until now. . . . Shall I drive you out to the west end? " Then Elisabeth could not help laughing: now, in the middle of the night! What would the people in the hotel think? " Why not just go to bed, Joachim. We can discuss all that in peace and quietness to-morrow. You must be tired too." Joachim said like an obstinate child: " I'm not tired." The flickering flame of the candle lighted up her pale face, which lay between her loosened hair on the snowy pillows. A peak of the bolster rose in the air like a nose, and its shadow on the wall was exactly the same shape as the shadow of Elisabeth's nose. " Please, Elisabeth, smooth down the corner of that pillow, to the left of your head there," he said from the door. " Why? " asked Elisabeth in surprise, putting up her hand towards it. " It casts such a horrible shadow," said Joachim; meanwhile another peak of the bolster had risen, showing another nose on the wall. Joachim was irritated, he wanted to set this matter right himself and took a step into the room. " But, Joachim, what's wrong with the shadows that they annoy you? Is it right now? " Joachim replied: " The shadow of your face on the wall is like a mountain range." " But that's nothing." " I can't stand it." Elisabeth was a little afraid lest this should be the prelude to putting out the candle, but to her pleasant surprise Joachim said: " We must have two candles for you, then there won't be any shadows and you'll look like Snow-white." And he actually went into his room and came back with the second lighted candle. " Oh, you're joking, Joachim," Elisabeth could not help saying, " where are you to put the second candle? There's no place for it on the wall. And besides, I would look like a corpse between two candles." Joachim studied the position. Elisabeth was right, so he said: " May I set it on the commode? " " Of course you may . . ." she paused for a moment, and said hesitatingly and yet with a slight feeling of reassurance, " you're my husband now." He held his hand in front of the flame and carried the candle over to the commode, reflectively contemplated the two lights, and the quietness and semi-darkness of this wedding night striking him he said: " Three would be more cheerful," as though with those words he were trying to excuse himself to Elisabeth and her parents for the quietness of the ceremony. She too gazed at the two candles; she had drawn the coverlet over her shoulders, and only her hand, caught at the wrist by a lace frill, hung languidly over the edge. Joachim was still thinking of the lack of display at their marriage; but he had held this hand in his in the carriage. He had become more composed, and had almost forgotten why he had come in here; now he remembered again and felt it his duty to repeat his offer: " So you don't want to go to your house, Elisabeth? " " But you're silly, Joachim; fancy my getting up now! I feel very comfortable here and you want to rout me out." Joachim stood irresolutely beside the commode; suddenly he could not comprehend the way in which things changed their nature and vocation; a bed was a pleasant article of furniture for sleeping on, with Ruzena it was a coign of desire and inexpressible sweetness, and now it was a thing unapproachable, a something whose edge he scarcely dared to touch. Wood was wood and nothing more, but still one shrank from touching the wood of a coffin. " It's so difficult, Elisabeth," he said suddenly, " forgive me." Yet he begged her forgiveness not merely, as she probably imagined, for expecting her to get up at that late hour, but because yet once more he had compared her with Ruzena, and—he admitted it to himself with horror —because he could almost have wished that Ruzena, and not she, were lying there. And he saw how deeply he was still stuck in the mire. " Forgive me," he said again, and he knelt down so as to kiss a good-night on the white, blue-veined hand on the edge of the bed. She could not tell whether this might not mean the dreaded approach of intimacy, and remained silent. His mouth was pressed to her hand, and he became aware of his teeth, which were crushed against the inner side of his lips, as the frontier of the hard bony skull which was hidden beneath his own skull and was continued in the skeleton. He felt too the warm breath in the cavity of his mouth, and the tongue embedded in the trough between his lower teeth, and he knew that now he must quickly remove all these, so that Elisabeth might not become inwardly aware of them. Yet he would not concede Ruzena this quick triumph, and so in silence he remained stubbornly on his knees beside the bed, until Elisabeth, as though to indicate that he should go, very gently pressed his hand. Perhaps he intentionally misunderstood this hint, for it gave him a remote memory of Ruzena's caressing hands; so he did not free Elisabeth's hand, although he was actually very impatient to leave the room. He waited for the miracle, the token of grace which God must grant him, and it was as though fear stood between the gates of grace. " Elisabeth, say something," he begged, and Elisabeth replied very slowly, as though the words were not her own: " We aren't strange enough, and we aren't intimate enough." Joachim said: " Elisabeth, do you want to leave me? " Elisabeth answered gently: " No, Joachim, I think we'll go the same road together now. Don't be unhappy, Joachim, it will all turn out for the best yet." Yes, Joachim would have liked to answer, and that's what Bertrand said too; but he was silent, not merely because it would have been unseemly to suggest such a thing, but because in her mouth Bertrand's words were like a Mephistophelian sign from the demon and the Evil One, instead of the sign from God that he had expected and hoped for and prayed for. For a moment Bertrand's image was faintly visible as at the bottom of a brown box, visible and yet hidden, and it was the Devil incarnate whose face and form threw the shadow of a mountain range upon the wall. And immovable and frozen as it was when it appeared, and swiftly, as at the tinkling of a bell, as it vanished again, yet it was a warning that the Evil One was not yet overcome, and that Elisabeth herself was still in his power, seeing that with her own words she had called him up, and seeing that she had not succeeded in scaring away those phantoms and sick fancies with words from God. But even if this was disappointing, yet it was also good, filling him with a sense of the pathos of the earthly and the human and of human weakness. Elisabeth was his heavenly goal, but the way on earth to such a goal he had himself, in spite of his great weakness, to find out and prepare for both of them: and meanwhile where in this loneliness was a guide to be found to that knowledge? Where could he find help? Clausewitz's aphorism came into his mind, that men act only from a divination and instinctive feeling of truth, and his heart was prescient with the knowledge that in a Christian household their

lives would be determined by the saving help of grace, guarding them
so that they might not wander on the earth unenlightened, helpless and
without meaning to their lives, and lose themselves in the void. No, that
could not be called a mere convention of feeling. He straightened himself and ran his hand softly over the silk coverlet under which her body
lay; he felt a little like a sick-room attendant, and distantly it was as
though he were stroking his sick father, or his father's deputy. " Poor
little Elisabeth," he said; it was the first endearment that he had
ventured to utter. She had freed her hand, and now passed it over his
hair: Ruzena had done that too, he thought. Nevertheless she said softly:
" Joachim, we're not intimate enough yet." He had raised himself a
little, and sat now on the edge of the bed and stroked her hair. Then
with his head on his hand he contemplated her face, which still lay,
pale and strange, not the face of a wife, not the face of his wife, on the
pillow, and it so happened that gradually and without himself noticing
it he found himself in a recumbent position beside her. She had moved
a little to the side, and her hand, which with its befrilled wrist was all
that emerged from the bedclothes, rested in his. Through his position
his military coat had become disordered, the lapels falling apart left his
black trousers visible, and when Joachim noticed this he hastily set
things right again and covered the place. He had now drawn up his
legs, and so as not to touch the sheets with his patent-leather shoes,
he rested his feet in a rather constrained posture on the chair standing
beside the bed. The candles flickered; first one went out, then the other.
Now and then they heard muffled footsteps in the carpeted corridor, a
door banged, and in the distance they could hear the sounds of the
great city, whose gigantic traffic did not fully cease even at night. They
lay motionless and gazed at the ceiling of the room, on which yellow strips
of light from the slits of the window-blinds were pencilled, and they
resembled a little the ribs of a skeleton. Then Joachim had fallen asleep,
and when Elisabeth noticed it she could not help smiling. And then she
too actually went to sleep.

IV

Nevertheless after some eighteen months they had their first child.
It actually happened. How this came about cannot be told here. Besides,
after the material for character construction already provided, the reader
can imagine it for himself.

Notes inspired by
The Sleepwalkers *(1986)*

MILAN KUNDERA

COMPOSITION

A trilogy composed of three novels: *Pasenow, or Romanticism*; *Esch, or Anarchy*; *Huguenau, or Realism* (in German, *Sachlichkeit*). The story of each novel takes place fifteen years after that of the preceding one: 1888; 1903; 1918. None of the novels is bound to another by causal connection: each has its own circle of characters, and its construction is unlike that of the two others.

It is true that Pasenow (protagonist of the first novel) and Esch (protagonist of the second) meet on the stage of the third, and that Bertrand (a character in the first novel) plays a role in the second. However, the story that Bertrand lives through in the first novel (along with Pasenow, Ruzena, Elisabeth) is completely absent from the second novel, and when Pasenow appears in the third novel he carries with him not the slightest memory of his youth (which is treated in the first novel).

There is thus a radical difference between *The Sleepwalkers* and the other great twentieth-century 'frescoes' (those of Proust, Musil, Thomas Mann, etc.): *In Broch, it is continuity neither of action nor of biography (a character's or a family's) that provides the unity of the whole. It is something else, something less apparent, less apprehensible, something hidden: the continuity of one theme (that of man facing the process of a disintegration of values).*

POSSIBILITIES

What are the possibilities for man in the trap the world has become?

To answer this, one must first have a certain idea of what the world is. One must have an ontological hypothesis about it.

The world according to Kafka: the bureaucratized universe. The office not merely as one kind of social phenomenon among many but as the essence of the world.

Here lies the resemblance (a curious, unexpected resemblance) between Kafka the hermetic and Hasek the popular. In *The Good Soldier Schweik*, Hasek does not describe the army (in the manner of a realist, a social critic) as a milieu of Austro-Hungarian society but as the modern version of the world. Like Kafka's Court, Hasek's army is nothing but an immense bureaucratic institution, an army-administration in which the old military virtues (courage, cunning, skill) no longer matter.

Hasek's military bureaucrats are stupid; the pedantic and absurd logic of Kafka's bureaucrats is also devoid of wisdom. In Kafka, stupidity is swathed in a mantle of mystery and takes on the quality of metaphysical parable. It intimidates. Joseph K. does his utmost to make some sense of its actions, its unintelligible words. For, terrible as it is to be condemned to death, it is intolerable to be condemned for nothing, to be a martyr to senselessness. Despite his innocence, K. therefore consents to his guilt and searched for his offense. In the last chapter, he shields his two executioners from the eyes of the municipal police (who might have saved him) and, moments before his death, reproaches himself for not having the strength to plunge the knife into his own chest and spare them the dirty job.

Schweik is just the opposite of K. He mimics the world around him (the world of stupidity) in so perfectly systematic a fashion that no one can tell if he is truly imbecilic or not. He adapts so easily (and with such delight!) to the reigning order not because he sees some sense in it but because he sees it has none at all. He amuses himself, he amuses other people, and by his extravagant conformism, he turns the world into one enormous joke.

(Those of us who have experienced the totalitarian Communist version of the modern world know that these two attitudes – seemingly artificial, literary, exaggerated – are only too real; we've lived in the realm bounded on one side by K.'s possibility, on the other by Schweik's; which is to say: in the realm where one pole is the identification with power, to the point where the victim develops solidarity with his own executioner, and the other pole the nonacceptance of power through the refusal to take seriously anything at all; which is to say: we have lived in the space between the absolute of the serious – K. – and the absolute of the non-serious – Schweik.)

And what about Broch? What is his ontological hypothesis?

The world is the process of the disintegration of values (values handed down from the Middle Ages), a process that stretches over the four centuries of the Modern Era and is their very essence.

What are man's possibilities in the face of this process?

Broch finds three: the Pasenow possibility, the Esch possibility, the Huguenau possibility.

THE PASENOW POSSIBILITY

Joachim von Pasenow's brother dies in a duel. The father says: 'He died for honor.' These words are writ forever in Joachim's memory.

But his friend Bertrand is amazed: How is it possible that in the age of trains and factories, two men can stand stiffly face to face, arms extended, revolvers in hand?

Upon which Joachim thinks: Bertrand has no feeling for honor.

And Bertrand goes on: Sentiments resist the changing times. They are an indestructible underpinning of conservatism. An atavistic residue.

Yes, the sentimental attachment to inherited values, to their atavistic residue, is Joachim von Pasenow's attitude.

Pasenow is introduced by the uniform motif. In earlier times, explains the narrator, the Church, as Supreme Judge, ruled over man. The priest's robes were the mark of supraterrestrial power, whereas the officer's uniform, the magistrate's gown represented the profane. As the magical influence of the Church gradually faded, the uniform replaced the sacerdotal habit and rose to the level of the absolute.

The uniform is that which we do not choose, that which is assigned us; it is the certitude of the universal as against the precariousness of the individual. When the values that were once so solid come under challenge and withdraw, heads bowed, he who cannot live without them (without fidelity, family, country, discipline, without love) buttons himself up in the universality of his uniform as if that uniform were the last shred of the transcendence that could protect him against the cold of a future in which there will be nothing left to respect.

Pasenow's story culminates on his wedding night. His wife, Elisabeth, does not love him. He sees nothing ahead but a future of lovelessness. He lies down beside her without undressing. That 'twisted his uniform a little, the coat skirts fell open and revealed the front of his black trousers, but as soon as Joachim noticed, he hastily set things right again and covered the place. He had drawn up his legs, and so as not to touch the coverlet with his glossy boots, he strained to keep his feet on the chair beside the bed.'

THE ESCH POSSIBILITY

The values handed down from the time when the Church completely dominated men's lives had long been shaken loose, but for Pasenow their content still seems clear. He has no doubt about what his country is, he knows to whom he should be faithful and who is his God.

In the presence of Esch, values have hidden their faces. Order, loyalty, sacrifice – he cherishes all these words, but exactly what do they represent? Sacrifice for what? Demand what sort of order? He doesn't know.

If a value has lost its concrete content, what is left of it? A mere empty form; an imperative that goes unheeded and, all the more furious, demands to be heard and obeyed. The less Esch knows what he wants, the more furiously he wants it.

Esch: the fanaticism of the era with no God. Because all values have hidden their faces, anything can be considered a value. Justice, order – Esch seeks them now in the trade union struggle, then in religion; today in police power, tomorrow in the mirage of America, where he dreams of emigrating. He could be a terrorist or a repentant terrorist turning in his comrades, or a party militant or a cult member or a kamikaze prepared to sacrifice his life. All the passions rampaging through the bloody history of our time are taken up, unmasked, diagnosed, and terrifyingly displayed in Esch's modest adventure.

He is discontented at the office where he works, he has a quarrel, he is dismissed. That is how his story begins. He believes that the cause of all the disorder that upsets him is a man named Nentwig, a book-keeper. God knows why him in particular. In any case, Esch decides to denounce him to the police. Isn't it his duty? Isn't it a service he owes everyone who, like himself, wants law and order?

But one day, in a bar, the unsuspecting Nentwig genially invites him to his table and offers him a drink. Beside himself, Esch tries to remember Nentwig's offense, but 'by now it was so bizarrely insubstantial and vague that Esch suddenly saw the absurdity of his project, and with a clumsy gesture, a little ashamed after all, he seized his glass.'

For Esch the world divides into the kingdom of Good and the kingdom of Evil, but, alas, both Good and Evil are equally impossible to identify (he has only to run into Nentwig and each no longer knows who is righteous and who wicked). In the great masquerade that is the world, Bertrand alone bears the stigmata of Evil forever on his face, because his crime is beyond all doubt: he is a homosexual, a disturber of the divine order. At the start of his novel Esch is ready to denounce Nentwig; at the end he mails a letter denouncing Bertrand.

THE HUGUENAU POSSIBILITY

Esch denounced Bertrand. Huguenau denounces Esch. Esch did it to save the world. Huguenau does it to save his career.

In a world without shared values, Huguenau, the innocent arriviste, feels perfectly at ease. The absence of moral imperatives is his freedom, his deliverance.

There is a deep significance in the fact that it is he who – without the faintest sense of guilt – murders Esch. For 'it is always the adherent of the smaller value system who slays the adherent of the larger system that is breaking up; it is always he, unfortunate wretch, who assumes the role of executioner in the process of value disintegration, and on the day when the trumpets of Judgment sound, it is the man released from all values who becomes the executioner of a world that has pronounced its own sentence.'

In Broch's mind, the Modern Era is the bridge that leads from the reign of irrational faith to the reign of the irrational in a world without faith. The figure who appears at the end of that bridge is Huguenau. The cheerful, guilt-free murderer. The end of the Modern Era in its euphoric version.

K., Schweik, Pasenow, Esch, Huguenau: five basic possibilities, five lodestars without which I believe it impossible to draw up the existential map of our time.

UNDER THE SKIES OF THE AGES

The planets that wheel in the skies of the Modern Era are reflected, always in a specific configuration, in the individual soul; it is through this configuration that the character's situation and the sense of his being are defined.

Broch speaks of Esch and all at once compares him to Luther. Both belong to the rebel category (Broch analyzes it at length). 'Esch is a rebel like Luther.' We tend to look for a character's roots in his childhood. Esch's roots (his childhood remains unknown to us) are to be found in another century. Esch's past is Luther.

To understand Pasenow, that man in uniform, Broch had to place him in the midst of the long historical process during which the profane uniform took the place of the priest's habit; immediately he did that, the whole celestial vault of the Modern Era lit up over this paltry officer.

For Broch, a character is conceived not as a uniqueness, inimitable and transitory, a miraculous moment fated to disappear, but as a solid bridge erected above time, where Luther and Esch, the past and the present, come together.

It is less in his philosophy of history than in this new way of seeing man (seeing him under the celestial arch of the ages) that Broch in *The Sleepwalkers* prefigures, I think, the future possibilities of the novel.

By Broch's light, I read Thomas Mann's *Doctor Faustus*, a novel that examines not only the life of a composer named Adrian Leverkühn but several centuries of German music along with him. Adrian is not only a composer, he is the composer who brings the history of music to an end (his greatest work is, incidentally, called *The Apocalypse*). And he is not just the last composer, he is also Faust. His gaze fixed on his country's diabolism (he wrote the novel toward the end of the Second World War), Thomas Mann ponders the contract that the mythical doctor – the incarnation of the German spirit – made with the devil. The whole history of his country suddenly looms up as the single adventure of a single character: a single Faust.

By Broch's light, I read Carlos Fuentes' *Terra Nostra*, in which the whole great Hispanic adventure (European and American) is encompassed in a wonderful telescoping, a wonderful oneiric distortion. Fuentes transforms Broch's principle, *Esch is like Luther*, into a still more radical principle: *Esch is Luther*. He provides us the key to his method: 'It takes several lives to make one person.' The old mythology of reincarnation materializes in a novelistic technique that makes *Terra Nostra* an immense, strange dream in which History is made and continually traversed by the same characters endlessly reincarnated. The same Ludovico who found a hitherto unknown continent in Mexico turns up several centuries later in Paris, with the same Celestina who centuries earlier was the mistress of Philip II. And so on.

Only at the end (the end of a love, of a life, of an era) does the past suddenly show itself as a whole and take on a brilliantly clear and finished shape. For Broch, the moment of the end is Huguenau; for Mann, Hitler. For Fuentes, it is the mythical frontier between two millennia; seen from that imaginary observatory, History – that European oddity, that smudge on time's pure surface – looks finished already, abandoned, lonely, and suddenly as humble, as touching as some little personal story we'll forget by tomorrow.

Indeed, if Luther is Esch, the history that leads from Luther to Esch is merely the biography of a single person: Martin Luther-Esch. And all of History is merely the story of a few characters (a Faust, a Don Juan, a Don Quixote, a Rastignac, an Esch) who have .traversed Europe's centuries together.

BEYOND CAUSALITY

On Levin's estate, a man and a woman meet – two melancholy, lonely people. They like one another and secretly hope to join their lives together. All they need is the chance to be alone for a moment and say so. Finally one day they find themselves unobserved in a wood where they have come to gather mushrooms. Ill at ease, they are silent, knowing that the moment is upon them and they must not let it slip by. The silence has already lasted rather a long while when the woman suddenly, 'involuntarily, reflexively,' starts to talk about mushrooms. Then silence again, and the man casts about for a way to declare himself, but instead of speaking of love, 'on some unexpected impulse' he too talks about mushrooms. On the way home they go on discussing mushrooms, powerless and desperate, for never, they know it, never will they speak of love.

Back at the house, the man tells himself that he did not declare his love because of the memory of his dead mistress, which he cannot betray. But we know perfectly well: It is a false excuse he invoked only to console himself. Console himself? Yes. Because we can resign ourselves to losing a love for a reason. We would never forgive ourselves for losing it for no reason at all.

This very beautiful little episode is a kind of parable for one of *Anna Karenina*'s great feats: bringing to light the causeless, incalculable, even mysterious aspect of human action.

What is action? – the eternal question of the novel, its constitutive question, so to speak. How is a decision born? How is it transformed into an act, and how do acts connect to make an adventure?

Out of the mysterious and chaotic fabric of life, the old novelists tried to tease the thread of a limpid rationality; in their view, the rationally accessible motive gives birth to an act, and that act provokes another. An adventure is a luminously causal chain of acts.

Werther loves his friends wife. He cannot betray his friend, he cannot give up his love, so he kills himself. Suicide with the transparent clarity of a mathematical equation.

But why does Anna Karenina kill herself?

The man who talked about mushrooms instead of love wants to believe that he did so out of loyalty to his vanished mistress. The reasons we might give for Anna's act would be worth just as little. True, people are treating her with contempt, but can she not do the same to them? She is barred from seeing her son, but is that a situation beyond appeal and beyond hope of change? Vronsky is already a little less infatuated, but after all, doesn't he still love her?

Besides, Anna did not come to the station to kill herself. She came to meet Vronsky. She throws herself beneath the train without having taken the decision to do so. It is rather the decision that takes Anna. That overtakes her. Like the man who talked about mushrooms instead of love, Anna acts 'on some unexpected impulse.' Which does not mean that her act is senseless. But its sense lies outside rationally apprehensible causality. Tolstoy had to use (for the first time in the history of the novel) an almost Joycean interior monologue to reconstruct the subtle fabric of fleeting impulses, transient feelings, fragmentary thoughts, to show us the suicidal journey of Anna's soul.

With Anna, we are far from Werther, and far from Dostoyevsky's

Kirilov too. Kirilov kills himself because he is forced to it by very clearly defined interests, carefully delineated intrigues. His act, however mad, is rational, conscious, meditated, premeditated. Kirilov's character is based entirely on his strange philosophy of suicide, and his act is merely the perfectly logical extension of his ideas,

Dostoyevsky grasped the madness of reason stubbornly determined to carry its logic through to the end. The terrain Tolstoy explores is the opposite: he uncovers the intrusions of illogic, of the irrational. That is why I mention him. The reference to Tolstoy places Broch in the context of one of the great explorations of the European novel: the exploration of the role the irrational plays in our decisions, in our lives.

CON-FUSIONS

Pasenow is seeing a Czech whore named Ruzena, but his parents arrange his marriage to a girl of their own milieu: Elisabeth. Pasenow loves her not at all, yet she does attract him. Actually, what attracts him is not Elisabeth herself but all that Elisabeth *represents* for him.

When he goes to see her for the first time, the streets, the gardens, the houses of her neighborhood radiate 'a great and insular security'; Elisabeth's house welcomes him with its happy atmosphere of 'a safe and gentle existence, filled with friendship' that will someday 'give place to love,' which in turn will someday 'die away into friendship.' The value Pasenow desires (the friendly security of a family) presents itself to him before he ever sees the woman who is to become (without her knowledge and against her nature) the bearer of that value.

He sits in the church in his native village and, eyes closed, imagines the Holy Family on a silver cloud with the ineffably beautiful Virgin Mary in its midst. Already as a child he had been carried away by that same image in that same church. At the time he was in love with a Polish servant girl on his father's farm, and in his reverie, he confused her with the Virgin and imagined himself sitting on her lovely knee, the knees of the Virgin turned servant girl. This time, his eyes closed, he sees the Virgin again and, all of a sudden, notices that her hair is blond! Yes, Mary has Elisabeth's hair! He is startled, he is shaken! It seems to him that through the device of this reverie, God himself is telling him that Elisabeth, whom he does not love, is his true and only love.

Irrational logic is based on the mechanism of con-fusion: Pasenow has a poor sense of reality; the causes of events escape him; he will never know what lies hidden behind the gazes of other people; yet although it may be disguised, unrecognizable, causeless, the external world is not mute: it speaks to him. It is like Baudelaire's famous poem where 'long echoes ... are confounded,' where 'the sounds, the scents, the colors correspond': the one thing is like another, is confounded with it (Elisabeth is confounded with the Virgin), and thus through its likeness makes itself clear.

Esch is a lover of the absolute. 'We can love only once' is his motto, and since Frau Hentjen loves him, according to Esch's logic she must not have loved her late husband. This means the man misused her and can only have been a villain. A villain like Bertrand. For the representatives of evil are interchangeable. They become con-fused with each other. They are only different manifestations of the same essence. It is when Esch glimpses Herr Hentjen's portrait on the wall that the idea comes to his mind: to go immediately and denounce Bertrand to the police. For if Esch can strike at Bertrand it will be like wounding Frau Hentjen's husband – as if he were ridding us, all of us, of a small share of the common evil.

FORESTS OF SYMBOLS

We must read *The Sleepwalkers* carefully, slowly, linger over actions as illogical as they are comprehensible, in order to perceive a hidden, subterranean *order* underlying the decisions of a Pasenow, a Ruzena, an Esch. These characters are not capable of facing reality as a concrete thing. Before their eyes everything turns into a symbol (Elisabeth the symbol of familial serenity, Bertrand the symbol of hell), and it is to symbols they are reacting when they believe they are acting upon reality.

Broch shows us that it is the system of con-fusions, the system of *symbolic thought*, that underlies all behavior, individual as well as collective. We need only examine our own lives to see how much this irrational system, far more than any reasoned thought, directs our attitudes: a certain man who, with his passion for aquarium fish, evokes some other who in the past caused me some terrible misery will always excite insurmountable mistrust in me ...

The irrational system rules political life no less: along with the last world war Communist Russia won the war of symbols: it succeeded for at least a half-century in providing the symbols of Good and Evil to that great army of Esches who are as avid for values as they are incapable of discriminating among them. This is why the gulag will never supplant Nazism as a symbol of absolute evil in the European consciousness. This is why people hold massive demonstrations against the war in Vietnam and not against the war in Afghanistan. Vietnam, colonialism, racism, imperialism, fascism, Nazism – all these words correspond like the colors and sounds in Baudelaire's poem, while the Afghanistan war is, so to speak, *symbolically mute*, or at any rate beyond the magic circle of absolute Evil, the geyser of symbols.

I also think of those daily slaughters along the highways, of that death that is as horrible as it is banal and that bears no resemblance to cancer or AIDS because, as the work not of nature but of man, it is an almost voluntary death. How can it be that such a death fails to dumbfound us, to turn our lives upside down, to incite us to vast reforms? No, it does not dumbfound us, because like Pasenow, we have a poor sense of the real, and in the sur-real sphere of symbols, this death in the guise of a hand-some car actually represents life; this smiling death is con-fused with modernity, freedom, adventure, just as Elisabeth was con-fused with the Virgin. The death of a man condemned to capital punishment, though infinitely rarer, much more readily draws our attention, rouses passions: confounded with the image of the executioner, it has a symbolic voltage that is far stronger, far darker and more repellent. Et cetera.

Man is a child wandering lost – to cite Baudelaire's poem again – in the 'forests of symbols.'

(The criterion of maturity: the ability to resist symbols. But mankind grows younger all the time.)

POLYHISTORICISM

In discussing his novels, Broch rejects the aesthetic of the 'psychological' novel in favor of the novel he calls 'gnosiological' or 'polyhistorical.' It seems to me that the second term, especially, is ill-chosen and mislead-ing. It was a compatriot of Broch's, Adalbert Stifter, founding father of Austrian fiction, who created a 'polyhistorical novel' in the precise sense

of the term when in 1857 (yes, the great year of *Madame Bovary*) he wrote
Der Nachsommer (*Indian Summer*). The novel is well known, Nietzsche
having ranked it among the four great books of German prose. To me it
is barely readable: we learn a great deal about geology, botany, zoology,
about all the crafts, about painting and architecture, but man and
human situations stand way off at the margins of this gigantic instructive
encyclopedia. Precisely because of its 'polyhistoricism,' this novel completely lacks the novel's specificity.

Now, this is not the case with Broch. He pursues 'what the novel alone
can discover.' But he knows that the conventional form (grounded exclusively in a character's adventure, and content with a mere narration
of that adventure) limits the novel, reduces its cognitive capacities. He
also knows that the novel has an extraordinary power of incorporation:
whereas neither poetry nor philosophy can incorporate the novel, the
novel can incorporate both poetry and philosophy without losing thereby
anything of its identity, which is characterized (we need only recall
Rabelais and Cervantes) precisely by its tendency to embrace other
genres, to absorb philosophical and scientific knowledge. So in Broch's
perspective, the word 'polyhistorical' means: marshaling all intellectual
means and all poetic forms to illuminate 'what the novel alone can
discover': man's being.

This, of course, implies a profound transformation of the novel's
form.

THE UNACHIEVED

I shall take the liberty of speaking very personally: I like and admire the
last novel of *The Sleepwalkers* (*Huguenau, or Realism*), in which the tendency
to synthesis and the transformation of form are most advanced, but I also
have some reservations:

– the 'polyhistorical' purpose demands a technique of ellipsis that
Broch has not completely worked out; architectural clarity suffers for it;

– the several elements (verse, narrative, aphorism, reportage, essay)
remain more juxtaposed than blended into a true 'polyphonic' unity;

– even though it is presented as a text written by one of the characters, the excellent essay on the disintegration of values can readily be
taken for the author's own thinking, for the novel's truth, its statement,

its thesis, and thus may damage the relativity that is indispensable to novelistic space.

All great works (precisely because they are great) contain something unachieved. Broch is an inspiration to us not only because of what he brought off but also because of what he aimed for and missed. The unachieved in his work can show us the need for (1) a new art of *radical divestment* (which can encompass the complexity of existence in the modern world without losing architectonic clarity)' (2) a new art of *novelistic counterpoint* (which can blend philosophy, narrative, and dream into one music); (3) a new art of the *specifically novelistic essay* (which does not claim to bear an apodictic message but remains hypothetical, playful, or ironic).

MODERNISMS

Of all the great novelists of our time, Broch is, perhaps, the least known. It is not so hard to understand why. He had scarcely completed *The Sleepwalkers* when he saw Hitler in power and German cultural life annihilated; five years later he left Austria for America, where remained until his death. In such conditions, his work – deprived of its natural audience, deprived of contact with a normal literary life – could no longer play its proper role in its time: gather to itself a community of readers, supporters, and connoisseurs, create a school, influence other writers. Like the work of Musil and Gombrowicz, it was discovered (rediscovered) after a long delay (and after its author's death) by those who, like Broch himself, were possessed by the passion for the new form – in other words, who were 'modernist' in orientation. But their modernism did not resemble Broch's. Not that it was later, more advanced; it was different in its roots, in its attitude toward the modern world, in its aesthetic. That difference brought about a certain embarrassment: Broch (like Musil, like Gombrowicz) was seen as a great innovator, but one who did not conform to the current and conventional image of modernism (for in the second half of this century, we must reckon with the modernism of fixed rules, the modernism of the university – establishment modernism, so to speak).

This establishment modernism, for instance, insists on the destruction of the novel form. In Broch's perspective, the possibilities of the novel form are far from being exhausted.

Establishment modernism would have the novel do away with the artifice of character, which it claims is finally nothing but a mask pointlessly hiding the author's face. In Broch's characters, the author's self is undetectable.

Establishment modernism has proscribed the notion of totality – the very word that Broch, by contrast, uses readily to say: In the age of the excessive division of labor, of runaway specialization, the novel is one of the last outposts where man can still maintain connections with life in its entirety.

According to establishment modernism, an impregnable boundary separates the 'modern' novel from the 'traditional' novel (this 'traditional novel' being the basket into which they shovel all the different phases of four centuries of the novel). In Broch's view, the modern novel continues the same quest that has preoccupied all the great novelists since Cervantes.

Behind establishment modernism there is a residue of ingenuous eschatological belief: that one History ends and another (better) one begins, founded on an entirely new basis. In Broch, there is the melancholy awareness of a History drawing to a close in circumstances that are profoundly hostile to the evolution of art and of the novel in particular.

Biographical Note

Hermann Broch was born on 1 November 1886 of Jewish parents from the textile quarter of Vienna. The family background – his father was a wholesale textile merchant from Moravia, his mother the daughter of a Viennese wholesale leather dealer – singled him out, as the first of two sons, for a career in the family firm. Between 1904 and 1906 he studied at the city's Technical College for Textile Manufacture and at the Spinning and Weaving College at Mühlhausen (Mulhouse, Alsace) in preparation for running the Brochs' textile concern at Teesdorf near Vienna. The following year he went on a fact-finding mission to the USA to study methods of cotton production and patented a cotton-mixing machine of which he was co-inventor. Volunteering in 1909 for service in the Austro-Hungarian Imperial Army, he was obliged to discontinue his training with the artillery in Zagreb because of ill health. Later the same year he joined the board of directors of the family spinning works. Having been declared unfit for military service during the First World War, he acted as director of a Red Cross convalescent home for soldiers within the grounds of the Teesdorf factory, while continuing to manage the family business. Broch once self-deprecatingly referred to himself as a 'captain of industry', yet his organizational skills and the constructive paternalism with which the Teesdorf plant treated its work-force had come to the attention of the Austrian business establishment and he was invited to serve in the Arbitration Section of the Austrian Trades Court and the State Anti-Unemployment Bureau.

By the age of forty, Broch had established a reputation not just as a successful industrialist, but also as a formidable autodidact with growing interests in modernist literature and philosophy. Even before the outbreak of the First World War he had begun publishing essays in the prestigious Viennese journal *Der Brenner*; his first work of fiction, the 'Methodological Novella' (later to become part of his 1950 novel *The*

Guiltless), had appeared in Franz Blei's *Summa* (1918); and he had a string of literary, philosophical and cultural essays and reviews to his credit by the mid 1920s. These, together with the fact that he began moving in Viennese *Kaffeehaus* circles, brought him to the attention of Stefan Zweig, Karl Kraus and Robert Musil. Between 1925 and 1930, he enrolled for courses in philosophy, mathematics and psychology at the University of Vienna. His decision to sell the family firm in 1927 and devote himself to intellectual pursuits came as a shock to his family. Broch was no doubt primarily responding to the economic warning signals of the time, but the coincidence of this radical *volte-face* with his intensive work on the first draft of *The Sleepwalkers* suggests that what he called the 'terrible strain' of his 'double existence' had also been instrumental in bringing about the biggest change of direction in his entire life.

The next decisive event in his life was not to be of Broch's own making. In 1938 Hitler's forces invaded Austria and Broch found himself on a Gestapo list. Whether this was because of his Jewishness or his politics remains unclear. His postman is rumoured to have denounced him on account of a subscription to the Moscow journal *Das Wort*, but Broch's voluminous international correspondence with leading pacifists and socialists on behalf of his proposed 'League of Nations Resolution' would have been equally incriminating. Broch spent three weeks in 'protective custody' before being released and instructed to report to the Viennese authorities. He was astute enough to evade further Gestapo attention before successfully fleeing to Scotland where, thanks to the good offices of his English translators Willa and Edwin Muir, he eventually obtained a US visa. Broch arrived in New York in October 1938 and was destined to stay in the United States until he died of a heart attack in May 1951.

'One thing at least I have in common with Kafka and Musil', Broch once remarked, is that 'none of us has an actual biography; we lived and wrote, nothing more.' Certainly, by the time Broch arrived in the United States he was inclined to identify his life exclusively with his writing. He had successfully completed the transition from man of industry to internationally acclaimed writer, mentioned alongside Joyce, Gide, Musil, Huxley and Thomas Mann. *The Sleepwalkers* had enjoyed instant recognition in the early 1930s, although an unfortunate combination of adverse economic circumstances and National Socialist pressures meant that the novel would now be more helpful to him in his new host country than in Europe. Although he had written a number of other works since the appearance of the *Sleepwalkers* trilogy in 1931–2 – including *The Unknown Quantity* (1933), a complex of stories that would become the core of *The Guiltless* (1950), as well as drafts of *The Spell* and *The Death of Virgil* – his principal calling-card was still his first novel; MGM and Paramount were interested in film rights to it, people of the stature of Albert Einstein, Thornton Wilder, Aldous Huxley and T. S. Eliot thought highly of the trilogy, and its theoretical sections on the disintegration of values would, it was hoped, help Broch gain a post at one of the Ivy League universities. However, like many exiles of his generation, he was to remain on the margins of academe. A number of awards (from the Bollingen, Guggenheim and Rockefeller Foundations) enabled him complete his *magnum opus*, the novel *The Death of Virgil*, as well as a long cultural essay on *Hugo von Hofmannsthal and His Times* and, most important of all, to continue working on his Theory of Mass Hysteria, the major project of his final years. While the parallel German and English publication of *The Death of Virgil* in 1945 had benefited from a highly favourable reception, for the following six years Broch was to resume his intolerable 'double existence': having to devote himself – now reluctantly – once more to literary work (above all, his two incomplete novels *The Guiltless* and *The Spell*) in order to placate his publishers and re-establish himself in Europe, while struggling against the passage of time and various illnesses to complete his project on mass hysteria. Broch died, in the eyes of the outside world as the author of two literary masterpieces, but in his own view as someone whose main sociological, political and humanitarian work remained unfinished.

John White

PENGUIN CLASSICS

www.penguinclassics.com

- *Details about every Penguin Classic*

- *Advanced information about forthcoming titles*

- *Hundreds of author biographies*

- *FREE resources including critical essays on the books and their historical background, reader's and teacher's guides.*

- *Links to other web resources for the Classics*

- *Discussion area*

- *Online review copy ordering for academics*

- *Competitions with prizes, and challenging Classics trivia quizzes*

PENGUIN CLASSICS ONLINE

READ MORE IN PENGUIN

In every corner of the world, on every subject under the sun, Penguin represents quality and variety – the very best in publishing today.

For complete information about books available from Penguin – including Puffins, Penguin Classics and Arkana – and how to order them, write to us at the appropriate address below. Please note that for copyright reasons the selection of books varies from country to country.

In the United Kingdom: Please write to *Dept. EP, Penguin Books Ltd, Bath Road, Harmondsworth, West Drayton, Middlesex UB7 0DA*

In the United States: Please write to *Consumer Sales, Penguin Putnam Inc., P.O. Box 12289 Dept. B, Newark, New Jersey 07101-5289.* VISA and MasterCard holders call 1-800-788-6262 to order Penguin titles

In Canada: Please write to *Penguin Books Canada Ltd, 10 Alcorn Avenue, Suite 300, Toronto, Ontario M4V 3B2*

In Australia: Please write to *Penguin Books Australia Ltd, P.O. Box 257, Ringwood, Victoria 3134*

In New Zealand: Please write to *Penguin Books (NZ) Ltd, Private Bag 102902, North Shore Mail Centre, Auckland 10*

In India: Please write to *Penguin Books India Pvt Ltd, 11 Community Centre, Panchsheel Park, New Delhi 110017*

In the Netherlands: Please write to *Penguin Books Netherlands bv, Postbus 3507, NL-1001 AH Amsterdam*

In Germany: Please write to *Penguin Books Deutschland GmbH, Metzlerstrasse 26, 60594 Frankfurt am Main*

In Spain: Please write to *Penguin Books S. A., Bravo Murillo 19, 1° B, 28015 Madrid*

In Italy: Please write to *Penguin Italia s.r.l., Via Benedetto Croce 2, 20094 Corsico, Milano*

In France: Please write to *Penguin France, Le Carré Wilson, 62 rue Benjamin Baillaud, 31500 Toulouse*

In Japan: Please write to *Penguin Books Japan Ltd, Kaneko Building, 2-3-25 Koraku, Bunkyo-Ku, Tokyo 112*

In South Africa: Please write to *Penguin Books South Africa (Pty) Ltd, Private Bag X14, Parkview, 2122 Johannesburg*

READ MORE IN PENGUIN

Published or forthcoming:

Ulysses James Joyce

Written over a seven-year period, from 1914 to 1921, *Ulysses* has survived bowdlerization, legal action and bitter controversy. An undisputed modernist classic, its ceaseless verbal inventiveness and astonishingly wide-ranging allusions confirm its standing as an imperishable monument to the human condition. 'Everybody knows now that *Ulysses* is the greatest novel of the century' Anthony Burgess, *Observer*

Nineteen Eighty-Four George Orwell

Hidden away in the Record Department of the Ministry of Truth, Winston Smith skilfully rewrites the past to suit the needs of the Party. Yet he inwardly rebels against the totalitarian world he lives in, which controls him through the all-seeing eye of Big Brother. 'His final masterpiece . . . *Nineteen Eighty-Four* is enthralling' Timothy Garton Ash, *New York Review of Books*

The Day of the Locust *and* The Dream Life of Balso Snell
Nathanael West

These two novellas demonstrate the fragility of the American dream. In *The Day of the Locust*, talented young artist Todd Hackett has been brought to Hollywood to work in a major studio. He discovers a surreal world of tarnished dreams, where violence and hysteria lurk behind the glittering façade. 'The best of the Hollywood novels, a nightmare vision of humanity destroyed by its obsession with film' J. G. Ballard, *Sunday Times*

The Myth of Sisyphus Albert Camus

The Myth of Sisyphus is one of the most profound philosophical statements written this century. It is a discussion of the central idea of absurdity that Camus was to develop in his novel *The Outsider*. Here Camus poses the fundamental question – Is life worth living? – and movingly argues for an acceptance of reality that encompasses revolt, passion and, above all, liberty.

READ MORE IN PENGUIN

Published or forthcoming:

The Chrysalids John Wyndham

Genetic mutation has devastated the world. In the primitive society that has emerged from its ruins, any sign of deviation is ruthlessly hunted out and destroyed. David lives in fear of discovery, for he is part of a secret group who are able to communicate with each other through their thoughts. As they grow older they feel increasingly isolated. Then one of them marries a 'norm' with terrifying consequences.

The Waves Virginia Woolf

The Waves traces the lives of a group of friends from childhood to youth and middle age. While social events, individual achievements and disappointments form its narrative, the novel is most remarkable for the poetic language that conveys the inner life of its characters: their aspirations, their triumphs and regrets, their awareness of unity and isolation.

Heart of Darkness Joseph Conrad

In Conrad's haunting tale Marlow, a seaman and wanderer, recounts his journey to the heart of Africa in search of the enigmatic Kurtz. He discovers how Kurtz has gained his position of power over the local people, and radically questions not only his own nature and values, but those of his society. '*Heart of Darkness* seemed to reach into the heart of Conrad himself' Peter Ackroyd, *The Times*

The Garden Party and Other Stories Katherine Mansfield

Innovative, startlingly perceptive and aglow with colour, these fifteen stories were written towards the end of Katherine Mansfield's short life. Many are set in the author's native New Zealand, others in England and the French Riviera. All are revelations of the unspoken, half-understood emotions that make up everyday experience.

READ MORE IN PENGUIN

Published or forthcoming:

Seven Pillars of Wisdom   T. E. Lawrence

Although 'continually and bitterly ashamed' that the Arabs had risen in revolt against the Turks as a result of fraudulent British promises, Lawrence led them in a triumphant campaign. *Seven Pillars of Wisdom* recreates epic events with extraordinary vividness. However flawed, Lawrence is one of the twentieth century's most fascinating figures. This is the greatest monument to his character.

A Month in the Country   J. L. Carr

A damaged survivor of the First World War, Tom Birkin finds refuge in the village church of Oxgodby where he is to spend the summer uncovering a huge medieval wall-painting. Immersed in the peace of the countryside and the unchanging rhythms of village life, Birkin experiences a sense of renewal. Now an old man, he looks back on that idyllic summer of 1920.

Lucky Jim   Kingsley Amis

Jim Dixon has accidentally fallen into a job at one of Britain's new redbrick universities. A moderately successful future beckons, as long as he can survive a madrigal-singing weekend at Professor Welch's, deliver a lecture on 'Merrie England' and resist Christine, the hopelessly desirable girlfriend of Welch's awful son Bertrand. 'A flawless comic novel . . . It has always made me laugh out loud' Helen Dunmore, *The Times*

Under Milk Wood   Dylan Thomas

As the inhabitants of Llareggub lie sleeping, their dreams and fantasies deliciously unfold. Waking up, their dreams turn to bustling activity as a new day begins. In this classic modern pastoral, the 'dismays and rainbows' of the imagined seaside town become, within the cycle of one day, 'a greenleaved sermon on the innocence of men'.

READ MORE IN PENGUIN

Published or forthcoming:

Swann's Way Marcel Proust

This first book of Proust's supreme masterpiece, *A la recherche du temps perdu*, recalls the early youth of Charles Swann in the small, provincial backwater of Combray through the eyes of the adult narrator. The story then moves forward to Swann's life as a man of fashion in the glittering world of *belle-époque* Paris. A scathing, often comic dissection of French society, *Swann's Way* is also a story of past moments tantalizingly lost and, finally, triumphantly rediscovered.

Metamorphosis and Other Stories Franz Kafka

A companion volume to *The Great Wall of China and Other Short Works*, these translations bring together the small proportion of Kafka's works that he thought worthy of publication. This volume contains his most famous story, 'Metamorphosis'. All the stories reveal the breadth of Kafka's literary vision and the extraordinary imaginative depth of his thought.

Cancer Ward Aleksandr Solzhenitsyn

One of the great allegorical masterpieces of world literature, *Cancer Ward* is both a deeply compassionate study of people facing terminal illness and a brilliant dissection of the 'cancerous' Soviet police state. Withdrawn from publication in Russia in 1964, it became a work that awoke the conscience of the world. 'Without doubt the greatest Russian novelist of this century' *Sunday Times*

Peter Camenzind Hermann Hesse

In a moment of 'emotion recollected in tranquility' Peter Camenzind recounts the days of his youth: his childhood in a remote mountain village, his abiding love of nature, and the discovery of literature which inspires him to leave the village and become a writer. 'One of the most penetrating accounts of a young man trying to discover the nature of his creative talent' *The Times Literary Supplement*

BY THE SAME AUTHOR

The Anarchist

The second in Broch's masterly trilogy, *The Sleepwalkers*, *The Anarchist* follows the destiny of August Esch, who faces an uncertain future after he is wrongfully dismissed from his job as a book-keeper. He becomes enmeshed in the attempt to avenge Martin, a political activist, imprisoned by the authorities; but his personal battle is with his own lust, which he seeks to channel into marriage with Frau Hentjen. *The Anarchist* is a brilliant depiction of German society as it approached the First World War.

'In this new way of seeing man ... Broch in *The Sleepwalkers* prefigures ... the future possibilities of the novel' Milan Kundera

The Realist

In this final volume of *The Sleepwalkers* trilogy, forty years have passed since the events of *The Romantic* took place and Joachim is now the commandant of Kur–Trier, in the final years of the Great War. Making his escape to the little town is Wilhelm Huguenau, a deserter and a ruthless exploiter, who finds himself in the newspaper office of August Esch. Huguenau and Esch become business partners, but Esch soon becomes something far worse – his victim. *The Realist* paints a chilling portrait of the disintegration of moral values.

'With unerring precision Broch finds the fault lines that run from the late nineteenth century into our calamitous age' W. G. Sebald

The Death of Virgil

Hermann Broch, an Austrian Jew imprisoned by the Nazis who managed to escape to America in 1938, became obsessed with literature's tendency to prettify suffering, and its impotence in the face of political terror. Broch explores these themes through the story of the dying Virgil, his relations with the Emperor Augustus and his desperate decision to burn the manuscript of his unfinished *Aeneid*. *The Death of Virgil* ranks among the boldest and most powerful attempts to confront the horrors of the twentieth century.

'One of the most extraordinary and profound experiments ever to have been undertaken with ... the novel' Thomas Mann